Praise for *Hard Cider*

"In this moving, compelling novel, a character who makes cider from a variety of different apples says, 'I can't help but feel that there's some magic in the mixing.' Barbara Stark-Nemon reminds us this is true for families, too. Through its exploration of the many forms family can take and the possibility of new beginnings in midlife, *Hard Cider* is easy to love."
—Gayle Brandeis, poet, essayist, and award-winning author
of *The Art of Misdiagnosis* and *The Book of Dead Birds*

"In this absorbing and thoughtful novel, the alchemy of turning apples into hard cider becomes a potent metaphor for the way in which time blends and distills the characters into a family. With grace and compassion, Stark-Nemon examines the forging of relationships under the pressure of shocking revelations. A deep valuing of connection to land, work, and loved ones emerges from this beautifully written story."
—Jessica Levine, author of *The Geometry of Love*
and *Nothing Forgotten*

"*Hard Cider* is a coming-of-age story for women of a 'certain age' finding their own paths after the kids are raised, unlocking their own dreams. Barbara Stark-Nemon woos her readers to fall in love, but not with a romantic notion of idealized marriage and family and not with the blush of new infatuation. Instead, we are immersed in the sensual details of her glorious Michigan landscape, where we are defenseless against falling in love with the natural world she so vividly paints. When I closed the last page, all I wanted to do was book a flight to Michigan in the autumn."
—Betsy Graziani Fasbinder, author of *Fire and Water* and
Filling Her Shoes: A Memoir of an Inherited Family

"I just flew through Barbara Stark Nemon's new novel *Hard Cider*. Well written and easy to read, with loving descriptions of northern Michigan, this is a story of Abbie Rose Stone, who strikes out on her own to create a cider business. In the process, she meets an intriguing young woman with secrets to uncover, secrets that could blow Abbie's cherished family apart—or enrich it. Abbie is an expert by experience as the true center of her family, navigating the subtle challenges of her loved ones. This character gives credit to women who hold their families together by sheer goodwill and small and large acts of love. A book that celebrates family."

— Caitlin Hicks, author of Readers' Favorite award winner and iBooks Best New Fiction pick *A Theory of Expanded Love*

"*Hard Cider* is magical in its rootedness even as it explores the way we seek home and community and the lives of our dreams."
—Andi Cumbo-Floyd, author of *The Slaves Have Names: Ancestors of my Home, Steele Secrets*, and *Love Letters to Writers: Encouragement, Accountability, and Truth-Telling*

"*Hard Cider* is the intriguing story of a strong woman struggling with the psychological fallout of infertility decades after achieving motherhood. Just as she is opening a new chapter in her life by beginning a business of her own, a seemingly harmless encounter leads to a revelation that threatens her hard-won confidence and the cohesion of her family. The reader follows with interest this vividly told story of a woman fighting to regain her bearings, master a major personal challenge, and protect her already-challenged family."
—Monica Starkman, MD, Psychiatrist, University of Michigan Medical School, author of *The End of Miracles*, and columnist for *Psychology Today*

"In *Hard Cider*, I enjoyed how we are dropped immediately into a story—and a family—that we are eager to know. The story guides us through the amazing landscape of Michigan, the details of making cider, and Abbie's family and other characters who are well drawn and full of surprises. I loved getting to know this family, and found it easy to empathize with the struggles and challenges that arise with the sons. We see how history is always coming to tap us on the shoulder, and we have to find ways to cope with it. As the deeper emotional story started unraveling, I couldn't turn the pages fast enough."
—Linda Joy Myers, president of the National Association of Memoir Writers and author of *Songs of the Plains* and *The Power of Memoir: How to Write Your Healing Story*

"A lyrically told, powerful story of a middle-aged woman who has the courage to pursue a long-held dream on her own terms while still grappling with the emotional push-pull of mothering adult children whose lives and dreams are not hers to control."
—Jenni Ogden, author of Sarton, Readers' Favorite, and IPPY award winner *A Drop in the Ocean*

"*Hard Cider* is a fabulous novel about starting a business, taking on challenges, and building a family. The real treat was spending time with protagonist Abbie Rose. Multi-talented and capable, she's the type of woman one admires from afar. Forced to reckon with potentially shattering news, she is human to the core. I so enjoyed being on this ride with her, watching her gain acceptance and eventually find grace. Not just a great story, it's a beautiful example of how to live."
—Jeanne McWilliams Blasberg, author of *Eden*

"*Hard Cider* is a beautifully written novel that will make Stark-Nemon your next one-click author!"
—Nicole Waggoner, author of *Center Ring* and *The Act*

HARD
CIDER

A NOVEL

BARBARA STARK-NEMON

SHE WRITES PRESS

Published September 18, 2018
Printed in the United States of America
Print ISBN: 978-1-63152-475-2
E-ISBN: 978-1-63152-476-9
Library of Congress Control Number: 2018940392

For information, address:
She Writes Press
1563 Solano Ave #546
Berkeley, CA 94707

Interior design by Tabitha Lahr

She Writes Press is a division of SparkPoint Studio, LLC.

To Everywoman- maker and keeper of families,
especially when it isn't easy.

"I have never written a book that was not born out of a question I needed to answer for myself."

—May Sarton

Prologue

"There would have been no rescue here!" The Ann Arbor fire marshal held my arm as fiercely as my gaze, neither of us paying attention to the breast milk leaking through my shirt. I tore my eyes away from his and tried again to look at the house, still reeking of wet char, a crazy perimeter of crime tape separating the ugly remains of our home from the brilliant June morning.

I stepped back and out of the chief's grasp as he turned to my husband and began again his obsessive relating of this fire story. It had raged so fast and ferociously during the night that the house was lost before the first pumper truck arrived. An accelerant placed under the car, my car in the garage, had exploded into the second story, spawning an inferno that raced through all the bedrooms until their floors collapsed into the rooms below.

An accelerant? Placed under my car? Who placed it? This was arson? I looked up. What remained was a shell with blackened eyes where once the windows had stood.

Our next-door neighbor had called in our fire, but another fire close by had caused a mix-up.

"We've responded to that fire, ma'am, we have a truck on the scene," the dispatcher had said.

"There's no truck here!" my neighbor had yelled.

More addresses, more time . . . and then the problem with the hook-up at the hydrant . . . I was only half-listening, and it was my husband, Steven, who the fire marshal was clutching.

"There would have been no rescue here! It was so fast!"

That I heard again. Without a word or a look, Steven placed baby Seth in my arms. Automatically I began to sway and twist from side to side, a little bounce at each knee like an insurance policy against the baby's waking. He'd slept all the way from the remote cottage in Canada where we'd been staying with friends when the Provincial Police had knocked at the door. We'd dropped our older children, Alex and Andrew, at my parents' an hour earlier.

Seth's warm body lay nestled over my swollen breast. I'd need to nurse him soon. *I should go inside and . . .* The wave of nausea hit me like the hot air that wouldn't come until later in the day. There was no inside, only the burned house behind the smoky façade.

I began to make eye contact with neighbors and strangers on the street behind me; horror was writ large on their faces. Their looks separated us, the people whose house had been torched, whose worldly goods had vanished, along with our peace of mind, from them—the people to whom this had not happened.

I looked back to Steven, staring at the house. He wore old basketball shorts and a ragged T-shirt, his long arms hanging at his sides, sandals planted on the sidewalk. His oversized, horn-rimmed glasses tilted slightly more than his head did. I saw the lawyer in him rapidly assessing the damage, the crime.

I didn't want to go into "do" mode. Steven had already gotten us here, starting six hours ago. Another hit of nausea. In twenty-four hours, he would go to work. He had a big hearing.

He wouldn't try to get a continuance, or have a junior partner substitute. He would rely on me to move forward.

He doesn't have clothes. We need a place to sleep . . . STOP! One thing at a time.

Seth pulled his knees up reflexively, a grunt of discomfort muffled by the breast his baby face was pressed into. I loosened my hold slightly and dipped my nose across the top of his fuzzy head, inhaling the baby sweetness as I adjusted his tiny body onto the shelf of my front. His once-more-contented head rested quietly under my chin.

Seth was nine weeks old. Thirty-six hours of labor, followed by a C-section, was still too close to have recovered any sense of my body apart from his. After six years of agonizing infertility treatments, in vitro fertilizations, and adoption proceedings, we finally had our family, and now we were supposed to get to live our dream life. *Arson?*

" . . . We will continue to consider this a crime scene until we have completed our investigation, at which time we will determine which areas of the structure are safe to enter for recovery purposes." The fire marshal watched me as he spoke and I guessed he knew I hadn't heard the first half of whatever he'd been saying. The chief pressed a business card into my hand and I turned away, looking behind me as though I knew what I needed or wanted to see. I did not.

The numbers of people had at least tripled. Gawkers—those who averted their eyes and those who stared, fascinated—were drawn like magnets to the awful spectacle. Again, I recognized that look in their faces—dread and fear. I'd seen it on so many faces along the bumpy road of my life. Would I ever be free from its sucker punch? Would I ever get to simply live my dreams?

"Abbie Rose!" A friend's slender arm went around the bulk of Seth and me. I hugged her but did not cry. I had work to do.

Chapter 1

Twenty years later.

A lex is coming. Let there be sun or snow. January thaw is more often a cruel joke than a welcome reprieve from winter freeze in this microclimate at the tip of Michigan's Leelanau Peninsula.

Abbie, Abbie Rose, I thought. *This is what you asked for.* And it was. I stared out into the light, steady rain, nearly invisible for the gray mist that rose from soaked ice on the long driveway. The haze softened the shoreline, dulled the green waters of the bay, and fed the lichen on the split-rail fence surrounding the overgrown orchard.

It wasn't as though Alex didn't know about January in northern Michigan. We'd been vacationing in this spot for more than twenty years. Shortly after our house fire, we brought our three boys to a cottage on this stretch of Lake Michigan, perched on a dune not half a mile from here. It overlooked the expanse of the lake and a string of islands that beckoned a sailor toward the open water and the distant reach of Wisconsin's Door Peninsula on the other side.

That cottage was a beloved escape from the high pressure of upscale Ann Arbor. It eased each of us, in different ways, through the stressful years of recovering our lives and rebuilding our Ann Arbor home after the fire, then working around the demands of Steven's big legal career, and my smaller one teaching, as the boys grew up.

The two-hundred-year-old farmhouse in which I now stood was another story. When I retired at fifty-three, a year earlier, I'd purchased the tract of land with a farmhouse, a log cabin, and five lake lots. Situated north of the town of Northport, surrounded on three sides by lake, the parcel was ideal for my dream of producing high-quality hard apple cider.

I gazed out the kitchen window at what would become the cider shed, leaden in the mist. Settled into the side of a hill where the driveway swept around the back of the house, the old brown building's reinvention was visibly underway with a new roof, repaired and finished with scalloped shingles. I'd saved the surrounding trees and therefore given up on photovoltaic roof tiles, so solar energy wouldn't power the works. The grey day made that bet seem like a good one. A familiar tug of anxiety at the money I'd spent on this project momentarily took hold of my gut, but resolution reasserted itself with the will I'd learned to summon like a trusted dog. I had a plan. My dream was worthwhile.

I turned back to the kitchen, preparation of Alex's favorite dishes in various states all over the large space. Piles of chopped vegetables, waiting to become minestrone soup, covered the island countertop with its dated blue Corian. The steam and earthy smell of simmering kidney beans already filled the open room. Beef brisket lay roasting in beer and ketchup in the oven, and the pastry for lemon meringue pie sat rolled between sheets of waxed paper in the refrigerator.

Suddenly, the tattered cover of my grandmother's *Settlement Cookbook* floated into my mind's eye. *The way to a man's heart . . .* printed under the title. Was I trying to charm Alex with my life in northern Michigan by making his favorite food? He was my son, after all. It was okay to make a special meal for him, even if talking about my business would be on the agenda.

My stomach fluttered with a mixture of anticipation and nerves at his visit. Raising him was the toughest challenge in my life of many challenges. Brilliant but moody and strong willed, he tested boundaries early and often, teaching Steven and me the need to cancel our expectations and love the child we had, not the one we thought we wanted.

His fascination and skill with technology at the dawn of its use in schools, combined with his intense dislike of a teacher, had led to his removal from one school for "threatening" the teacher online. His refusal to allow a bully to act unimpeded in a middle school lunchroom had resulted in his sending the bully flying across the room, and both boys were suspended. When we were no longer able to safely manage his behavior at home, we'd survived by sending him to boarding school. Instead of going straight to college after high school, he'd enlisted in the army, where he'd distinguished himself in the honor guard but then felt compelled to challenge a superior on behalf of a sexual harassment victim. Finally, after training to become a physician's assistant, he'd tried to rescue a young single mother with children in foster care, getting himself into trouble in the process. He'd moved to Iowa for a job so he could get on with the life he envisioned: working as a PA, going fishing, and drinking a beer or two on the back porch while his dog ran amok on the back forty.

Alex's troubles had forced him to reckon with demons reaching back to his stormy adolescence and then move forward with his life. It had been hard on him. It had nearly killed me, as grown children's problems do their parents. But we had stuck with Alex, and he had stuck with us, and he seemed to have emerged into adulthood with his talent, intelligence, and life skills intact. Still . . .

The phone startled me out of my reverie with a jolt.

"Hey Mom, what's up?" Alex's voice was calm but, as always, tinged with challenge,

"Hi, honey. Where are you?"

"Just passing through Chicago. I'll be on 94 in under an hour. God I love the speed limits in Michigan. I should see you by dinner. What's it like up there?"

No use pretending with Alex. "Well, the British would call this 'filthy' weather, but I'm cooking you one hell of a good dinner."

"No snow?! It's January in northern Michigan! What the fu . . . Okay. Well, whatever. Is Dad up there?"

Resist, Abbie Rose, resist. The "yeah, right" stayed where it belonged. Steven would not be part of this visit with Alex, or any discussion about my business. Though he still worked as an attorney, he'd recently given up many of his partnership administrative duties, with an eye toward retirement. He didn't know exactly what retirement would mean for him, but he'd made it clear he wouldn't be throwing his energy into a hard cider business in northern Michigan. If and when the time came, he would help with any legal documents I needed, as he had for dozens of friends and family members before me, but he was leaving it to me to pursue this dream on my own. If I decided to proceed, I'd be in the deep without him, to sink or to swim.

"No, sweetie, he's hanging out downstate this weekend, catching up on paperwork. He may make it up by midweek." I waited a scant conversational beat for a sign of Alex's response to this information, but no clues were forthcoming. "I hope you have some energy left for tomorrow, after all that driving," I continued. "We have an appointment to see Charles Aiken."

"And I'm supposed to know who that is?" *There it is. He is irritated. Does he want to see Steven, or has he forgotten about tomorrow?* I looked longingly at the scotch bottle at the end of the counter.

"Remember I told you about Manitou Brewing Company? I've gotten to know the owner and I'm going to meet with him and his son tomorrow. They've planted five acres of hard cider apples. In another three years, he thinks they'll be ready to process commercially."

Silence. The Indiana road noise and the rumble of Alex's Dodge Ram combined with the slap of windshield wipers to create a considerable sound barrier, making it hard to detect the meaning of the barely audible sigh that whispered from the phone.

"And I suppose you've got several PA job interviews scheduled for me too?"

I smiled and shook my head, for no one else's benefit. "No, honey, but that's a good idea." *Two people can play this game.*

"All right. Well, I tried to call Shawn, but he hasn't gotten back to me. I may text him as I head up 31, but even if I stop to see him, I should be up there before seven or eight. Although it's probably snowing like crazy where he is."

"Okay, just drive carefully. Take your time. I'll be here when you get here."

Stopping to see Shawn. Of course. He's probably nervous. Why didn't I think of that before? Alex's birth father lived on the west side of Michigan, and Alex would drive right through his town to get to me.

Five years earlier, after his stint in the army and just shy of his twenty-second birthday, Alex had found Shawn. We had always told our two older boys, both adopted, that we would help them search for their birth parents as soon as they turned eighteen if they wanted to. Ultimately, Alex acted on his own and wrote a brief, neutral email to Shawn Field, announcing that he believed Shawn was his biological father and politely requesting contact. It was a classic, gutsy, Alex move. He prepared us for it, especially asking if Steven would be okay with Alex's finding this "other" father.

The encounter went improbably well. Shawn immediately said all the right things: "I've thought of you every day since I learned you were born"; "I never knew where you were or who adopted you"; "we'll take it at whatever pace works for you"; and especially, "Your parents must be amazing. You're such a great kid."

The images from the night Alex and Shawn traveled

across the state to Ann Arbor to introduce us to each other are burned into my mind's eye forever. Body types: check. Eye and hair color: check. Mannerisms, facial expressions, charm: check.

Steven had been brilliant. Warm, funny, easygoing, unthreatened. It had been an incredibly healing evening all the way around. Two fathers and a mom, all putting out the love for this complicated boy. It was the first time Alex had his biological and adoptive family together in one place.

Then came all the changes.

Alex got caught up in the young woman's disastrous problems. Shawn's own complicated web of divorce, another son, and a girlfriend got messy for Alex. They stayed in touch, but at this point I wasn't sure where their relationship was headed. I hoped their visit today, if there was one, would be good.

The phone startled me again. I grabbed it, thinking Alex had forgotten to tell me something, but instead, I heard an older man's voice.

"Hey Abbie, it's Charles."

"Hey Charlie, how are you?"

Charles Aiken and his son James had started Manitou Brewing Company nearly ten years earlier. Now they successfully produced craft beer. If all went well, I would be working with them to create my hard apple cider.

And if Alex would consider it, and if he could find the PA job that he liked, he might be the trusted technical advisor to help me move this project forward. There were many "ifs," and Charlie was one of them.

"You coming down tomorrow?" he asked. "James can't be here, but you come on anyway."

"Absolutely! Alex is on his way and I hope he'll come with me. You tell James he'll miss a good lemon meringue pie."

Charlie's chuckle was deep and warm.

"Is there a cider tasting possibility?" I ventured. Manitou's first test batch was in the barrel.

"Mmmm, not likely, but we'll see."

"Okay, I'm figuring about two. Does that work?"

"Yep."

"Thanks, Charlie."

I sighed as I hung up. Tomorrow would be an interesting day.

I walked across the kitchen and into the small office facing the front of the property. This had been the original bedroom in the core structure of what, with additions, had become a sprawling farmhouse. I moved to the window of the tiny room and sat on the wrought iron bed that had likely been in the same spot for most of the house's existence. My hand traveled absently over the quilt as I looked down the long field that bordered the quarter-mile driveway, all the way down to the brick gateposts at the entrance from the road.

A subtle movement caught my eye. It wasn't one of the area's ubiquitous deer. I squinted into the darkening mist. A slender figure, hunched slightly against the drizzle, walked slowly back and forth at the posts, stopping occasionally to look up the length of the driveway. It looked to be a young woman—a girl, even—and if she was one of my scarce year-round neighbors, I didn't recognize her. Tourists were rare at this time of year. She looked as if she couldn't decide whether to come up to the house or not. *What now? I should hop in the truck and see if she needs help.*

The oven buzzer sounded and I returned to the kitchen to baste the brisket. When I got back to the window, the girl had retreated down the road.

Weird. I guess I don't need to chase her.

Chapter 2

I sometimes wonder if parenting isn't like what a famous novelist once said about writers—that they are anti-therapists who figure out the characters in a book and then give them damage, so they do whatever it is they need to do. Perhaps parents engage in a similar and dangerous creative process with their children, only in a less intentional, more convoluted way.

Alex and I were sliding down M-22 in my Ford Flex, trying to stay on the curving road along the west coast of the peninsula. Spare beauty filled the bleak and frosty landscape, a beauty that made me love to be here when others my age were basking in Arizona sunlight. The unseasonable rain of the previous two days had given way to a sudden freeze and windswept blue sky as high pressure dipped down from the north. Even through my Maui Jims, the ice sparkled on bare tree branches as the cold pulled all the moisture from the air, candy-coating every tree and shrub with a million prisms.

I knew better than to wax poetic with Alex. It was enough that he sat by my side, his knee bobbing incessantly, releasing the rest of his body to relax. He stared at the mesmerizing rows of orchard, occasionally interrupted by a snug farmhouse up a hill or down a snaking road from the two-lane. Maybe it would have been better to take the route through Suttons Bay, where the most activity on the peninsula happened, but I loved this stretch of road.

"How'd the visit with Shawn go?" I ventured. I'd not asked the previous evening when Alex arrived, not wishing to pounce on this other world of his the minute he showed up.

"He's okay." Alex's voice was unguarded, and I waited for him to continue. "He and his girlfriend are heading out to California to see her daughter. I guess there's a new grand-child. She will stay out there for a while, but Shawn's coming back after a few days. Looks like his business is finally picking up some."

"That's cool. Did you see Rob?" I kept my voice entirely casual. Rob was Alex's half brother, the son Shawn had raised. Rob was ten years younger than Alex, and the process of their getting to know each other had been tentative on both sides.

"Nope, he's at school and couldn't get away on short notice. Shawn seemed disappointed, but we're in touch with each other when we want to be."

I waited for Alex to say more, but he was finished.

I had spoken to him over dinner about the pressing, storage, and fermentation process I had in mind for the cidery and how helpful I thought he could be with his extraordinary skills at organizing spaces and maximizing efficiency. Now I wanted him to know more about Charles Aiken.

"So this guy Charlie—I think he'll still be Mr. Aiken to you at this point—he knows all about the history of hard cider. It's kind of interesting, actually. I want to go see this museum he's been to in England. It's in Hereford. You know that's where I used to live, that year I spent in England."

"Mm-hmm."

"He's had his apples planted for four years now, and what I'm proposing, like I told you last night, is that they'll do the growing, I'll get into the pressing and fermenting part of the business, and they'll do the bottling and distribution from their operation downstate. You remember, they have a beer brewery there."

"Why would you truck the cider downstate when there's so much wine bottling and distribution up here?" Even at twenty-seven, Alex could sometimes talk to me like a long-suffering teenager. It was the tone.

"Because they already have the business down there. Maybe one day they'll decide to bring it all up here. I don't think we're there yet."

"We? Sounds like you're already in it for sure. I mean, you re-roofed the shed, you're talking like it's already part your business. What does Dad think of all this?"

"He's nervous. You know he thought I was nuts when I first started talking about it, but he's gone over parts of a business plan with me and asked me good, hard questions, and I promised not to tie up any of our family money beyond what we decided I could put in from my inheritance so there won't be pressure on him to support the business."

"Oh, so your inheritance doesn't count as family money?"

"Excuse me?"

"No, I think I have the right to ask! I'm trying to understand if Dad really supports this or if you just bypassed him by using the money from Grandma and Grandpa. It seems an awful lot like you've just imagined this whole business the way you want it to be, and you're forcing everyone and everything around you to fit your little fantasy."

My God, when is this son of mine going to blunt the razor edge of his inquiries? Why does he need to flay every deed to expose a perverse intent?

"So you obviously need to talk to Dad directly if you really want to know what he thinks," I said. "The inheritance is money we didn't ever count on, and so wasn't part of our planning for our future. I don't think Dad would have made the choice to put it into this property, but he didn't strenuously object to it either. The land itself is a good investment."

My hands tightened on the wheel. "And yes, it's been a dream of mine, Alex, and people should fulfill their dreams if they can do so responsibly." I didn't mean to get preachy with him, but goading gets me there quickly.

Alex wasn't quite done. "So are you just going to live up here all the time without him? Is this some kind of separation or something?"

"Alex!" I shot a look at him before turning back to the road. His steady gaze appeared more provocative than disturbed. "Seriously? No! I'm traveling back and forth a good bit, with a preference for being up here, and Dad comes up too. He loves it here also, he's just not ready to move here permanently. He's just started scaling back his practice, but he's not retiring yet."

I slowed the Flex as we entered the town of Leland, sleepy on a winter afternoon, Christmas decorations draped lazily on the tree planters. I pulled over in front of a small shop and turned to fully face Alex.

"This is a time of exploration for us—a next chapter. This cider thing is something I really want to try—"

"Why?" Alex interrupted. "What's the big deal with cider? And it doesn't sound like 'us,' it sounds like only *you* exploring."

I dropped my hands from their grip on the steering wheel and stared at them in my lap. Leave it to Alex to worry a sore spot. I knew what I had to say about the business was true to my core. I hoped what I had to say about Steven and me wasn't only "fitting my little fantasy," as Alex had just suggested.

I turned toward him again. "You know I've always been into gardening and growing fruit. Ever since I lived in England and learned to love hard cider, I've been fascinated with its making. I promised myself I'd find a way to make the farmhouse and the land pay for itself. And I love living in Northport. I don't think I need to explain that to you after all these years of spending time here. I feel like I have another big life project in me, and creating a business out of these deep interests seems to pull it all together."

Alex was still listening, so I continued.

"Dad is anxious about my getting into something that's, from his point of view, so out of my wheel house. I recognize that starting this business is somewhat risky, as any new business would be, but I am being careful, and I'm doing my homework. And I'm enjoying everything I'm learning." I sighed. "Sometimes in a marriage, you have to let the other person stretch, and this is definitely a stretch for us, but I would not do this if I thought it would damage our family. How all the arrangements work out is definitely a work in progress, and you know Dad and I are both pretty independent."

Alex's knee began to bob up and down again, signaling that I'd said more than enough. "All right," he said.

Reflexively, I searched the window of the shop across the sidewalk. New sweaters, but nothing for spring yet. Fine with me. I wasn't done with winter by a long shot. I needed some more time to think, to deliberate on what lay ahead.

I pulled the Flex out onto the road and quickly left the town behind.

Global warming aside, the Leelanau Peninsula was far enough north in Michigan that mother nature, the locals, and the tourists seemed to share an understanding that spring, summer, and fall were short, brilliant, and demanding, requiring energy and speed and a frantic level of growth and activity. I met and enjoyed that challenge when the time came, but for me, winter's reward included long stretches of time for contemplation, and quieter activities of hand and mind. Even now, as we crossed the bridge over the Leland River and left the little town, part of me longed to be back in my sewing room, arranging yellow flannel triangles on a background of stylized clouds. I visualized the half-made sailboat quilt for a niece's baby.

Deciding to lighten the conversation, I told Alex, "You know, thirty years ago, on our first trip together, Dad and I stayed at the inn where Charlie Aiken lives now."

We were passing the road that bisected the peninsula; it was time to slow down and start looking for the Blue Heron Inn. The old white farmhouse appeared around a bend in the road and we turned into the dirt driveway. The Flex picked its four wheels over the crunch of ice and stones and came to a rest at the side of the inn.

I didn't open the door right away; instead, I continued my story. "It was an October weekend, at the height of fall color. We'd spent a night farther south at a resort just north of Sleeping Bear Dunes and had a spectacular hike on the dunes and in the forest, with one magnificent view of Lake Michigan after another. We drove up the coast to Leland, where I'd sailed into the harbor before but never explored by land. We found this inn and stayed here."

The Blue Heron had been cozy and our hosts friendly, though Steven and I had eyes for little more than each other at that point. We began that weekend as lovers and ended it engaged to be married. Now, a complicated lifetime later, I was greeting the inn again, possibly to enter another life project originating from this ramshackle but lovely old structure.

Alex swung his tall, strong body out of the Flex and surveyed the property. I saw in his eyes an appreciation of the neatly stacked woodpile between the house and the outbuildings and a critique of the outbuildings, solid but worn-looking. I led the way to the back of the inn and the staircase to the kitchen. Charlie had instructed me that only inn guests used the veranda entrance at the front facing the road.

Charlie's daughter Melissa answered my knock with the tired smile of a woman with more to do than time allowed, but with a light in her pale blue eyes that signaled satisfaction in the challenges she faced.

"Hey Mel. This is my son Alex. We're here to talk cider with your dad. Is he around?"

"Hi, Melissa Aiken." Mel stuck her hand out to Alex as she leaned into the door to let us in. "Dad's in the orchard checking on the ice. You can head out there if you want, or wait here and have a cup of coffee. He won't be long."

I looked at Alex. "I left the pie in the car. I'll go out and get it. You want to take a quick look at the trees?"

Alex gave me the 'You're not leaving me here with a stranger' look and said casually, "Sure."

We stepped back into the icy afternoon and I led the way around the back of the inn, our boots crunching toward the five acres of cider apples Charlie and James had put in. We ducked between well-trimmed trees with strong central leaders and horizontal branching at two-foot intervals. I loved the vigor and order of an orchard, with mesmerizing rows marching across the landscape. I noted that the ice that had coated roadside branches farther up the peninsula hadn't settled on this protected grove of trees.

Charles Aiken smiled as he strode up a path toward us. A handsome man of medium height, he was blessed with a full head of sandy hair streaked with gray. Trim and clean-shaven, dressed in upscale gentleman farmer style, he sported solid jeans, thick wool socks turned over leather boots, a good parka, and an Irish wool bucket hat.

"Hi, Charlie! Out checking the children for frostbite?" The shouted question died in the crackle of approaching boots and Alex's silent scrutiny.

"I sure didn't bring them this far to lose them to ice, I hope." Charlie stuck his hand out, much as his daughter had done. "Charles Aiken."

"Alex Stone. I'm pleased to meet you." Alex grasped Charlie's hand. Alex was always good at handshakes and eye contact, a skill that belied his innate shyness and basic premise that most people were fools that he wouldn't suffer gladly.

I stepped back, quashing my usual urge to jump into the connection, facilitate commonality, and smooth transitions. I had a new mantra: *Let things happen the way they're supposed to.* They would ultimately anyway.

"So these are the cider apple trees?" Alex asked.

"Yep. Don't know if your mom told you or not, but we ordered these five years ago from a nursery in Virginia that's been working on apple varieties going all the way back to colonial times. Some of the trees here are likely descendants of trees Thomas Jefferson cultivated at Monticello. We've got some russets, some Paula Reds, and Macouns. The first years are all about cultivating and pruning to establish a good fruiting tree. We got a decent crop this fall and are betting on an even better one next year. C'mon and have a look at the old pressing equipment we've salvaged."

Everyone turned and headed back around the inn to the ad hoc cider house, the first of several outbuildings to our right. They strode together like manly men about the business of finding or fending off common ground and mining the entropy that would tell them whether they might work together. I tripped along behind the two of them, thinking, *Men! These two either will or won't get along, but in either case, it'll be interesting to watch.*

Charles slid the door to the small barn open and we stepped into the sweet dank warmth and the powerful smells of a packed earth floor, crushed apples, and hay. I couldn't help myself: I broke into a delighted smile and tucked my hands into my jacket pockets. I'd arrived at the next step in a grand adventure.

Chapter 3

The late-afternoon sun ignited an orange and blue light show on the sand along the lakeshore as I drove the three miles into Northport.

I'd succumbed to the guilty pleasure of a single pork chop for lunch, compromising my otherwise pork-free life—in deference to Steven's kosher background, I never bought it when cooking for him—and had just settled, with a glass of pinot noir, into our well-worn Norwegian recliner for some last moments of peace and quiet when I noted the flashing light on the answering machine.

There were three voicemails. The first two were solicitations but the third message revealed a soft, unfamiliar voice.

Hi Mrs. Stone, This is Julia Reiss at Dolls and More. The sock yarn you ordered is in. You can come in and pick it up . . . or I could bring it out on my way home one day . . .

Her voice dropped off to a lengthy pause. Then she left the store's number, as well as her cell number. The message ended. Puzzled, I settled back into my chair. Who was Julia Reiss?

On the face of it, this was just an ordinary message, but I thought I knew all the people who helped the owner of the local knit shop. And the message seemed to go beyond simple customer service. I sipped my wine and wondered about her offer. I resolved to pick up the yarn at the store on my way down to Ann Arbor this afternoon—they'd be open for at least another hour.

I drained my wine, grabbed what I needed for the week in Ann Arbor, and headed toward town.

My first purchases were a newspaper and a few groceries that I knew Steven wouldn't have stocked. Next, I stopped for a mail pickup at the old house that still held sway as the town's post office. I moved on to the neighboring library, where I stopped to chat and return DVDs I'd borrowed. Down Nagonaba, the main street with the unpronounceable name, I stopped at the hardware store where Joseph, the ancient sales clerk, knew every piece of merchandise and had a ready answer or explanation suited to my skill level for any problem I posed. Today he helped me troubleshoot a dripping sink faucet. Next, I stopped into my favorite bookstore, a classic old shop with beautiful wooden shelves, a wide and quirky selection of used books reflecting the whims of the philosopher proprietress, and interesting new releases. I'd ordered a mystery written by a local author for Steven's birthday.

Finally, I grabbed a steaming cup of coffee at the North Country Cafe, tucked back in the rehabbed corner retail space that anchored the town. Danielle, the owner, caught me up on recent events, asked about my trip downstate, and prepared my hazelnut cappuccino. As she steamed the milk, I began my informational fishing expedition.

"Well, I guess I better get over and pick up my new yarn. I cooked up a project for the Guild Bazaar. I've also made some darling little baby dresses for all my friends who are having granddaughters. Not that I'll ever get one . . ."

Danielle, also the mother of three boys, hadn't improved the gender balance with her two grandsons. "You can always dream." She laughed.

"I promise I'll make you two when you hit the jackpot, Dani . . . pink and purple! By the way, what do you know about the new girl working for Sally? How'd she land here?" My question was direct, but that was how Danielle rolled.

"Don't know, exactly. She just showed up here looking for a job a couple of weeks ago. She never found me, but she went to Dolls and More and a couple of other places in town." Danielle paused long enough to fill and slide a coffee cup across the counter and retrieve the dollar bills from someone behind me before I even realized he'd come in.

"Sally says she's from somewhere in Ohio. No one seems to know why she wants to be up here, especially in the winter. But apparently she can really knit and sew. Sally says she'll be a godsend when it gets busy at the store. She's staying somewhere out by you, I guess."

"Interesting. Thanks, Dani," I said before heading for the door, cappuccino in hand.

The sun was making a brave appearance for a February afternoon. Shining through the hazy sky, its hint of heat gave the lie to the dullness of the landscape. The quiet inwardness of winter that suited me so well would eventually give way to the hubbub of summer. I'd be drawn to the outdoors and physical work in my garden and orchard. The desertion of residents during winter would yield once more to traffic and crowding. For now, though, I could stand in the street with my face turned upward for a daily fix of vitamin D without attracting the slightest notice. Thus fortified, I crossed over to Dolls and More.

From my first moment of entry through the door with its burnished brass handset, it was clear to me that this small shop featured much of what I loved best about small-town fiber art shops. The front section contained bins of yarn on one side and bolts of fabric on the other, the center crammed with racks of pattern books, doll-making tools, needles, hooks, and other crafting paraphernalia.

I walked through the shop front to the wide door at the back and down three steps into the studio, where Sally, the energetic owner, held classes and where more fabric and yarns were displayed. I'd spent many a pleasant hour taking specialty classes with Sally and other members of Northport's vibrant local fiber arts community.

"Sal?" I called. Evidence of her machine embroidery business lay scattered over the counter at the register, and the display of antique and homemade dolls and supplies she sold to would-be doll makers graced the opposite counter. Since Sally had opened the store nearly fifteen years earlier, the scope of her retail endeavors had expanded.

"Sally?" I called again.

From the storage room at the other end of the studio, a young woman's long, dark curls appeared in the doorframe. Her cerulean blue eyes met mine immediately. "Sally's coming in later. It's just me right now. Hi, I'm Julia. Julia Reiss. I just started working here."

Julia Reiss was arrestingly beautiful. I thought she must be in her mid twenties. Taller than I, and very slender, she was also very shapely. Her dark hair framed an oval face with creamy skin.

"Hi Julia, I'm Abbie Rose Stone." Julia's gaze became pensive. "Thanks for your phone call. I thought I'd just stop in to pick up my yarn."

"Sure. I'll get it for you. It's in here." Julia stepped back down into the stockroom. I stayed in the studio to have a look at what had gone on since I'd been there last.

Set on the corner of the table closest to the window facing Mill Street lay a nearly completed child's sweater still on its fine needles. I recognized the pattern immediately, having knit a nearly identical one myself. Colorful toys, numbers, and figures danced across a navy background. The work was fine and even. I reached for the needles and instinctively checked the reverse side of the work, the true test of a knitter's skills. All the connections between different colored yarns were expertly woven and the transitions were smooth and tidy.

Julie Reiss's voice spoke hesitantly behind me: "I've got your yarn."

"Is this yours?" I asked, surprised at the mild embarrassment I felt. The culture at Dolls and More was one of continual sharing and support, yet I didn't know how far into that artistic fold Julia had been drawn and here I stood, inspecting her work.

"Yeah, Sally asked me to make it as a sample. We've got the Debbie Bliss book with the pattern and all the right yarns." Julia was quietly matter-of-fact.

"I love this sweater. You've done a beautiful job." I hoped I sounded as genuinely admiring as I felt.

"Thanks. I want to do the rosebud teddy and the ducks and boats sweater. I like the projects in this book."

"Me too. Looks like you've been knitting for a long time. Where did you learn?" While the question gave me a natural way to begin satisfying my curiosity about the girl in front of me, it was one I could rarely resist posing to any other knitter or quilter. I found a woman's path to working with her hands endlessly interesting, as well as an informative key to the nature of her muse.

Julia thought for a moment. She seemed neither skittish nor impulsive. "I actually learned first from my great-grandmother. My mom was pretty young when she had me and she didn't marry my dad until later. She and my grandma both worked, so I spent a lot of time with my great-grandma. She did cross-stitch tablecloths and crocheted lace, and she knit whole suits for herself out of silk yarn. When my grandmother retired, she started working in a knit store in Ohio. She still does. My mom knits too. I started doing spool knitting when I was four and then learned to crochet and knit. I guess I've always liked making things."

"That's quite a pedigree. I can see why you'd like working here." It was on the tip of my tongue to go on to ask Julia why she'd come to Northport, but I wanted both of us to stay in the comfort of artistic sharing for a while longer. "One of my grandmothers was also a master knitter, but we weren't that close so I had to learn a lot more on my own," I volunteered. "My other grandmother did beautiful cross-stitch."

Julia looked down at her sweater, lying on the table between us. "Do you have a daughter that you've taught?" Her deep blue eyes turned back up to mine.

My sigh escaped before I could hold it in. I didn't typically discuss how I mourned a daughterless existence, or the deprivation of female intimacy that was grounded in my Prussian Germanic mother and the age span between my younger sisters and me. *Such intimate questions* . . .

"Nope, three boys. I do have a daughter-in-law, and she's a talented knitter, but they aren't nearby and she's really busy, so we don't get much fiber art time together." To my own surprise, I kept right on talking. "We almost adopted a baby girl once, but it was so close to the time my youngest boy was born, and the other two were still small, and the birth mother of the little girl changed her mind anyway, so it didn't work out." *Why am I blabbing like this?* "So I spent a lot of my parenting time building with Legos, coaching soccer, and going to rowing regattas, basketball, and water polo games. My husband still occasionally threatens to go and find three little girls to adopt."

I said this last part lightly, with an eye roll, but Julia, who'd been listening intently, seemed to think seriously about my comments, and a stricken look passed over her lovely features.

"So you adopted kids," she said quietly. "My brother is adopted."

Her brother, but apparently not her. "Two of my three boys are adopted," I said.

Now we'd each exposed our private lives, so I changed the subject, hoping to move away from whatever had disturbed Julia, and ask what I'd been curious about.

"What made you decide to come here to Northport? Especially in the winter? And you offered to bring my yarn out to me, which is very nice. Do you live north of town?"

Before Julia could answer, her cell phone rang on the table next to where we stood.

"Sorry," she said quickly, "but I have to check this."

"No problem, I'll just browse," I said, giving the girl points for not assuming I'd be okay with the disruption. I moved back to the children's sweater sample I'd admired previously and fingered yarns in nearby bins while Julia carried on a brief, urgent-sounding conversation. She listened more than spoke for a short while, then raised her voice slightly and said into the phone, "Mom, I have to go."

"Sorry," she said again when she came to stand next to me. She could have used the interruption to ignore my questions, but instead spoke quickly and intensely. "I'm giving myself some distance from my family right now, and it's been hard for my mom." Something changed in her posture as she handed me my yarn. She straightened her shoulders, stood tall. "In fact, that's kind of why I came to live here. I have some family issues to sort out, and I thought this would be a good place to do it. The Leytons, out on Sugarbush Road, needed someone to house sit for the winter, and Sally wanted some extra help here, so it all worked out."

I saw a fierceness in Julia's expression, but also felt myself retreat from an inclination to sympathize or ask for any more information. As a parent, I'd struggled with well-meaning advisors questioning my decisions and giving unasked-for advice to my children. I had no desire to step into that role with another family.

"Family issues can be tough to sort out," is all I said.

Julia glanced around the store. Another customer had come in. Turning back to me, she asked in a bright voice, "You have kids who rowed? I'm a rower. I rowed in high school and college, and I'm actually running a rowing camp in Ohio this summer, so I'll be gone for a couple of weeks."

Her tall, slender figure and broad shoulders made for a great rowing body—no surprise there. But most people who moved up to Northport were retirees or, less often, young families. Twenty-something singles with no apparent ties to the area rarely chose this small town. "Oh," I said, "so you're thinking of staying in Northport for a while?"

"Let me know if you need anything," Julia called to other customer. Then she looked at me with an odd expression. "Yeah, I guess I am thinking of staying around for a while." She pointed to my yarn. "What are you planning for this?"

"I'm looking to make the baby shoes and the rabbit from that Debbie Bliss book, actually. I'm doing them for the Fiber Arts Guild show." I watched her mentally flip through the pattern book and arrive at the sweet photo of rabbit booties and a knitted animal with a blue vest and pink undersides on his floppy ears.

"That'll be adorable," she said. "You'll have to come in and show us when you finish."

Julia might be very good for Sally's business. She knows how to engage a customer. "Oh, I'm sure I'll be in long before I'm done. I'm kind of a regular here," I said, with more assertiveness than I'd intended.

"Then I guess I'll see you again soon." She smiled.

"Yeah, that'll be nice. If you want to ring me up, I'll head out."

I followed Julia to the register at the front of the store, where she efficiently completed my purchase.

I settled into the Flex for the long ride to Ann Arbor. Julia Reiss had given me a lot to think about. It intrigued me that she lived at the Leytons'. On my way into town, I'd stopped at a stand of stag-horn sumac to gather branches of the crimson dried fruit; it always looked lovely on a table or sideboard. Near there, through the shrubs and the sleeping apple orchard, the home of Stan and Gina Leyton rose on a hill.

They had moved to the area fifteen years earlier. Gina had nearly single-handedly revived the artistic community at this remote end of the peninsula, spearheading the construction of a shared school and community theater for which she directed plays. The Leytons had also created a Celtic maze in the field next to their house that drew tourists and new age devotees alike. Gina had convinced locals to come to yoga and Pilates classes who had never tried either, and, recently, introduced and marketed edible serviceberries to the fruit-raising culture of the area.

I wondered how Julia had found them, or they her. I wondered about the mother at the other end of the phone conversation at the knit shop. *A girl of many questions.*

Chapter 4

Satellite radio and audio books rescued me from the travel hell of switching from radio station to radio station as I drove down the center of the state to Ann Arbor. Even so, the in-depth news programs I normally loved on public radio sounded foreign and even a little obsessive after a stint of living off the media grid in Northport.

The drive from door to door took, at minimum, four hours and forty-five minutes. Today the roads were clear and I had time to think of what lay ahead: Steven's birthday, and the organizing touch I was sure the house in Ann Arbor needed after weeks of his living there alone.

Winter twilight descended on the highway as I traveled south, the wrecked centers of mid-state cities shielded from scrutiny by those of us on the highway with other places to come from and go to. The snow began just south of Flint, a steady, dry, mesmerizing dance of flakes striking the windshield like sparklers from the gathering dusk. I loved snow, even when driving in it became a challenge. I loved being wrapped in the cocoon of white silence, and the softening of hard edges. I loved it even when, as now, one could have thoughts of winter aconites—harbingers of spring—poking their yellow blossoms through the snow.

The quiet midweek evening in downtown Ann Arbor still boasted after-work diners filling the Main Street restaurants and students, bundled head to toe, on their way across campus to libraries or bars after the day's classes. I had chosen to brave the elements and isolation at the farmhouse in Northport, but my rootedness in Ann Arbor was more complicated. I had attended college, married, made my adult life, conducted my career, and raised my children in this university town. Friends, community, family—it had all happened here. But so had an earlier failed marriage, problems with our children, and fallout from lives turning out differently from what we'd hoped and dreamed.

I recognized that my sense of "home" was in transition, but as I turned into the familiar driveway on the quiet street in the middle of town, I experienced a small surge of comfort in the face of our English cottage-style house. A copper beech towered in front and hemlocks shielded the property from the north wind. Steven and I had rehabbed this house when we first bought it and then rebuilt it after it burned, a phoenix rising into our lives and then sheltering us these last twenty years.

I often wondered how my children, all of whom lived elsewhere, thought about coming home. Seth still had an intact bedroom of his own here, and friends he liked to see when he was in town. Andrew and his wife, Carrie, visited, but home for them had become where they lived now, on the other side of Michigan. And Alex? Alex avoided coming to Ann Arbor like the plague.

I wondered if the house itself played into Alex's discomfort. He alone had been old enough to understand the loss of our home to an arsonist, and had been forced to contend with his own fear, and the fear and horror of the other children and adults around him, all as a six-year-old. Then he'd had a rocky adolescence, with the defiance and boundary violations that had forced us to send him away to school. Even after coming home to finish high school, he'd found life in this university town too rarified, liberal, and intense.

The insistent ring of my cell phone cut short my reverie. Steven's law firm number flashed as I answered.

"Abbie, hi," Steven said. "Where are you?"

"Just pulling into the driveway. How're you doing?"

"It's been really busy. I'm just going into a last meeting, and then I should be able to leave. How was the drive?"

"Good. The snow didn't start until after Flint, so I got here ahead of any problem, but the roads might be getting bad now."

"Okay, well, I have to go. I'll see you in about forty-five minutes."

"Good. See you soon, bye."

How many hundreds of times had we had this exact conversation? When the kids were little and I believed he'd get home in the forty-five minutes he promised, I'd kept the dinner warm and the children entertained during the disastrous time in late afternoon when they were cranky, tired, and hungry. I'd done so out of a belief that the family dinner was important. Then an hour, sometimes two, would go by, and I would give up; I'd feed, bathe, and put the children to sleep myself, leaving a lone place setting at the table and the detritus of dinner on the stove. No June Cleaver happy to see her hubby on those days.

The arguments were useless. *Why couldn't you call? Who did you stop and talk to in the hall while we were all waiting for you?* Steven had a big job and had always devoted himself to it. Everything else he had in him, he'd devoted to our family. We'd argued only about the proportions.

Now it didn't matter anymore. I'd see what was in the refrigerator, add in what I'd shopped for in Northport, and pull something together whenever Steven got home.

I opened the garage door and squeezed out of the car and into the house. I still couldn't help but listen for the dog tags clinking against each other and the click, click, click of claws on wooden floors when I opened the door. The ghost of our dog, Mickey, still informed the silence of the dark kitchen.

After setting my computer, backpack, and knitting bag inside the doorway, I walked into the kitchen, a space that opened into a great room and the rest of the main floor. Several days' worth of the *Wall Street Journal* and *New York Times* littered the kitchen table, and more were stacked along the counter near the door. I automatically started to straighten up, but stopped myself.

Don't, Abbie. Just don't . . . Instead, I moved to the refrigerator and, finding an old bottle of sparkling water, opened it where I stood and took a long draw, the cold effervescence bursting in my throat and into my chest. My eyes swept over the elevated counter behind the sink and into the great room. Looking up, I could see snow through the clerestory window. The counter held loose piles of mail, the hardy succulents I'd left to be tended here, and an ovoid art glass piece Steven had given me years earlier. In the least bit of light, it shone as if from within, and it did so now, the mysterious light a small beacon. I smiled and turned back to the refrigerator to find some dinner.

I woke from a dream of sailing on a south wind among the smooth rocks of the Benjamin Islands in Lake Huron's North Channel. I have an intimate relationship with the south wind, as I do with the rhythmic wash of waves on the sand heard through a lakeside window at night and the shadow of pine boughs on the forest floor in moonlight. These are secret sensibilities that ground me.

No south wind today, at least not that a person could feel wrapped in the heat of this buttoned-up house on a late winter day. I'd lived so much of my life with hopeful and dogged energy in this solid home with its many intricate spaces. Now I longed for the simplicity of water, wind, and sand. I craved cleaner lines, less clutter, an obvious metaphor for my wish to uncomplicate my life.

In this moment, the temple of the familiar felt languid and simple enough and I nestled into the quilts, the memory of making love with Steven after our time apart bringing a smile to my waking. I allowed the myriad tasks of the day ahead to float above the bed, at bay for now.

The ringing telephone brought these thoughts to an abrupt halt, as phones still did for me. Unlike my children, I felt obliged to answer phones, or at least attend to the intrusion. I reached into the shelf of the nightstand from which the multi-line intercom and phone system, now a dinosaur, still served our home.

"Hello?"

"Hi." The pause lasted longer than normal, and because of that I knew it was Andrew. No "Hi Mom," or "Hey Mom, it's Andrew." Just, "Hi."

"Hey Andrew." I paused. Under his rules, I now had the responsibility of leading the conversation. He never called without an express reason. So, I could maneuver the conversation to find out what he wanted, or mark time with news sharing until he was ready. I had long ago learned to ask for information I needed and wait for the rest. That Steven's birthday happened to be today complicated this ritual dance, but since I hadn't yet texted reminders to my sons, I questioned whether this could be a birthday call.

"How's Carrie?" I asked. My daughter-in-law had just begun her first placement as a nurse anesthetist graduate student.

"She's good. She's still working nights and I'm on all days right now, so we don't see much of each other. We both have next weekend off, so we should be able to have some fun."

"How did you get to be on all days?" Andrew's prior sheriff assignments had involved mostly night shifts.

"My promotion came through and they needed a marine officer."

"Already? Wow, that's great."

"Yeah, I guess. A couple of the new guys are kind of idiots."

"Well, that's what they're paying you the big bucks for, sweetie. Did your pay go up?"

"A couple of hundred dollars. It helps."

"That's wonderful, Andrew. Congratulations!" Pause. "Has Carrie been able to scrub into surgeries yet?"

"Yeah, I think so."

"Did she like it?"

"I guess."

I'd asked enough now, I could tell. I curbed my desire to say, *"What do you mean, you guess? Haven't you asked her?"* Whatever they did in the way of communicating with each other appeared to work very well.

Carrie was a woman with plans. She'd been a floor nurse in a large hospital while Andrew finished his Coast Guard enlistment, and now that they'd returned to Michigan, she'd begun an advanced degree in anesthesia. So far, her plans had proceeded as scheduled, and I was proud of and impressed with her accomplishments.

"Is Dad home? I need to ask him something."

Involuntarily, my heart sank. Not a birthday call. "I think he's down in his office."

"We're starting to think about what's going to happen when Carrie's done here. It's still seven months, but she thinks it's time to start looking for jobs for her, and if Dad has some contacts, people might pay attention faster."

"Good idea to get a head start on that. Is she looking in Ann Arbor? Does she want one of the big hospitals? Here, I'll let you talk to Dad about it so you don't have to repeat yourself."

"Oh, and Mom, I know you think I forgot, but we want to say happy birthday to him too."

Will miracles never cease? "Busted. You know your mother . . . Hang on." I transferred the call to Steven and swung my feet out of bed, an energy of hopefulness inspiring me to dress for a bundled run through the neighborhood to the arboretum. The Huron River would be dressed in winter white and black water ripples.

I never tired of this run. Through snow-covered plantings of spring-flowering shrubs, through a glen of rhododendron, azalea, and mountain laurel, the path wound its way for a whole mile down to the river. There it left the riverbank and wound into a broad field, maintained as prairie by the University School of Natural Resources. A controlled burn in the fall had left areas of stubble where wild grasses had grown, but now the whole of the landscape was softened by the copious snowfall of the past week. It sparkled with myriad snowflakes taking bows in the morning sunlight.

I settled into a slow, steady jog, grateful that all I had to think about and plan for today were final logistics for tonight's surprise birthday dinner for Steven. I'd invited a few friends to join us at a local restaurant. Steven hated attention drawn to him but loved socializing in an intimate setting, and I knew he'd enjoy himself tonight.

I came to a stand of aging pines, thick, solid trunks soaring to their needled crowns. So often in the past, I'd had to struggle with a heavy heart and overwhelming challenges on runs to this arboretum. When we'd had to send Alex away to school, I'd stumbled down the hill to this spot and wrapped my arms around a tree in the center of the grove, forehead against bark, beating heart to living wood, the connection producing sparks on the screen of my closed eyelids, and just cried. Bark prints forged on my forehead, I had shuddered through a final sob, willed a draft of energy from the lovely pines, and turned back to kick into uphill mode. That is how I got through those dark days: parceling out the energy to make it all the way, praying for the Zen to take over.

No matter that my pace had become slower now and my joints no longer contained well-oiled springs. I headed up the long hill to home, enjoying how the familiar strain called forth a rhythm, two short inhalations followed by a long exhale.

Halfway up, cell phone vibration rescued me from the out-of-breath climb and I slowed to a walk, letting the rings continue until I'd recovered enough to speak. I smiled as the screen flashed "Owen Moses."

Owen had hired me as an editor during graduate school, and we counted each other as lifelong friends of the soul mate variety. Different in background and living in different parts of the country for nearly all of our thirty-year friendship, the many streams of our connection ran deep: music, sailing, artisanship, complicated relationships, raising boys, northern homes that were heart centers, a fascination with words, and a wry belief in common decency. Fortuitously, Owen also had a friend with years of experience in the apple growing and processing business. I put the phone to my ear.

"Owen. Long time no talk to."

"Abbie Rose, where have I caught you?"

"I'm actually huffing and puffing my way up the big hill in the Arb in Ann Arbor. Where are you?"

"I'm in Annapolis. I tried you in Northport, where you'll find a message, so I thought I'd try your cell phone. I didn't know you were downstate. How's the cider research going?"

"I came down for Steven's birthday and I'm actually working on the trip to New Hampshire. Looks like it won't happen until the fall—that way I can go for a pressing, which is what I want to see most. Did you talk to your friend Sam?"

"Well, happy birthday to Steven. I did talk to Sam. I will email you both by way of introduction, and you can take it from there. He said he'd be happy to talk to you and even host you if you venture out east."

"You are the best. Thank you so much."

"Any plans to come out this way for some sailing? I'm about to put *Synergy* in the water."

"That sounds enticing. You may get two for the price of one. Steven is insisting that he wants to do more sailing this summer. I'm sorry to admit I'd rather watch the apples grow." I hadn't intended the wry complaint in my voice to sound so peevish.

"Sailing with Steven would be just wonderful. In fact, you can send him out here and stay back to meditate in the orchard." This is why I loved Owen. "Is Steven actually backing down on work?"

"He actually is. I'll pass along the invite."

By the time I'd caught up on Owen's life, I'd walked to the top of the arboretum and trotted the two blocks to home. *Another summer on its way. Time to gear up.*

Chapter 5

One who injures another is liable for five things—
damage, pain, healing, loss of time and disgrace.

—Mishnah

I'm sorry, I'm sorry, I'm sorry, I'm sorry, I'm sorry. I recited
the words over and over running on hard-packed sand, my
body tilting toward the water as I headed up the beach to the
point—like if I was sorry enough I might magically sail onto
the gentle waves and the pain in my joints, along with the
pain in my heart, would lift in the breeze.

My talk with Steven this morning about Alex hadn't gone
well. *Did I know it wouldn't? Did I sabotage it?* After four nice
days together in Ann Arbor, were we back to that old place of
fighting our way to a mutually acceptable decision on something important, having nicked another piece off the corpus
of our relationship as collateral damage? *Just run, Abbie.*

If only Mickey were here to distract me. Our Brittany span-
iel had died with grace at the age of fourteen a year ago, the
dog of all our hearts, but especially mine. Not a day went by

that I didn't miss her. In summer, she would bark at my heels until I found some piece of driftwood to throw into the water, the farther the better. For a field dog she was a remarkable swimmer, and had scared us more than once with the distance she was willing to swim to chase after a seagull or herd Steven or me back to shore from a long-distance swim. On a wintery day along the lake like this one, she'd be just off the edge of the beach in the dune grass.

Thinking of Mickey now brought sorrow front and center into my *"I'm sorry"* chant. Losing her had been true sorrow, and put to shame my current angry sarcasm.

I was truly only sorry that I hadn't been clever or controlled enough to keep the conversation with Steven this morning from becoming an argument, but even so, as with most of the arguments we'd had, important information had still passed between us that would reemerge in the future— with any luck, toned down and more reasoned.

It had begun well. I told him I'd spoken to Alex and that as a result of Alex's visit to Shawn in January, Shawn planned to travel to Iowa to see Alex in the spring.

"Good for him," Steven said. "It's healthy for Alex to maintain that relationship." He went on to talk about maintenance chores on the Ann Arbor house, and when he might next come north. We threaded our way through these exchanges with the familiarity of long-married people.

The basic business concluded, I broached the topic that Alex and I had spent more time talking about earlier that morning: " You know when Alex visited up here in January, he and I went down to see Manitou Brewing, but we didn't get to talk much about how he might get involved in the cider business. I wanted to hear his thoughts about my plans, so we had a good conversation about it today."

I rushed on, "I asked him what he really thought about a move back to Michigan. He said he knows he has a good job and a decent place to live in Iowa, and he's made some acquaintances, so he's not in a huge hurry to leave. And as you have been quick to point out to him, it doesn't make a lot of sense for him to come back here to join a business that's not even a business yet. He's checked out PA opportunities in Traverse City, and he'll wait to see what I'm going to get involved in."

Steven remained silent so I continued, "I told him that sounded about right to me. I reinforced to him that I'd love to tap into his organizational and mechanical skills and get his thoughts about any other part of the business, but I'm not asking him to consider running it, or being involved at all, if it doesn't interest him."

The continued pause on the other end of the phone told me that either Steven was reading email or he was choosing his words before responding.

"Alex needs to concentrate on figuring out what the best next move for *him* is," Steven began. "Are you sure you ought to be distracting him with all of this?"

"All of this" in Steven code meant my business proposition that didn't interest him, and that he apparently thought shouldn't interest our children, either. Still, I worked to stay measured and calm.

"Steven, I don't really look at this as a distraction but as an option for Alex, if he wants to be involved. He's not all that happy in Iowa on his own: there's no connection to family or friends or a relationship! You know he loves Northport and the whole area. How is he going to know if coming back here interests him if he doesn't explore it? He's just looking. It's not like he has to make a commitment to helping me with this business, and it's not as if he would give up being a PA." I censored my next thought, though it burned in my chest as an ember of anger that didn't bode well for the rest of our conversation: *At least he's looking at my business before rejecting the idea.*

In twenty-five years of marriage, I'd made and acted upon a major decision knowing that Steven was either outright against the idea or not solidly on board with it only

three times. One time was the day I'd torn up the enroll-
ment deposit in front of the parochial school we'd decided
to send Alex to, knowing that I wanted my children to go to
public schools. Another time, I'd decided to bid on the original ramshackle beach house on Lake Michigan, which I did
without Steven ever having seen it. He'd ended up agreeing to
purchase it, and now shared my view that the years we spent
in that funky little place had ended up being precious to our
family even beyond our expectations.

The most painful disagreement, however, had occurred
when all our fertility treatments hadn't worked and adoption
became more lengthy and problematic than we'd thought.
Steven had suggested hiring a woman to be a surrogate for
us—someone who could produce a child for us using Steven's
sperm through artificial insemination. Surrogacy would give
Steven a biological child, which he wanted. Much as I wanted
to make a baby with him, if that couldn't happen, a surrogate
arrangement would give us the possibility of a child with
Steven's deep brown eyes and dark, curly hair. The vision
pulled at my heartstrings. I thought I wanted to do this—for
him, and for us.

So Steven found a willing woman and arranged an
artificial insemination. That attempt didn't work, however—
making it another devastation to our torturous attempts to
overcome my infertility. Afterward, I realized that I couldn't
cope with having a child through a surrogate—the payments,
along with the intentionality of producing a child and then
taking it away from its natural mother, didn't sit well with
me. I told Steven I didn't want him to try again and he reluctantly agreed, though he argued strenuously that thousands
of people had had children through sperm donation and a
woman donating her egg and womb was no different. I just
couldn't get there.

Each time we'd come to a precipice of major disagreement in our lives together, we'd pulled back from rupture. I
worried we might be approaching another such crossroads.

Steven did not want to commit to a life and a business in Northport, and I did not want to wait any longer to give it a try. I wanted to pursue this business. I had bought this property, had sold three of its five lakefront lots to reduce taxes and restore the equity I would need to invest in a hard apple cider business. I had studied and researched and felt prepared to join forces with people who would help me get my project off the ground—possibly the Aikens, possibly Alex.

Steven was ready with his response, interrupting my reverie. "If you're trying to bring him back to Michigan, why up there, where it will be hard to find a relationship, let alone a PA job in orthopedics? Whose needs are you talking about here?"

"Alex is not a child, Steven. He isn't going to do this if it doesn't make sense for him. He's not interested in a life in Ann Arbor. I'm exploring whether he wants to be helpful on the business and organizational side of my project, but *he's* exploring making a desirable life move for himself."

"You aren't being a parent! Why are you pulling him toward something that isn't good for him?"

I lost my temper. "Did you just hear anything I said? You know, I think this conversation isn't going anywhere. I'll talk to you later." The ice in my voice matched the shards I felt in the pit of my stomach. I clicked the End button and banged the phone into the charger.

Moments later I let the phone ring through to the answering machine, knowing it would be an irate message from Steven. "Did you hang up on me? Don't call back unless you apologize!" I already had my hands in the potato chip bag.

I'm sorry, I'm sorry, I'm sorry . . . As if the cosmic punisher heard my thoughts, on my next long stride over the glistening sand, my shoe slid out from under me and I fell hard on a veneer of ice, wrenching my knee and losing my breath as my back hit the ground. I lay there for a long moment, the surge of pain further robbing me of breath. *I won't be able to move.*

I'll freeze to death before anyone finds me. The chill of the frozen beach found its way through my running jacket as I gasped for air. I cursed again the absence of cell phone coverage on this whole tip of the peninsula. Pain and fear forced out tears of anger and frustration that had been locked in my throat all morning. I sat up and worked to slowly bend the twisted knee. I could move; it didn't feel like anything was broken. Still, it took several minutes before the pain subsided enough for me to try standing.

The beach ended in a spit of rocks, displayed magnificently on this brilliant Sunday, all tumbled by the forces of wind, water, and sand. Above, bleached golden tufts of dune grass bent in graceful arcs from mounds of snow frozen onto the dune. I stopped to rest and dry my eyes. With a last look at the lake, lapping gently at the treacherous beach, I turned and scaled the dune past the log cabin standing sentry on Cathead Point. I'd rented the cabin out for most of the summer, but on some autumn nights, I'd come to sleep at this tip of solid land, listening to the rush of water on the windward side of the point and the lap of the waves as they rounded down on the other side into the bay to the east. The original bent-wood furniture and hand-drawn map framed in birch bark still graced the ample main room. Tiny bedrooms perched atop the steep oak staircase. Even though it was closed and boarded for the winter, I could feel the thrill of its long history—a history I now felt was mine. *I belong here now! I'm part of the place, and it's part of me.*

I limped through the final quarter of a mile to the farmhouse, down the center of the point on a flat, sandy road. Even in the March cold, the scent of pine and cedar greeted me as footfall after footfall crunched through the light snow. Alex might be at work and unavailable, but I'd try to Skype him with our lousy internet. He could at least look at my knee and tell me what I needed to do.

I determined not to bring my struggle with Steven into our conversation. Alex's precise radar for parental discord and his unerring sense of how to turn it back on us had trained me well to keep marital disagreement out of the conversation with all my children.

I rounded the bend of the road as it wound into the clearing where the house presided over acres of orchard and open fields. Clinging to the railing, I mounted the stairs of the back porch. Shedding shoes, hat, anorak, and fleece, I opened the door to the kitchen and welcomed the burn on my cheeks as they met the blast of warmth from the tile wood stove. I grabbed my laptop from the table, hobbled to the freezer for an icepack, and headed for the couch.

I was in luck; I reached Alex right away. He was perched on a kitchen stool in athletic shorts and a T-shirt, cold be damned. He leaned comfortably on the wide countertop, his large hands cradling a huge coffee mug.

I tried to keep my voice from quavering. "Hey Toot. The temperature took a nice drop here overnight. It's a little icy out there—and I just took a colossal spill at the beach. Would you take a look at my knee?" I leaned back and tilted the laptop to display my already-swollen knee.

Alex straightened. "Tell me how you fell." He bent toward the screen. When I didn't answer right away he looked up again, and I described the fall. He instructed me to palpate and move my knee in different directions, and then asked me to lie down flat.

"Can you bend it?" he asked.

I winced when I tried, but was able to bring my leg to a reasonable angle before the pain stopped me.

"I think you're in luck. I'm guessing it's just a sprain—but of course without feeling it myself, I can't be sure. It's unlikely that anything major tore. Lucky for you, I happen to have left a knee brace in the sports closet up there. It's probably on the big side, but it'll work for today. We'll see how it feels tomorrow and decide if you need x-rays or not.

You should definitely take some ibuprofen and ice it for a while. And prop your leg on some cushions. You're going to take it easy on that knee today, but every hour you need to move around a little."

"Okay, well can I at least get cleaned up? Can I take a bath?"

"Ice first."

Alex finished giving me instructions, then promised to check in later.

"Thanks so much, sweetie." He'd just saved me a forty-minute drive to the nearest ER.

After icing my knee as instructed, I filled the tub for a bath, though I knew it was too early to treat my knee to heat. As I settled into the warmth, I could still feel cold in the sting of my thighs. I stretched my lower spine in the soothing water.

Why do I want to go into business with Alex? Why not Andrew or Seth? I'd actually hoped that Andrew and Carrie would move up to Northport and join me some day. For now, Carrie had to finish graduate school and find work as a nurse anesthetist. If the business worked, Andrew might want to be a part of it eventually, but for now, after all his years of Coast Guard duty elsewhere, Carrie wanted to live downstate near her family, and there were many law enforcement options for Andrew where they were.

And Seth, who worked for an energy start-up firm in Chicago, loved to visit but found Traverse City too sleepy. He would go back to school to achieve his goal of striking start-up gold in the burgeoning energy field.

Alex was the only one potentially ready and available to help me with this cider project. But *was* he ready? Steven's objections weighed heavily on me as I slid underwater for a last soak.

Chapter 6

Two consecutive days of brilliant sunshine is a gift any time during a Michigan winter, but it is a special treasure for the fruit grower when it comes late in the season. Charlie Aiken had pruners in hand when I pulled into the orchard. Sunlight glinted off crusted snow on the two-track as I headed toward him from the Flex, which I left at the top of the road. I could not make my way delicately over the surface in my bulky boots, and amusement played in Charlie's eyes as he watched my feet crunch and lift each step of the way, as if I were walking on chewing gum.

"Every move a picture, huh Charlie," I called, trying not to sound breathless on top of it all. I didn't mind providing the morning's entertainment, since Charlie would provide the professional development. Winter into early spring is pruning and training time in the northern orchard. The five hundred four-year-old trees surrounding us were in the prime stage to establish a strong central leader trunk and three or four fundamental branches extending horizontally in different directions. This structure would maximize fruit bearing for the next twenty or thirty years. Charlie and I were going to prune and train—my first hands-on contribution to our prospective joint business venture.

Yarlington Mill, Dabinet, Kingston Black, Golden russet, Brown Snout, Galarina, and Medaille. The varietal names rolled off my mental tongue like old English sonnets. Charlie had eighty of each type, and I was interested to see if I could detect any differences at all in the young trees. The distinguishing characteristics I had learned to note between types of fruits—bark color and texture, placement of blossom cluster buds, suckering tendencies—I had yet to learn within apple varieties.

Charlie led the way to the top of a gentle rise at the east end of the five-acre orchard. "The height over here and the long day of exposure to western sun puts these trees at least a week ahead of the ones at the other end," he said, "so we'll start here."

I followed him, grinning to myself. I'd already figured out that the eastern side of the orchard would bloom first, and that these trees would also be most at risk for blossom freeze damage.

How would this work between Charlie and me? I had found myself in Abbie-the-warrior mode on the ride down this morning, with an unsettled stomach and quickened pulse, sensing that today would be a test. My skills as a pruner, and the development of a working relationship with Charlie, were on the line.

I decided to choose my tree first and see whether Charlie would join me to observe or comment, or work on his own. These were, after all, his trees, and the investment to date, both financial and in sweat equity, had been entirely his. If I were he, I would be watching my every move—from a respectful distance. And that's exactly what he did.

I stood back and studied the healthy young apple tree before me. The central leader and the three strong side branches were all there. I saw no dead wood to trim out. I noted new side branches, one of which stretched up from the trunk at almost a thirty-degree angle, and several straight vertical suckers that had to come out. I'd sharpened my pruners and lopper early this morning, and they hung, along with a small tree saw, from my tool belt. Though I'd never had my own orchard, I'd always had tree fruit in my home garden, and in my training as a Master Gardener, I'd learned the basics of fruit tree pruning. When I'd bought the farmhouse, I'd begun to work on the four ancient apple trees that remained from an old orchard that had once existed on the property.

The suckers and upright branches were the first to go, to maintain an open, airy shape that would increase the tree's disease and pest resistance. Next, the upper limbs had to be trimmed shorter than the ones below; the idea was to end up with a shape like a Christmas tree. I searched along for spots with well-shaped blossom cluster buds and trimmed immediately beyond them. I stepped back to judge my progress, and felt Charlie doing the same.

My last task was to cut out or place a spreader between the trunk and the new thirty-degree branch. The new shoot occupied a functional place in the overall shape of the tree; I decided to keep it. I turned back to Charlie, and without a word, he reached into his tool cart and handed me a forked plastic branch spreader, which I wedged between the trunk and limb while Charlie tied the center of the branch to stakes that he pounded into the frozen ground. When we were done, I looked at him as he surveyed the tree. He gave a clear nod, and we moved on. *If only children and husbands could be pruned to grow the way you want them to this easily . . .*

The morning flew as we worked, and despite the cold temperatures, we soon shed our heavy outer shells and wore only down vests. By noon, I was thoroughly hungry.

"How about some lunch?" I asked. "I made some sandwiches, if you're interested." I looked up at Charlie and could see he was tired too. We'd done a good bit of hard labor.

"Sounds great," he said. "Let's go in and I'll make you something hot to drink. Maybe even scare up a beer."

"Come on, Charles, winter is when you check out the competition and do some tasting," I said with a chuckle. "Haven't you got some cider to try?"

With Melissa at work and her kids in school, we were alone in the kitchen. The gorgeous Scandinavian masonry stove throwing heat at us from the far side of the room was what had inspired me to put one in my own kitchen. Charlie stoked it with a new log, and I went to work on the stacked turkey sandwich I'd made for myself. Charlie broke out a very dry cider from a maker on the west side of the state, and also poured us each a steaming cup of his special cleansing tea, before sitting and devouring the eggplant and feta I'd fixed for him. The cider he sipped at, but didn't really drink.

Charlie's stringent diet, begun after a cancer diagnosis ten years ago, involved a complex system of fasts and teas, as well as a lengthy list of allowed, required, and forbidden foods. He looked more a sophisticated, urban business type (which he had been for most of his adult life) than a holistic medicine advocate, but no one would argue with the success of the regimen. After being given only months to live, he had survived beyond the ten-year mark.

I liked the cleansing tea with its combination of herb, flower, and pepper flavors. I also figured that given my cozy relationship with the scotch bottle, some cleansing would work just fine for me too.

"I met with Lance Kupfer about renovating my small barn into a cider shed. I've already done the roof, and he'll have an estimate on the rest to me soon," I told Charlie.

He nodded.

"Then I'm heading downstate," I said. "Oh, and I've booked an October trip to New Hampshire to see how they're making cider out there."

Charlie looked up from his tea and smiled. "Well, good. Let me know if you need any contacts. Made that same trip myself about ten years ago now. Who you going to see?"

"I've arranged to meet David Waters and tour Framinghill Ciders. If I'm going to get into pressing and cider making, I want to scout out the best there is."

"Are you sure you want to get into the pressing?" Charlie's gaze turned penetrating. "You can mix and store and age the juice without getting into that whole mess."

"I know." Charlie's gentle challenge pricked the sore spot made by Steven's doubts and my own. "I'm not really sure, but I want to understand what would be involved. This other guy I'm in touch with in New Hampshire knows Waters pretty well. It's just research, Charlie. If it doesn't work for the whole operation, I won't do it, believe me." I knew we were feeling our way along this idea of joining forces, and the morning had gone well. We'd made it to another level of connection, and I wanted Charlie to trust me.

We finished lunch, and soon I was steering the Flex onto M-22 toward home. The winter day remained beautiful; wishing to share it, I dialed Seth's phone number while I still had a signal. To my surprise, he picked up immediately.

"Hey sweetie, I thought you'd be at work and I would leave a message."

"Hi Momma, yeah, I'm on my way back from a meeting, so I can talk for a few minutes." He sounded as though he was walking, and I imagined him on the streets of Chicago, tall and slim, his shearling coat and the wool scarf I'd knitted him keeping him warm in the windy freeze. "I actually planned to call you tonight," he said. "I have a friend here whose apartment got destroyed last night in a house fire. They're okay, but they're obviously freaked out and kind of don't know where to start. Didn't you put together a kit or something for people with fires? Do I remember that right?"

"Oh god, I'm so sorry. Yeah, I did, actually. Who is it?"

"I don't know if you remember Ashley—she's a friend from Northwestern. I think we took her out once with a big group for dinner. It's her and her boyfriend's apartment."

"Okay, so what I have might be a bit dated, but I'll

absolutely send it to you. I can't believe you remember that I've done this before."

"Mom, really?"

"Okay, right." But it was true. Our fire had happened when Seth was nine weeks old. He didn't remember sleeping in a dresser drawer for the first days until we replaced his bassinet and crib. He hadn't seen the file system and the nine-month procedure to inventory our possessions and file an insurance claim.

If he'd sensed the devastation the fire wrought on our physical and emotional lives, it had happened so early in his own experience that he'd hardly known anything different. Andrew, at three, and Alex, at nearly six, were a different story. They knew the trauma of lost possessions, the sight of the burned-out wreckage of their home, and the contrast of stressed parents having to cope with it all with how their lives had been pre-fire.

"I'll send a checklist and the suggestions for labels for file folders. Do you think they'll want digital files or physical ones?"

"These two might want the physical ones. Thanks, Momma."

"Absolutely. I'll send them to you tomorrow. And you? Everything going okay there? We're having a stellar winter afternoon here, and I just wanted to share."

"Yeah, work is going great, I'm playing some decent basketball. Life is good."

"Okay, well, I'm about to lose you—I'm in that hole between Leland and Northport. Love you, sweetie."

"Love you, Mom."

I drove through Northport and made my way toward the farmhouse, urging the Flex up the small hill from which I could see all the way to the stone pillars at the foot of our driveway. I noted movement in the middle distance. I let the car coast a few hundred feet, then pulled to one side. I recognized the dark curls peeking below the stocking hat of the girl walking up the road toward me. She hesitated.

What is Julia Reiss doing pacing in front of my driveway? Is she the person I saw here two months ago?

I returned the car to the road and drove slowly toward her. Julia stopped as I neared her and stood to the driver's side of the car. I rolled down the window.

"Hi, Julia."

"Hi, Mrs. Stone." She stood uncertainly, keeping a ten-foot distance between us.

"What're you doing out this way?" I asked. "We don't see many people walking on the road in the winter."

"Just walking." Her mittened hand brushed the tip of her nose.

"I guess we are practically neighbors."

Her silence gave me the feeling she wanted to say something more, but she didn't.

"Well, enjoy your walk." I waited a moment longer, then said good-bye and drove through the stone pillars onto the long driveway. *Should I have invited her in for a hot drink?* That would have been the neighborly thing to do, but I was tired and didn't really want to entertain. Also, Julia Reiss gave me an odd feeling. But I'd think about that another time. All I wanted now was a hot bath and a glass of wine.

Chapter 7

Spring arrived in the lurching, messy, but energizing manner of changing seasons in northern Michigan, and then abruptly turned into summer. Gardening, entertaining, and travel competed for my attention with plans for the hard cider business. Steven came to Northport for several weeks and filled the house with friends and family. The social contact gave him much pleasure, and he did his share of the work. Though I enjoyed connecting in vacation mode with those close to us, the amount of attention and constant face time with other people it required wore down my patience and goodwill. I used a regimen of running, swimming, and biking, along with a supply of scotch, to keep myself centered.

Whenever I could, I haunted Charlie Aiken's orchard—first in May, when the young trees burst into blossom, their sweet scent drawing bees to pollinate, and then as fruit set and the schedule of spraying and fertilizing marched into June and July. I helped out frequently, especially on the day after a vicious thunderstorm damaged orchards in a swath across the whole peninsula. The youth of the trees and our solid spring pruning kept the damage to a minimum, but Charles, James, and I spent a whole day trimming and clearing.

In late July, Steven and I took a break from northern Michigan for a five-day sail in the Chesapeake Bay with Owen Moses. True to his promise, Owen treated Steven to his first sailing outside the Great Lakes, teaching him the finer points of ocean navigating on the Chesapeake and accounting for tides. We sailed, talked, laughed, and drank. As a bonus, Seth joined us for two of the days on the back end of a business trip to DC. Our youngest son had a knack for fitting into any social environment. Steven had someone to talk sports with, and Seth caught us up with his company's progress in marketing solar energy. His genial comfort and ease with Owen, their common interest in the energy field, and Seth's willingness to share in the heavy lifting of sails and anchors made him the perfect addition to our crew. As reluctant as I'd been to make the time for sailing, the magic of wind, sun, and water, intensified by the pleasure of time spent with dear ones, made for a great vacation.

On his last evening, Seth and I relaxed on the foredeck of the stately thirty-six-foot sailboat, with Steven comfortably behind us at the helm and Owen smoking an after-dinner cigar on the rear settee of the cockpit. We sailed into the perfect evening, a ten-knot, steady breeze cooling the summer dusk. Seth handed me an icy beer, and after taking a long draw on his own, he said, "Dad says you're getting more involved in the hard cider business. What's happening with that? And is Alex really going to join in?"

The setting sun shone orange on our faces as we headed back toward the marina. "I'm learning as much as I can about the whole process right now," I said. "I've connected with a grower near Leland who's planted a whole orchard of heritage cider apples, and I'm looking into the pressing and fermenting process to do as a business—at least to start."

"But why cider? I mean, I know you like growing things and you said when you bought the farmhouse property you were looking at doing some kind of farm business. But why this one?"

I gazed at my tall, bronzed son, foot braced against the teak toe rail, his torso and curly head profiled against the wind-filled sail. He'd been gone from home for six years, and I realized now that he'd only ever heard periodic summaries of what occupied my life. What had Steven already said? Had he complained? Seth's question seemed free of criticism or objection. It sounded as if he simply wanted to know. I gathered my thoughts to explain to this mostly sympathetic son of mine.

"It started when I lived in England when I was just about your age." It startled me to realize I'd been exactly Seth's age when I spent a year on a teacher exchange program in London, coping with a marriage in the throes of rupturing—a marriage about which my children knew almost nothing. *Don't make this too long, Abbie.* "I spent practically every weekend traveling around Great Britain, and that's when I got my introduction to hard cider. There were as many cider makers in England as there are craft breweries now in the US, and I fell in love with it. Cider has a long and interesting history in this country, too. When water supplies weren't safe for drinking, cider became the go-to beverage. In colonial times, it sometimes substituted for currency and was used for barter. You know, the whole story of Johnny Appleseed is based in truth. There's this great book called *The Botany of Desire* that describes how—"

"Okay, I get it," Seth said. "You're into apple cider. But last time I checked, you didn't know how to work with a spreadsheet. Now you're talking about starting a business?"

I drew in a breath off the lovely breeze. "You have been talking to Dad! I know he thinks I don't know anything about running a business, and it's true I've never run one myself. But I worked in Grandpa's business for many summers, and shy of being absolutely cutthroat, I actually think I have the head for it." Maybe Seth could handle hearing his mother go deep. I would at least try to explain. "I'm looking forward to putting my energy into learning the skills I need to make a business that will fulfill a dream I've had for a long time. I know it'll be hard, but I'm committed to at least thoroughly exploring the possibilities, and this is a time in my life where I have some more freedom. That's why I want to pursue this project."

Seth looked at me for a long moment before smiling. "When you get into it, I can help with the nitty-gritty of the business plan."

I pulled my sunglasses down my nose, holding Seth's eyes with my own. His expression was sincere, though a hint of amusement flickered in his deep brown eyes.

"Thanks, sweetie. I'll keep that in mind."

"What about Alex?" Seth asked. "Is he really thinking about this move?"

"Let's just say I've asked him to be a technical advisor as I figure out if and how I want to establish a pressing and fermenting operation. You know he's really good at analyzing and organizing systems and anything mechanical. That's what I'm looking at right now. But Alex is in Iowa, and he has to decide if he wants to stay there or go somewhere else. Joining my business would only be a small part of a decision to come back to Michigan, and I think he'd only do it in conjunction with a PA job. I'd call it a distant possibility right now, but it is a possibility. Has he talked to you about it?"

"Not really. He mentioned he'd visited over the winter, and Dad mentioned it also, so I just wondered what you had in mind."

"I'm really looking forward to this trip in the fall to New Hampshire. I'll see some different operations that are well established and make really good cider. I'm hoping to have a better sense of what I want to do once I've seen all that."

Seth reached his nearly empty beer bottle toward me. "To Momma's new adventure," he toasted.

We clinked bottles and I settled back with a smile to enjoy the last of the evening sail.

The four summer weeks Steven had taken off work required him to put in intense hours at his firm in September and October, so once more, I found myself alone in the farmhouse after Labor Day. As the autumn progressed, the colors in northern Michigan turned neon yellow and orange, set off by the remaining green. As the time approached for my cider research trip east, I once again frequented Charlie Aiken's orchard, just entering its full bearing years. The trees had fared well during this growing season, adding height, significant branching, and stouter trunks.

Closer to my own house, I visited Kilcherman Orchard and got a look at their harvesting operation. Their mature, varied apple trees were a model of growing apples for cider production done right. Now I felt prepared to learn more firsthand about that production process.

Before I left, I prepared the farmhouse and gardens for winter, shutting down hose bibs and the outdoor shower, clearing the gardens of spent plants, pulling in porch furniture and kayaks, and switching out rakes for snow shovels in the garden shed. I even made sure the snow plow attachment fit properly on the lawn tractor.

Change-of-season chores always left me with a mixed feeling of accomplishment and poignancy, relinquishing the beauty and drama just past and anticipating what would soon come. When I left in a week's time, Northport would still be in the full glory of autumn, but when I came back in the second week of November, I could easily return to a blinding snowstorm.

My final errand took me to Dolls and More, for a purchase of sock yarn. Knitting socks works well on airplanes. Julia Reiss did not appear as I chatted with Sally. I'd seen little of Julia over the summer, as the Leytons had returned to their home, Julia had been gone to teach the rowing camp, and I hadn't frequented the knit shop much during the busy outdoor season.

I fingered the lovely lavender yarn I'd decided to purchase and looked over the flyer on the counter in front of me, which listed classes the shop would offer in the months to come. Julia was listed as the instructor for two of the knitting classes.

"I see Julia is staying on," I said to Sally.

"Yep, she's been a great asset here. The Leytons are heading back to Arizona after Thanksgiving, and she'll be house sitting there again. Having her teach knitting has allowed me to expand into more doll making, and the classes are filling nicely."

"That's great," I said, and pried no further. I was curious about Julia but more eager to complete my tasks, so I paid for the yarn and left.

Chapter 8

The prayer I'd learned to say every night before going to sleep as a child, about the oneness of God and all beings, floated into my mind, along with gratitude that I could be pressed into the window seat of a small jet at take-off. To this very day, taking off in an airplane signaled, to me, a momentary suspension between the end of exhausting preparation and extrication from the complexities of my life and the beginning of an adventure.

I'd had a childhood full of air travel in small single-engine planes, piloted by my parents and a family friend. During those years I'd gained a visceral sense of the mechanical insecurities of aircraft and the physical alarm systems offered by the human body to remind us that flight is not what we were designed to do. The prayer had always seemed to me like a perfect acknowledgment of my transitional state on every level. I tuned into oneness.

I settled back in my seat, ready to embrace this late-autumn trip to New Hampshire. I had hopes of recovering some sense of the self-determined life I wished for, which had vanished over the course of a hectic spring and summer.

"How are you liking *Seasons of Fire and Ice?*" The deep voice penetrated the roar of the jet engines and my early attempts at mind-clearing meditation, another favorite airplane trick. I opened my eyes and looked at the man seated two seats over. He was good-looking, and as relaxed as a tall person can be in the undignified confines of a coach seat on a small jet. His eyes met mine and then glanced at the book in my lap.

"Quite a bit, actually. Have you read it?"

"I wrote it. Donald Lystra." He offered his hand across the seat.

"You've got to be kidding!" I felt a whoosh of excitement, synchronous with the ascending airplane. I had thought a lot about how children survive less-than-ideal circumstances, and I'd been deeply moved by the book. "You portray so well this kid trying to navigate with parents who love him but don't really act in his best interest," I said, leaning toward him. "The fact that he finds his way despite them is comforting."

My comment suddenly sounded too intimate, too revelatory of my chronic worry that despite our hard work and best intentions, Steven and I might have failed our children, particularly Alex, by not giving him all the tools he needed to thrive as an adult. I quickly changed the subject. "Where are you going? Are you giving a book talk?"

"Nope. I have a reunion. What about you?"

"I'm going to see apple orchards and hard cider making. Business trip."

"Are you making cider in Michigan?"

I hesitated only a moment, and then said, "Yes, I am." I felt bold.

Donald Lystra and I parted company at the car rental desk in Boston. I was pleased to have handed him one of my sassy new business cards, though all it depicted was my contact information and a stylized image of an apple. It was a nice start to my first business trip.

Driving out of Boston, my least favorite city to navigate by car, I wended my way over the black ribbons of road into the countryside beyond Medford and toward New Hampshire. The autumn had been warm, and though the cider-pressing season was well underway, the apple harvest was predicted to extend far into November.

Blue sky radiated behind the shiny black of leafless trees on this brilliant day. I wanted to stop the car and tramp through the woods to a clearing, perhaps disturbed by resting deer during the night, or possibly, in another season, pristine with a new snowfall. Always, the image of high times in my twenties revisited me on beautiful days such as this one. In winter, we would ski into the woods, lean our poles into our buttocks, and turn our faces to the sun until they burned. Then we'd fall to our stomachs, chins resting on mittened hands, and look for snowflakes stacked across the surface before us, each a prism of light, scissor-cut by God into patterns that undulated in fantastic three-dimensional structures across the clearing. If we got cold, we simply got up and skied away into a rhythm that restored blood to every vital part of our young, strong bodies.

The memory of the bliss, the heady promise of those days, triggered a pang of loss and sorrow at the confusion and heartbreak that came out of that time. Distance and altered state had rendered so much of what happened then unreliable in my memory, but I remembered the snow.

The white stuff had not yet made an appearance in this part of New England, however, and I was grateful. My destination, a bed-and-breakfast in Antrim, lay near the center of New Hampshire. Staying there would put me an easy day's drive from the orchards and cider mills I wanted to visit. I'd been invited to a cider pressing that would have several luminaries of the hard cider renaissance in attendance.

I'd done my reading. Bob Walker's *Hard Cider Handbook* was still the bedrock bible of the field, and my contact with Rick Loudon of Loudon Hill Orchards had led me to Michael

Pollan's *The Botany of Desire* and its wonderful section on the apple. Finally, I had plowed through a winemaking tutorial, so I had some vocabulary and knew a little bit about the chemistry of fermentation. I loved that I'd learned so much history, science, and even philosophy on the road to mastering hard cider production.

The alchemy was what I really wanted to learn, and that I would try to do at the knee of David Waters, consummate cider maker at Orphan Lane Orchards in Lebanon, New Hampshire.

Antrim shared with other towns in the area a mixture of well-preserved, centuries-old brick buildings and ramshackle cobbled structures of indeterminate age and construction. The farms surrounding the town had faded barns rooted into the earth with fieldstone foundations. Though not lush, the landscapes looked productive and well tended. Upcountry Inn turned out to be a rambling brick house set high off a road outside the town. It overlooked a horse pasture and was backed up onto a steep hill.

Any misapprehension I had about my host being a native farmer quickly disappeared when Vincent, a transplanted New Yorker with iPhone in hand and laptop close by, greeted me. He and his wife were business consultants, and I guessed immediately that converting part of the house into a B&B paid the taxes.

"Welcome," he said. "I'll show you to your room and then perhaps make some suggestions of places to see in the area, if you like." He led the way from the large, modern sitting room into a smaller one filled with antiques and then up a narrow staircase to the second floor and a succession of small bedrooms. Each room contained a Victorian iron or brass bedstead, beautiful handmade quilts, a small writing desk, and a dresser. I took the smallest room, because it looked out over the back of the property onto the hills and forest above. Victor pointed out the bathroom and left me to settle into my base of operations for the next two days.

My appointment to see a cider pressing wasn't until the next morning, so I changed into workout clothes and descended to the kitchen to see what Vincent could suggest for a late-afternoon adventure. He was on the phone, so I wandered the common rooms and decided that this couple had a great gig going. They'd collected high quality antiques. A garden room of glass walls, which acted as both a greenhouse and a lounge area, opened off both sitting rooms. Out of the side windows, I saw a small orchard, and through an open door marked "private" a well-equipped, high-tech office—which, I assumed, was where Vincent and his wife ran their businesses. I shook my head. I still couldn't get Ethernet cable at the farmhouse in Northport.

"Is the room going to work for you?" Vincent asked, having quietly appeared at my side.

"Absolutely, thanks. I'd like to take you up on your offer to steer me to places of local interest. I have the rest of today free."

"Better yet, how about I take you on a little tour?" he suggested. "How are you on a bicycle?"

"A bike ride would be great, that's so nice of you."

An hour later, I'd heard much of Vincent's life story and experienced a strenuous hill ride along the banks of the Connecticut River. I had picked out Frank's Restaurant for a good home-cooked dinner and a beer, and Vincent had interviewed me regarding my breakfast choices for the next morning. As soon as he heard the purpose of my trip, I also got the offer to try his own hard cider, bottled the previous year and made from his homegrown apples, as well as instructions to hike up to the top of the hill behind the bed-and-breakfast to see a new orchard of hard cider apples that had been planted by a local landowner two years ago.

Pleased at this bonus, I felt a surge of confidence that my investment in this research mission would actually work to educate me in the way I'd hoped.

Breathless from the climb up the hill, I found the new mini orchard laid out in neat rows, the young saplings just beginning to branch. The Aikens' trees were giant by contrast. The steep hill provided a spectacular view over the town to the left and the valley meadows stretching into the distance to the right. A squeal of delight escaped me as I took in someone else's new foray into the fellowship of hard cider makers in this spectacular spot. I headed back down the hill. A perfect first day.

The cider mill in New Boston, New Hampshire looked like the classic image of an old New England mill. Set right next to the road, built into the side of a hill, its two-story, metal-roofed, aged gray timbers rose like a natural outcropping from the flinty soil. The sign fixed to its façade, CIDER MILL GALLERY, confirmed the new identity of the space.

Because health department codes had become so restrictive, commercial cider pressing was no longer an option for this two-hundred-year-old structure. Bob and Eileen, the mill owners, were transplanted New Yorkers who had bought and preserved the mill in the 1980s. They supported their habit with "real" jobs in the city and through consulting. Old-fashioned cider pressing, a life's dream for them, had led them to connect with the cider mavens in the area, many of whom were gathered on this warm October morning for a private pressing.

My host, Bob Walker, had welcomed my interest, given me some background, and extended the invitation to come. His email had been clear, however: he would be busy with an author whose book he was editing, and with the other friends and family members working for their share in the pressing. I got it. Look, ask questions, join in the work, but don't demand too much attention.

I parked my car and found the entrance at the side of the mill. After stepping inside, I took a moment to let my eyes adjust to the dark of the interior. Eight-foot tables bearing the contributions for a potluck lunch lined the only open space in the cavernous ground floor of the building. A gargantuan, belt-driven apple grinder and press, built of massive oak timbers and painted a cheery red, occupied two-thirds of the lofty space.

I'd seen a small modern press, which gleamed of stainless steel and efficiency and electronics, at Tandem Ciders in Michigan. I'd also seen the pieces of an old press in Charlie Aiken's barn. But I'd not seen an old-fashioned press in action since my childhood visits to a cider mill.

I located Bob Walker, whose solid, Flemish fairness complemented his air of brisk efficiency. He introduced a group of volunteers, all gazing up at a billowing canvas chute already feeding ground apples into the press's cloth-lined frame. The chute disappeared into the ceiling above. I located a staircase in the corner of the room and, climbing it, found myself in an airy gallery with lovely landscape paintings covering the walls. A sectioned-off area of the floor featured an ancient wooden hopper that sat atop a large grinder.

A tight group of workers, ranging from what looked to be a seven- or eight-year-old girl to a woman clearly in her eighties, bent over the hopper. At the center of the group, directing the activity of feeding apples into the grinder, stood a white-haired, white-bearded man in jeans and a work shirt sporting bright red suspenders.

Allen Swift. I was stunned. For years, I'd watched this man on his public television garden show, and now he patiently explained the virtues of the different apples stacked in bushels around the hopper to the small girl. I listened, transfixed by his presence, as he conducted my first real-time cider making training.

"We're starting here with the Baldwins, these bright red ones with the white stars," he began. "They've got good solid flesh and they'll guarantee some sweetness. Let's dump a couple of bushels of these in." Many hands helped the little girl's and the apples jumped in the hopper, where knives sliced and ground them, before they dropped through the chute below as pomace—apple mash.

"Next we want these Stayman Winesaps," Swift continued, warming to the audience. "They're the dull, greenish-red-looking ones over there. They're soft and yellow in the flesh, but they're tart and spicy tasting. They'll add a wine-like flavor to our cider." Strong arms lifted the heavy bushel to the edge of the hopper and soon the apples were being tossed into the grinder.

"Next we'll put in some Ribston Pippin. They're the yellow/orange ones right here. We need these for their rich, sweet aroma." The glint of the knives at the bottom of the hopper and the disappearing apples seemed to fascinate the girl much more than their flesh and flavor characteristics, but I hung onto Swift's every tutorial word. I grabbed at the next designated bushel to lend my hand to the effort.

"Does it much matter if you get all the balance of cider apples in at grinding time, or can you mix it up with the musts after grinding?" I asked as I heaved the last of the Pippins into the hopper. I suddenly wondered if my use of the word for extracted juice sounded pompous, but Swift didn't seem to mind; he paused and considered my question.

"I know people who do combine different juices after grinding, but I can't help but feel that there's some magic in the mixing right from the get-go. If you really want control of the taste or you're not sure of what you've got, you can mix single varietals."

I stood at his elbow and, as I lifted the next bushel from where he'd pointed it out, asked my next question: "Do you change up the type of apples each year?"

"That is part of the fun . . . every year we find different apples people are bringing back, or find substitutes for varieties we didn't like from last year, or just find ones we like better this year. Here, have a look." He pulled out a piece of lined, coffee-stained paper, smoothed it out onto a clipboard lying on a table by the doorway, and passed the clipboard to me. Then he was gone, back to directing apples into the maw of the grinder.

Varieties, read the title. A list of apple varieties and amounts in bushels identified the stacks of baskets and boxes crowded into the grinder loft. *Liberty, Gravenstein, July Red, Manning Miller, Kingston Black, Cortland, Chisel Jersey, Ashton Bitter, Yarlington Mills*—all were varieties I had read about in orchards going back to Thomas Jefferson's. Charlie Aiken and I had discussed nearly all of them. I was surprised to see two different varieties of pears listed on the paper. I filed a question on my mental list. Allen returned to my side with his pocketknife open and sliced a wedge of a small orange apple with juicy yellow flesh. I popped it in my mouth as a burst of aroma filled the air.

"Mmmm, Pippin," I guessed cautiously.

"Cox Orange Pippin, to be exact," he shot back, grinning, as he turned away again.

I silently thanked the Kilchermans and their orchard of antique apples, located down the road from the farmhouse in Northport. For years I'd stopped all through the fall and tried small boxes and bags of different apples, some so bitter it took hours to lose the sour memory from my tongue. I'd learned to ask, "Cooking or eating?" of the senior Kilchermans before purchasing, and to make sure the paper sacks were labeled. I'd now progressed to a point where I could taste-identify some varieties, but I had a long way to go.

The first load of pomace had filled the press frames below, so I returned to the first floor and watched as Bob Walker and three assistants raked the mash evenly around the cloth-lined, square frame. Four such frames, called a cheese, would be stacked for the next step—the pressing. I'd done my homework.

The massive hydraulic press switched on, and belts whirred above me around pulleys the size of semi tires. As the press began to do its work, juice poured through the slats of the frames and into the tray at the bottom, where it flowed to a low corner and down through a large plastic tube leading to a tank outside the lower doors of the mill. This fine old machine, in all its glory, did what it was meant to do, with knowledgeable stewards of the process ensuring that each step happened as it should.

I had joined into the work next to a petite woman named Ona, whose well-behaved thatch of grey-streaked hair, swept up in a pair of combs, framed her classically pretty face. It turned out that she owned the orchard above my B&B in Antrim. She described the pressing procedure going on in front of us in detail.

I learned that apples needed to stay above twenty-eight degrees, that Stayman Winesap and Castle apples are incredibly delicious, Porter is great for pie, and that Thomas Jefferson cultivated Esopus Spitzenburgs. Furthermore, as a cider maker, bleach is your friend; all parts of production and storage equipment have to be thoroughly cleaned, as bacteria can produce mold. Ona recommended three-gallon carboys rather than five- or eight-gallon glass jugs, as the latter were heavy and unwieldy. Camden tablets, she said, killed natural yeast so champagne yeast could be used to get controlled fermentation. I also learned that a fermentation lock lets gas out but no oxygen in so the cider won't "turn."

Three pressings later, with lunch and cleanup behind us, we were offered samples of the juice—not yet cider—from the tank. The cider makers brought their carboys to be filled with the spoils of the day. As I stood in the loose line waiting my turn, I watched the faces of those before me light up with pleasure. When my turn came, I took my first sip as Bob Walker smiled close by.

The cider's taste and aroma were like the visual effect of an Impressionist painting—bursting with light and colorful flavor and intensity. I'd never tasted anything this wonderful derived from an apple. It made me giddy. And this was just the beginning. Next the juice would be strained, and in twenty-four hours it would oxidize and cloud, dropping sediment to the bottom of the container. After that, the juice would be transferred to containers to drink or set up to ferment for hard cider.

"How'd you like your first cider pressing?" Walker asked.

"Pretty fascinating—and delicious," I replied, returning his smile. "If I squint my eyes a little, I can see this happening a couple of hundred years ago."

"With Allen, you don't have to squint much." Walker put his arm around Swift, who had joined us but still had an eye on the containers being filled, one by one, from the tank. "If you want to see the cider making process in its highest form, from apple to bottle, go see Orphan Lane Orchards and have a sit-down with David Waters," he continued. "He's a real master and has been in this business for a long time now. It's only about an hour and a half from here."

"It's on the docket for tomorrow, and I'm really looking forward to it," I said, pleased that my plan anticipated Walker's advice.

"What made you decide to get into this business?" he asked.

I'd been asked this question before, mostly by skeptical friends and family members, my husband not the least of them. But Bob Walker seemed more genuinely curious than skeptical, and had, after all, hosted me and sponsored this event, so I decided to tell him the simplest truth I knew.

"I fell in love with hard cider during a year I lived in England. Then I fell in love with a little piece of heaven on the Leelanau Peninsula in northern Michigan, where apples grow, and where a robust wine production and distribution network are already in place. I needed a business to support a real estate purchase and my desire to make a life in that area. And I'm looking to partner with someone who's already invested in a cider apple orchard. There you have it. Not an elegant business plan, but I'm hoping to wrap some pieces of my life into something that works with my dreams."

I had said more of my truth than I'd planned but felt a defiant pride in my response; I felt there had been a tacit permission to respond as if the question were more than perfunctory.

"You'll need a lot more than luck," Swift said, "but I wish you luck and I wish you well. The power of passion is formidable."

"That it is. I thank you both. It's been a real pleasure meeting you." With a last look around the mill, I took my leave and found my way back to Antrim for an evening of rest.

Chapter 9

It took only a single warning light to scare me out of my false sense of independence, born of complacency and the fantasy that I could manage everything on this trip by myself. Driving the back roads of New Hampshire on a fall day gone cold and windy, the rental car's "check engine" light illuminated with a ping. My cell phone read "no service," and I hadn't seen another human being or habitation for miles.

This followed the previous night's version of travel's underbelly. Owen's contact, whose one-hundred-year-old family apple business had brought me to this area to begin with, had called yesterday morning with the news that he'd received an unexpected visit from a child in crisis and had to beg off hosting me at his home at the last minute. I had spent the night at the only available motel in a fifty-mile radius. For a hundred dollars I'd gotten a musty, run-down room overlooking a parking lot filled with at least a dozen motorcycles, with more roaring engines arriving periodically. Steven's concerned voice over the telephone had been a comfort, but the last thing I wanted to do was worry him. I'd not slept much.

Now I began to make my way toward the town of Lebanon, where I hoped the car could be repaired or switched out so I'd be on time for my one o'clock appointment at Orphan Hill Orchards. The endless arch of trees over the well-tended two-lane road, which moments ago had felt like an enchanted bower, now looked like menacing arms overhead. *On Star!* Relief flooded my veins and went to every prickled nerve ending. If I had to stop, On Star would find me.

Fear receded, replaced by the larger questions that had nagged at me in solitary moments on this trip: *What am I really doing? How have I come to invest so much time and energy and resources into this potentially risky business?* Steven's concerns, never far from the ruffled surface of my equanimity, pulled at my confidence like an undertow.

"At this age we shouldn't be making risky investments," he'd said when I first seriously talked to him.

"I'm only investing money we never counted on having," I countered.

"You don't know the first thing about starting a business, much less running one. Do you really want to be working this hard at setting up a business at this time in your life?" he retorted.

"I do!" I answered. "I'm excited to be trying something totally different and interesting to me."

We'd been having versions of this conversation ever since.

The morning's coffee started to burn in my gut. My defense of my plan played in my head as I sped through the deserted countryside. *What do you mean "at this age"? I'm fifty-four years old, I ran the Chicago Marathon last year, I've had successful careers as a teacher and speech therapist, and now I want to apply my love for growing things to an upscale market for artisanal drinks and foods in a place I want to live. Works for me!* The fierceness of my solitary defense amused me. Steven had, after all, agreed to my pursuit. I'd gotten agreement if not enthusiasm from him, and it was up to me to maintain the courage of my own convictions.

I finished the drive without incident.

Orphan Hill Orchards sat atop a steep hill above the town of Lebanon. An article I'd read about the property remarked that it had everything you'd expect from a multi-generational, family-owned apple farm: a quaint old farmhouse, a barn, open outbuildings filled with tractors and other equipment, and, of course, miles of well-tended orchard.

My hosts for the afternoon's interview were a huge golden Labrador retriever and a tall, handsome man with salt-and-pepper curls topped by a bright turquoise stocking cap.

David Waters wore denim work pants and a brown plaid flannel shirt under a red-and-black-checked wool vest. His intense blue eyes lit on mine for a nanosecond as he greeted me and then scanned back and forth around the farmyard as we walked and he talked, pointing out the nuts and bolts of the apple operation and the award-winning hard cider he'd staked the business on ten years earlier. Our email correspondence leading up to this visit had established that I wasn't just politely interested—that I had invested in this trip to learn what I could from a master cider maker.

"What got you interested in all of this?" he asked me abruptly.

I repeated the explanation I'd given Bob Walker and Allen Swift the day before. David stopped and looked directly at me after I mentioned having learned to love hard cider when I lived in England.

"When were you in England?" he asked.

"1988."

"Where?"

"London and St. Albans, but I spent a fair amount of time in the West Country and particularly in Somerset." I suddenly cared that he approve of my British tasting credentials.

"We got our first graft varietals after a visit in '84 to orchards in Somerset and Hereford," he said. "We planted our first orchard of pure cider apples in '89." He stopped as a cell phone went off in his pocket. He excused himself and dug it out, giving me a chance to observe him.

I'm a hand person. I notice people's hands right away, and I make snap judgments based on what I see. David Waters had great hands: workingmen's hands that also bespoke grace and class. Mismatched plaids and turquoise stocking cap notwithstanding, this Harvard man had come back to the family farm and made good in the business of growing apples and making hard cider. I knew that for him, it all started and ended with the apple. Growing carefully chosen varieties of apples to perfection and bringing their distinctive tastes directly to the cider he made was his passion, and like any true visionary, he had collected the right people to help him make it happen. His hands told a story of hard work, finesse, and confidence.

"Sorry, I had to take that. Where were we? Right." He stopped and looked straight at me with a hard expression. "Do you realize how complicated this is? A lot of people are interested in dabbling, but this isn't a business you can just dabble in. Do you have a source for apples?"

The harshness of this questioning momentarily stunned me. True, I'd asked to take up this man's time. Perhaps he wanted to test whether I was serious enough to warrant an in-depth look at his operation.

"The person I'm planning to work with has planted a small orchard of Yarlington Mill, Dabinet, Kingston Black, Golden russet, Brown Snout, Galarina, and Medaille. We're looking to see how they do in Michigan and expect our first full harvest two years from now. It'll be more like five before we can be in full production." I was standing my ground. This wasn't like going up against Steven's generic criticisms of my lack of business acumen. This man knew what I didn't yet—exactly what it would cost in time, energy, finances, and expertise to make good hard cider. I wanted him to know that I understood it all started with the apples.

David's gaze appeared to go inward as he thought. After a moment, he strode toward the cider barn, beginning a rapid-fire tumble of information. I stumbled after him, notebook and pen in hand. "Medaille d'Or is high in tannins and it'll contribute a strong, fruity flavor. Galarina's fruiting zone moves out from the trunk quickly; we harvest it here between the Macs and the Cortlands. Honestly, if I were you, I'd look into Esopus Spitzenburg and Calville Blanc d'Hiver." My afternoon mentor was off to the races, unleashing his expansive generosity and knowledge. I had apparently passed a test.

As I hurried along behind David, I took in the orchards falling away from the stone wall that surrounded the farmyard and bordered the road. Mesmerizing rows of perfectly pruned, mature trees receded into the distance; the still-green leaves set off the sparse remains of bright red fruit, and brilliant orange foliage on the hills in the distance created a stunning backdrop. Steely cloud streams were scattered against the clear blue of the New England sky, but for the moment, the sun shone brightly. As if cued, a lovely young woman drove a vintage red tractor up the path between tree rows, hauling apples to the barn.

David began talking again as we passed a row of picturesque wooden bins filled to their brims with yellow apples tinged with a blush of pink. *Some variety of Cox Pippin . . . this late in the season?* I thought, but there was no time to ask as we reached the cider barn and stepped in. My eyes took a moment to adjust. In front of me lay a modern, high-tech cider operation, with a vast mill, plastic vats, oak aging barrels, and a stainless steel bottling machine. I snapped photos while workers conferred with David, and we made our way to the tasting room and the refrigeration coolers at the back of the barn. Ten-foot stainless steel tanks with spigots at their bottoms and floor-to-ceiling rows of oak casks filled the cooler.

In the tasting room, benches with test tubes and beakers lined the wall, and I waited as David fielded another phone call and more questions from workers who came and went. In between, he brought me wine glasses with tastes of semi-dry, extra-dry, Roadhouse, and the new Farmyard, one-of-a-kind cider series. They were all delicious; real hard ciders, absent the cloying sweetness that foretold a subsequent headache. Instead, the tastes hinted of the special fruits that had gone into the mix.

After David pointed out the remaining functions of different areas of the barn, we re-emerged into the sunlight and crossed over to the storage shed, where bins were filled with apples waiting to be pressed. The immensity of the process and the expertise required by this man and his team of colleagues dizzied me. I filled five pages of my pocket notebook with names, ideas, and topics to learn about.

I had now taken an hour of David Waters's time, and he certainly hadn't signed up to give me a personal seminar on cider making. Even so, I couldn't make myself leave quite yet.

"What's your one best piece of advice for someone who is serious and willing to put the work into learning this business?" I asked.

David thought for a moment. "First, don't spend a lot of time imitating other ciders. It's a common beginning mistake. Research apple varieties. Do the horticultural job of figuring out what to grow and how to grow it in your soil. Take a course on cider making; the best ones are still in France or the UK. Work to capture the unique qualities of what you've grown. Understand that batch chemistry has its own features and problems. Don't undercapitalize and don't be overeager."

I had to laugh. I, no doubt, was both overeager and undercapitalized. "Points taken." I looked down at the rocky ground, then up to meet his eyes again. "Thanks so much for letting me see how it's done right."

"Good luck," David said.

We shook hands, and I turned back toward my car. *Good luck indeed.*

Chapter 10

Down the mountain I drove, head full of orchards and cider making and possibility. Lebanon reminded me of a midsize town in the Upper Peninsula of Michigan. The commercial strip was repeatable anywhere in a northern climate: wide roads with orange plastic poles already placed to appear above snowplowed drifts during the impending winter, and fast food restaurants, chain motels, truck stop gas stations, and a VFW hall neatly line up at roadside. Blessedly, I'd found a car rental office willing to swap my car out for another. I checked into my motel room, and no sooner had I lain down on the striped bedspread than my cell phone rang. I grabbed it and sat up. Alex.

"Hey sweetie." I tried to keep concern out of my voice.

"Hey. How's the trip?"

This was a good beginning. Nothing disastrous.

"It's been pretty incredible. I've been going from one fascinating cider venture to another. I just got back from visiting what I think is the premier cider maker in America at the moment. The farm is beautiful and I learned a lot. How're you doing?"

"Check your email when you get a chance. Susan Shear sent me a bit of family medical history."

"Okaaay . . . Do you want to give me some idea?"

"No, I need to sit down and make some sort of family tree. I don't quite understand it all yet."

"Right. I'll look at it. But are you okay?"

"Yes, Mom. I'll talk to you later."

"Okay, love you." I had learned long ago that when Alex was ready to be done with a conversation, the conversation ended.

"Love you too, Mom." This recent intimacy Alex had allowed during the period of time immediately after the mess he'd gotten himself into with the young woman and her children. He'd relied a great deal on Steven and me for emotional support, and had finally begun to understand that we really did love him. While we didn't always agree with his behavior or decisions, we were in it with him for the long haul, even when it wasn't clear that he was in it for himself.

I lay back on the bed for another moment, closing my eyes and summoning a deep, cleansing breath from the high orchard I'd left earlier in the day, trying to ignore the stale motel room air. Then I slipped my shoes back on, grabbed my room key and laptop, and found my way to the lobby and Wi-Fi.

The day's emails poured into my inbox. I scanned until I saw the forwarded note from Alex.

Susan Shear, Alex's birth grandmother, had recently responded to Alex's request for contact. Alex had told Steven and me about this but hadn't shared any of the specifics. From the email, it was clear they'd corresponded a number of times, and also clear that Alex had asked Susan about family genetics and illnesses. I looked at the address bar and saw that Alex had also forwarded this email to Steven.

Within the first paragraph, Susan, apparently close to my age, revealed that she had worked in a special education preschool and liked to knit and garden. With a loose and irreverent tone, she quickly got down to the business of the email. One after another, she listed names, genetic connections, and diseases: bipolar disorder, developmental delays, allergies, and alcoholism. My chest tightened. Susan had no direct contact with her daughter, Alex's birth mother, but another family member reported that she'd struggled with obesity, neurological problems, and other unnamed medical issues. She had married and had five children.

We'd never been apprised of this medical history in the home study done during Alex's adoption. Stunning information should not be delivered in the faceless lobby of a Days Inn. Plain papered walls, metal breakfast room furniture, and the ubiquitous breakfast bar, sadly empty in the gathering dark of an October afternoon, provided me no place to anchor my attention or look for inspiration.

I reached for my cell phone and texted Alex: *WOW . . . un-f—ing-believable! What are your thoughts?*

He responded a moment later. *Need to map out family tree and re-read some emails. It's all a little confusing to be honest. I'm thinking about the weight problem.*

I sat back. *Weight problem? That's what he's worried about?* I was thinking about his years of highly charged anxiety, and his superhuman efforts to focus his talents and intelligence in positive ways—the mixture of successes and defeats he'd experienced.

The cell phone rang and I fumbled to answer it. Steven's, not Alex's, name appeared on the screen. More than likely, he had just read the email too.

I tried to answer, but the weak phone signal caused a failing connection. I texted him that I'd call when I was en route to Boston in the morning, and stumbled back to my room.

I phoned Steven as soon as I started toward Boston.

"Where's he going with this?" Steven's voice held concern and irritation in equal parts. "I mean, I can understand wanting to know a familial medical history—"

"That's exactly where I think he's going with this. He wants to know where he came from. Really. It's not Toledo this time."

"Toledo" was shorthand for not telling a child more than he wanted to know. It came from a joke about a little boy who asks his mother where he came from and the mother gives him the whole birds and bees lecture, after which the child says, "Yeah, but where did I come from, Mom? Timmy comes from Toledo." I hoped Steven would at least smile at this, but if he did, I couldn't feel it over the phone.

I resisted the urge to fill his silence by saying any more. Instead, a memory slipped into my thoughts like a little parable. When Alex was six, a scheduling snafu had resulted in his having to come to a school meeting with me. It was a deposition on a child custody case involving one of my students. Adoption had been an issue. I'd set Alex up with crayons and paper at a table across a partition from where the adults sat, and he'd been good as gold. In the car afterward, I'd thanked him for being so patient, and after a moment he'd abruptly asked me, "Am I ever gonna meet the mother whose tummy I came out of?" Apparently, he'd understood more of the content of the meeting than I'd realized. There, on the highway circling town, I'd launched into a carefully crafted explanation of a future time when Mommy and Daddy would help him find his birth mother if he wanted to, and we could go to the people who helped us adopt him to get information, and on and on. When I thought I'd assured him, I looked over to his seat and he was fast asleep. All he'd needed to know was that it was okay to ask.

He still needed to know that, but now he wanted the content as well.

At last Steven spoke. "I'm worried this could derail him. What did he sound like to you?"

"A little tense. I think he's shocked. It would have been nice if we'd known all of this when he first had to struggle with his own stuff." Another silence returned the high-speed highway noise to my attention. No traffic to speak of yet.

"You can say that again." Steven said, his tone more gentle. All the years of coping with Alex's intensity, his need for structure and for scaffolding to support his discomfort in social situations, though he masked it well with his charm, intelligence, and ability to talk to anyone one on one—it all flowed into the car with me, and another silence told me Steven was being similarly visited. We had done our best from situation to situation as Alex had rocketed between wonderful successes and abysmal disasters. He had often chosen relationships to save others, forgetting, at times, to save himself.

In a well-practiced short-circuiting of the painful descent into which Alex's problems could plunge me, I visualized the windswept beach of the Lake Michigan. I summoned the rosy horizon of a winter twilight defining the slate blue of the lake, a steady wind carrying a gull in the fading light, the white noise of rhythmic waves calming my spirit.

"I just don't want him to go down another hole," Steven said at last.

"I know," I said. "I think he's actually in a pretty good place."

There is a comfort in sharing the distinctive trauma of a child's trouble with the one other person who is also forced to reckon with it, even when the burden has at times commandeered the relationship. Steven's gentleness, and the depth of his essential warm-heartedness, mitigated the old weariness of having to represent our son's position to him then defend it, whether I agreed with it or not. I punched the seat warmer switch and drew in a protective breath.

We knew few other people whose children had run afoul of the law, or of the commonly accepted values of our upper middle-class existence—or who had ricocheted between opportunities, accomplishments, and disasters in quite the spectacular way that Alex had.

"I know," I said again. "He's done a lot of work, Steven, and maybe this all has to be a part of it."

"If he would only talk to me about it, I could help him understand."

This was an old complaint and we both knew it.

"It's not the help he needs from you right now, Steven. He has to make this his own territory, you know?" I focused on keeping my voice gentle. Steven bristled when I edged into advising him on what to say to his sons—something I did frequently. I wished Alex would say these things to his father himself. Then it occurred to me that perhaps he had.

A sliver of moon appeared in the afternoon sky as I approached the outskirts of Boston. I was still twenty miles away from the airport. I longed for a cold black night sky by the lake with this very moon vying with a million stars for attention. *Soon enough.*

"I've got to go, hon, or I'll lose my way," I said. "I'm getting close to Boston, and you know I hate driving around Boston."

"You haven't told me anything about your trip!" Steven answered. "I want to hear."

"It's been fascinating. I really learned a lot. I'll tell you about it when I get home." *Asked and answered.* Though I knew Steven's interest didn't match my own in this endeavor, and that I should focus what I said on the evidence of my increasing expertise, he did have a very good head for business, and I hoped he would hear me out on all that I'd learned.

"Okay, well, I have to finish paying bills and then I have a meeting." Steven often ended a phone call with a recitation of what he needed to be doing that our conversation was keeping him from. I no longer assumed he was chiding me for keeping him on the phone. I recognized that he had to orally organize himself by listing tasks, and all that was required from me was to wait for him to finish.

At the pause that meant a switch from looking at the calendar on his computer to checking email or a stock quote, I said, "I'll be home around seven. I'll see you then."

"Okay, have a good flight," came the distracted reply.

I'd scored a window bulkhead seat for the flight back to Detroit and I settled into the corner formed by the seat and the window frame, neck pillow in place, eyes closed, drifting off to sleep in the roar of the plane gaining altitude. I didn't want to think about Alex, but in twenty-seven years, I hadn't mastered the ability to park my worries about him at will— especially when a small kernel of undefined dread rolled in my gut like a hot marble, as it did now. I always knew when there was something I didn't know . . .

The drone of the airplane engine and the gentle bumps of ascending altitude lulled me into the waking dream state I loved. Conscious enough to observe mentally but unbound by time, perspective, and judgment, I had open access to an amalgam of memory, dreaming, and thought.

I began to dream of my father, and the days preceding his death. I knew how much he loved his life and those of us in it, and that he would not relinquish a single moment of it until his time came. His impending surgery had been minor, but the risk to him from failing heart muscle was not. Funny how the muscle failed long before the heart itself.

From childhood, I had rehearsed how to behave around things sad and painful—imagined the event, set up all the relevant characters, mentally executed the unhappy details, and then separated myself from the scene to orchestrate the correct response. When my father had to go, I'd rehearsed staying calm, focusing on organizing the necessary tasks, keeping the anguish within, caring for others.

So I wasn't ready for the shock and distress that came from another quarter during my father's final illness. Already navigating treacherous emotional shoals with Alex, I learned that in the final year of his Army Reserve duty he would be deployed to Iraq. Within weeks.

As had happened before, I grabbed on to the tail of this tiger and held on for dear life. I did not cry. I had practiced.

What practice did the dread in my gut require now? I didn't know . . .

The days in Ann Arbor went well. Mail, family contacts, good dinners with Steven, and the organizational and seasonal chores of home and garden got done. I took my leave guilt-free. Steven looked forward to coming north for Thanksgiving in a week. Only my sleep had suffered; early-to-bed evenings had been stymied by a wakefulness that discounted the fatigue I felt. When I went to bed, a continuous movie played on the screen of my resolutely shuttered eyes in brick red, popping images, like slowly boiling soup. These images reminded me of an old-time science movie about cellular activity magnified many times over, like an India print pattern gone wild. Steven snored contentedly for the first brief hours that he could sleep, his apnea causing a clamorous struggle for oxygen. It seemed we each had a little shortage of some vital calming nutrient. I longed for the peace of the farmhouse.

The road back to Northport unfolded into bitterer weather than I'd left, but the beauty of an early snowfall and rare, brilliant sunshine dressed even the simplest farmland in enchanting sparkles, softening the harsh simplicity of lonely farmhouses and second-growth forest. But for the cold, the landscape begged to be touched, like the old German advent calendars my grandmother imported for us every year when I was young.

I marked the freeway exits that brought me closer to my refuge and wondered exactly when the center of my spiritual gravity came to rest at the top of the remote peninsula that forms the pinky finger of the Michigan mitt. There were the years of sailing and Nordic skiing, when my love of water, natural beauty, and the seasons found full expression in the Great Lakes northern woods and waters of Michigan, Wisconsin, and Ontario. But it wasn't until Steven and I made a family and found the little corner of beach that we kept returning to year after year that I felt the deep, centering calm of a true home—one reliably able to bring me back to myself. Heading toward it now, head filled with ideas about hard apple cider, my satisfaction index mounted.

Chapter 11

The next morning dawned cool and cloudy, focusing my attention on the Thanksgiving countdown. Not unlike training for an athletic event, I planned for this holiday with a conscious delegation of time and energy, meted out over a number of days. I made shopping and to-do lists and a day-by-day timeline detailing the preparations on all fronts: sleeping accommodations, pantry stocking, baking, cooking, and entertainment. I scrutinized the farmhouse's living space through the lens of other family members and decluttered stacks of reading material, knitting projects, extra layers of clothing, and the collections of objects and knickknacks I seemed to attract like a magnet. I rearranged a selection of photos to maximize their appeal to my husband and sons.

Greeting Steven Stone at our home in the north country was like trying to catch a whirling ball of barbed wire. The best strategy was to allow him to land and have some time to slow down. After a day or two he would become calmer, let go the stresses of work, and then begin seeing and doing useful tasks that I hadn't.

A phone call from him mid-morning confirmed what I knew would happen; he'd gotten a late start and wouldn't arrive until close to dinnertime. Andrew and Carrie would roll in tomorrow, and Alex and Seth would drive in early Thursday morning. Everyone had the weekend off, and the weather report was brilliant: sunny, with highs in the forties to fifties. The recent snow would soon be gone.

It had been years—three, to be exact—since our whole family (and *just* our whole family) had been together for Thanksgiving anywhere, and more than that, since we'd been able to celebrate together in Northport.

Untethered to religious observance or obligations and focused on home and family, Thanksgiving was far and away my favorite fuss of the year. I loved the food and never minded preparing it. I traced the origin of my gratitude to my maternal grandparents, who had always hailed this holiday as their particular welcome to America. Arriving in New York in November of 1938 after escaping Nazi Germany at the last possible moment, they found themselves whisked in a limousine to the home of the woman who had given them an affidavit to enter the country. She was the German wife of a vice president of Macy's Department Store in New York, and she'd invited my elegant but penniless grandparents and my thirteen-year-old mother to a multi-course Thanksgiving meal, replete with white-gloved waiters, fine china, and classic American dishes. Then and there, my attorney grandfather, who would start his working life on this side of the Atlantic on the assembly line in a paper box factory, embraced America as a land of freedom and opportunity and converted the devastation of all he'd lost to pleasure and anticipation for what he dreamed lay ahead. As long as he lived, he retold the story of this first Thanksgiving each year at the family table, and I'd found a way to continue the tale long after he was gone.

My grandparents' china and sterling were stored in their antique breakfront in my dining room downstate, but their ceramic turkey candlesticks, salt and pepper shakers, and table decorations had accompanied me on the trip north, and

I lovingly unpacked them as I started readying the house for the family.

This would be a one-table Thanksgiving; all of us would fit into the dining alcove around the extended cherry table. I pulled the heavy leaves from the wooden racks Alex had built for me in the pantry so I could keep the huge slabs accessible without using up precious floor space. He'd also mounted birch-bark-framed photos of all the family pets, past and present, on the exposed undersides of the table leaves so that while stored, they were decorative. As I struggled with the thirty-inch bulk of one of the leaves, I marveled at the subtle ways in which Alex chose to express his artistry.

Next, I retrieved the cross-stitched tablecloth I'd found in a local yard sale from its drawer and shook it out over the table. Talented hands had devoted hours to the design that covered the extensive border. I'd spent some hours myself repairing a tear and removing most of the stains that bespoke other families' celebrations. I fingered the gold threads of the embroidery and summoned the memory of the smaller, deep-blue work that had graced the tablecloth my grandmother made for my wedding and that we'd lost in the house fire. Even at twenty-two years' remove, the loss of her precious gift, along with the innocence of dreams from that time, washed over me like an ill wind. With a final snap, I smoothed the cloth over the table.

The bay windows in the alcove that faced the lake were anchored with storage benches, and as I withdrew a basket from one of them I gazed toward the water. During the summer months it was not unusual to see morning walkers on the stony beach, headed a quarter of a mile to the northwest point that formed one "ear" of Cathead Bay. But now it was November, and I was surprised to see a lone figure jogging across the rocky shore, dark curls flowing in the sharp wind. Julia Reiss moved with the easy gait of a natural runner.

On impulse, I turned toward the patio door and stepped out into the bracing morning, watched as the girl approached, and then called to her. Wind and waves drowned my voice so I employed the fierce, four-finger whistle that had served me well in corralling the attention of years' worth of boys' soccer teams. *If she's not blasting hard rock through those earphones, she'll hear that*, I thought—and sure enough, she slowed and turned toward my exaggerated waving, pulling her earphones out as she trotted toward the house.

She could have just waved back.

"Morning!" I called. "You're up and out early."

"I told Sally I'd come in early today. She says it's going to be a busy one. I guess people are already coming up for Thanksgiving and looking to beef up their knitting projects. A run felt like a good idea before I spend all day hunched over needles and yarn."

I liked the way she thought. "You can run down the center road on your way back," I offered. "It says it's private, but you have my permission. Stop in for something hot if you want."

Julia's look of surprise turned quickly into a smile. "I don't really have time this morning, but I would love to another day."

"Ok, well, enjoy it out here," I said as I waved her off. She resumed her run and picked her way back to the rocky shore, planting her feet with care between the boulders that increased in size as the point narrowed.

I turned back to my preparations. I pulled the giant branch of driftwood from the living room mantel and placed it in the center of the table. Alex had dragged it home years ago, and it had stayed with me since. In its center, the wood divided around a hole formed by a knot or burl that the elements had removed sometime in the branch's watery history. It wrapped perfectly around an ivory pillar candle. The silver shimmer and downy texture of the piece, worn by sand, wind, and lake, added natural grace to the artfulness of the hand-wrought table linen, a duality of beauty I found particularly satisfying.

I continued to set the table. We were six people, unless, as often happened, I invited last-minute strays—like Julia.

A batch of brownies in the oven followed dozens of chocolate chip cookies. With the exception of the run I'd need to make to Leland for fresh-caught lake trout later in the afternoon, the shopping and gathering was complete. I opened the door to the second-floor staircase and made my way up to check the four bedrooms and three bathrooms we would occupy over the next five days. I was grateful for my longstanding habit of restoring clean linens and towels to all bedrooms and bathrooms after visitors left; it meant I had little to do on days like this one.

Opening shades and curtains to views of the orchard land, woods, and lake, I paused to once again consider the wisdom of pursuing the hard cider business. Steven had frequently suggested operating a bed-and-breakfast at the farmhouse instead. The six bedrooms and five bathrooms that had been built and renovated by previous owners made that a legitimate possibility, and I had seriously considered it as part of the business plan when we purchased the property. I'd told Steven the B&B idea remained an option, but hospitality wasn't the business I wanted to commit to. As I looked around at the quilts, furnishings, and decorating touches I'd made to the rooms, however, I recognized that it wouldn't be a bad way to pay the taxes.

I turned the thermostats to a comfortable temperature and returned to the kitchen, where, for the next ninety minutes, I worked like a machine to churn out the chopped garlic and paprika rub for the turkey, form dough balls for the crusts of the lemon meringue, pumpkin, and apple pies that were my various sons' Thanksgiving favorites, peel sweet potatoes, trim green beans, and mix the doughs for whole wheat honey and cinnamon breads we'd be eating all weekend.

As a satisfying array of bowls and containers filled the refrigerator and oven smells filled the house, a nagging malaise settled into the center of my body, weighing in my chest and pulling at my guts like the fingers of an ugly scar.

Alex. Something is wrong with Alex. It came to me like this always, bubbling up from the ever-uneasy plateau of ignorance and denial that allowed me to think he was okay until he wasn't. *He's drinking too much. He's gotten into trouble at the hospital pushing some boundary too far. Something.*

Breathe, Abbie Rose, breathe. I grabbed a bag of potato chips. *No scotch . . . Float the duck.* I called up a meditation I'd learned to quell my anxiety. In my mind's eye, I put a duck on the November lake, calmer today than on most days, but vast and powerful. I would float the duck on the water of the many things I couldn't control and not add my fear to the mix. The duck wouldn't mind waves and would stay afloat. I could too.

Chapter 12

Andrew and Carrie's late-model Ford Explorer passed between the stone pillars at paved road speed and never slowed on the gravel until it swung around the back of the house and lurched onto the grass near the kitchen door. Steven and I had lingered over our late lunch, hoping Andrew and Carrie would join us before we finished, and we both sprang toward the door to help them unload.

After scraping his way through high school, Andrew had found, in Carrie, the shy, pretty girl of his dreams. Her closeness to her large family still allowed for a warm relationship with us that was an enormous comfort to me. Andrew had always been independent and more emotionally reserved than our other children. I had long ago chalked up his distance from the family to a combination of a few things: suffering through a house fire; his older brother's explosive ride through adolescence; having a younger brother to whom everything came easily; and, most important, finding himself with family members whose temperaments were wildly different from his own. I tried to celebrate the fun, distinctive, and deceptively intelligent strengths that Andrew possessed. I'd given up trying to mediate or fix his challenges.

With Carrie, I had proceeded slowly; I never wanted her to feel responsible for interceding with Andrew on our behalf. Her willingness to devote time and effort to a connection with us had helped us stay linked to Andrew, however, and for that I remained grateful.

"Hi," Carrie sang as we loaded ourselves with bags and suitcases. Her natural beauty centered on her enormous blue eyes and infectious smile. Her features were wide and open, and though she was petite and fundamentally shy, she was formidable, and I found myself getting lost in her calm loveliness. She wore it like a fairy princess in low-rise jeans.

"Hi Mom, hi Dad," Andrew chirped as he squeezed past me into the kitchen toward the hall and rear staircase. "We in the usual room?" I grabbed around his broad chest for a hug as he fumbled, trying to hold on to the bags.

"Yeah, but why don't you leave your stuff for a few minutes and join us for lunch? Have you guys eaten at all?"

"We've been sitting for the last five hours and we stopped in Traverse City for something to eat. I think we're good for now."

"All righty then, up you go. Let me know if you need anything up there."

Steven reached for Carrie and put his arm gently around her shoulder as he relieved her of her suitcase. "Here, let me take that." The sounds of suitcases bumping against the narrow staircase walls receded as the three of them climbed the stairs.

When Steven reappeared in the kitchen, he hesitated.

"Let's just finish eating and let them settle in," I suggested.

"Right." Steven sat down.

It wasn't two minutes before Andrew and Carrie joined us.

"Hey!" I said, half rising as they entered the kitchen. "You sure you don't want something? There's lots to eat here."

"No Mom, I told you, we just ate. Sit down . . . So, you guys want the good news or the better news?"

I felt myself flush. Surprises weren't my favorite thing,

but Andrew wasn't often the bearer of any news at all, so I sat heavily and tried a bright, "Oooh . . . either one!"

"So Carrie's been asked back for a second interview with an anesthesia group at the University of Michigan. It's not a sure thing—there were a ton of applicants—but she felt really good about how the interview went. And since she's at the top of her class, we think it's looking good. My boss has a good buddy in the sheriff's department in Washtenaw County, and they think there'll be an opening next spring, so there's a good chance I could get that job too."

The way he beamed at Carrie made me grin. "Wow," I said, "That's excellent. This is exactly what you wanted, right?"

"Yeah. None of it's certain, but for our first round, it's pretty encouraging." Andrew sent a sidelong glance to Carrie, who was blushing furiously. "So that's the good news. The better news is . . ." Andrew paused and then blurted out, "Carrie's pregnant, so there's going to be a little Stone running around here pretty soon!"

I was shocked into silence. Steven's editor, meanwhile, failed to show up for active duty.

"Really? Are you guys ready for this yet?"

Nearly simultaneously, I jumped up and shrieked, "Yes! That's fantastic!"

I certainly related to Steven's concern. Andrew and Carrie had married very young and weren't finished with their educations. The last months of Carrie's clinical training would be grueling. On the other hand, Andrew had always had magic with children, and Carrie was the consummate mother type.

Andrew looked stricken by Steven's reaction. His face hardened. "Well, that says it all, doesn't it? Dad says, 'Oh no,' and Mom screams, 'Fantastic.'"

"No, no," Steven jumped in. "I'm just a little shocked. That's great news. Did you guys plan this?"

"No!" Carrie broke in. "But we thought about it, and we decided we both really always wanted kids, and I should be able to flex my schedule when the baby comes. I'll be able to graduate and take my boards, and Andrew will get paid a little more . . ."

Carrie's uncertain look brought me to my feet and I pulled her into my arms, not looking at Andrew or at Steven. "Oh honey, this is great! You're going to be a great mom, and if anyone on this earth can figure it all out, it's you." I'd said the truest words I could think of with a mind still reeling. Retaking my seat, I looked more carefully at Carrie. "You look beautiful. How do you feel? How far along are you?"

"Fourteen weeks. I'm a little sick in the mornings, but it's not bad," she said. Both she and Andrew were looking at Steven, who had the deer-in-the-headlights, forced smile on his face that got stuck there when he didn't know where to go in a situation and couldn't say what he really felt.

A rescue was in order.

"What I think you're trying to say here, hon," I said with mocking exaggeration, my palms up, hands bobbing with every word, "is that you're in a state of shock, but this is really exciting news, right? This isn't what they thought would be happening now, but they've considered it, and they've decided it's what's meant to be, so we get excited with them, right?"

"Yeah, Dad, you've always wanted more babies, remember? Now you can stop bugging Mom about adopting little girls, okay? Only this one is going to be a boy."

"Really?" I turned back to Andrew. "You don't think I deserve a little girl baby?"

Andrew's good humor was restored, Steven was genuinely smiling, and I figured this might be my one and only chance to put in a pitch with the fates for a girl.

"Andrew wants a boy for the first one." Carrie was chatty now that the tension had been cut. "I'm thinking the first two will be boys and then we'll have girls."

"Whoa . . . how many are you thinking of?" I asked.

"I'm thinking four. Andrew is thinking two, but we'll see," Carrie answered brightly.

A tidal wave of poignant hope washed over me in that kitchen tableau. The confidence of youth and young love fed Andrew and Carrie's belief that plans could be made and followed and the future could be navigated on the sunny side of the street. They were willing to work hard, they thought they were the captains of their ship, and all we needed to do was get on board.

Okay, I can get on board.

I beamed up at my son, and when I rose to hug him this time, he hugged me back.

By the time Andrew stumbled down to the kitchen and poured himself a giant mug of coffee the next morning, I'd finished my holiday preparation chores.

"I always know I can get a big cup of good coffee here. I can make okay coffee at the post, but it's not as good as this," he offered.

"We aim to please . . . Glad you like it," I said. "What's your plan for today?"

"You mentioned that new hard cider place last night. Should we go down and check out the competition? Carrie's just going to sleep in and take it easy today."

"Wow, that's a great idea," I said. "He's not exactly competition. I mean, he could be if we ever decided to go into full production and have a retail space, but right now I'm working with an apple grower, and I'm interested in getting into the juice pressing and fermenting. If our business thrives, we might eventually be a supplier for Tandem Ciders. But we're a long way off from that, of course." I grinned. "Do you want to go now? I could get them to open up if they're not already."

Steven walked into the kitchen and started rooting around in the cupboard.

"If you're looking for cereal, you're not going to find it there," I told him, pointing to the cupboard on the other side of the island where the cereal had always been stored.

"Andrew and I are talking about going to the new cider place down toward Sutton's Bay. You want to come?"

"I think not," he said. "The right man for the right job, I always say. Andrew's your guy to test cider, as long as you're not trying to talk him into giving up his career for this business. I've got my jobs around here to attend to." Steven's remarks were made with good humor, but they cut nonetheless.

"Be nice, Mr. Stone," I said, unable to resist a retort. "It's Thanksgiving."

"I do want to try some hard cider," Andrew cut in. "I've never had it on this side of the Atlantic. And I'm not going into this business, Dad. I'm perfectly happy being a sheriff." Andrew's easy response obviated any need for me to say more.

He turned toward the stairs. "I'll be back down in ten minutes, Mom. I'm gonna take a shower."

"Okay, honey." I moved to wash the few dishes in the sink.

"Are you just going to taste ciders, or are you looking to get involved with this place?" Steven asked.

I kept my voice casual. "Well, Charlie Aiken is looking to supply hard cider producers with his artisanal apples. I would get into the pressing and storing—maybe all the way to finish, or maybe we'll provide equipment to let people make their own and supply places like Tandem. I don't know yet, but it's a growing market across the country, and we're positioned perfectly here to take advantage of that. The owners of Tandem want to work with local growers. They're into the local, sustainable thing and right now, even Christmas Cove Farm can't keep up with their prospective demand."

Although his voice was calm, Steven's words irked me. "Just remember, Abbie, this is your fantasy, not Alex's or Andrew's. Alex should be a PA. He's good at it and it's a great achievement for him. And Andrew still needs to think about going to school."

"You know, you need to stop lecturing me, Steven. You just heard Andrew say he's not interested in this for himself. He just wants to go down and try some cider. And I know how you feel about Alex. Everyone knows! You and I have agreed that I'm going to explore getting into this business on some level. I have a lot to learn about running a business, and I hope you'll consult with me, but it infuriates me that you act as if I can't learn what I need to know. If you can't be enthusiastic about what I'm doing, at least stop being chippy and negative! You have a right to share your concerns, and I have heard them, and believe me, I take them into account. At this point all you're adding to the conversation is negativity. Stop!" I could feel myself getting angrier, but I kept my tone measured. "Our boys are adults. Alex is only looking at moving here as one possible option for himself. And he's just *looking* at it. That's all. He is not giving up being a PA. Period." I wiped the counter in what I hoped was a conversation-ending flourish and headed to the back hall.

"I'm going to stay here with Carrie, and maybe take care of some email before everyone else shows up," Steven said. He didn't blow up.

"Great," I answered brightly. "Have a good morning." I headed out into the sunshine.

It was a twenty-minute drive to the cider bar. A little surprised and a lot happy to be on an adventure with this middle son of mine, I waited to see if he wanted to talk before beginning my own musing. Some things never changed, and we drove in contented silence for a few miles, turning south off the access road, away from the lake and toward Northport. Orderly rows of young fruit trees stretched to the horizon on both sides of the road.

"Don't these guys have enough apples to supply Tandem Ciders?" Andrew asked amiably. We were passing row after row of the Kilchermans' apple trees: different varieties, sizes, and shapes.

"Yeah, they do have a lot of antique varietals, but they're not set up to grow a lot of the cider varieties. Their biggest production goes for antique eating and cooking apples. We're ahead in that my would-be business partner got a small orchard planted with just the apples that would make really excellent Michigan hard cider." I was warming to the topic, but looked over to see if I'd already exceeded Andrew's interest. He continued to stare out his window, but I could tell I still had him.

"Who's fronting the money?" he asked. Nothing is subtle about Andrew.

"Well, I'm making a decision right now whether I want to be an investor or a partner with Charles Aiken. If it's a viable business, and if we think it could really go somewhere, it will be worth it to partner. That's more involvement than just passive investing."

"Which one does Dad think you should do?" Andrew asked.

"He hasn't weighed in on that issue. He's less certain about the whole idea than I am, to say the least," I admitted.

"But does he think it's a bad investment?" Andrew pressed.

"He hasn't really spent the time making that assessment. He's been pretty focused on not wanting it to interfere with Alex's career, or yours."

"So why are you doing this, then? Is Alex really that interested?"

Andrew's questions momentarily hung between us. I took my foot off the accelerator and pulled to the side of the road. He had the right to get the same answers as his brother and father. "You know, I feel like I have one more thing in me to do. I love it up here, and even though Dad won't admit it right now, we've both always wanted to have a business that our kids and all the stray people in our lives who need it or want it could join. And for me it's also about the uniqueness of this area, and about growing things, and about the history of this drink and the people I've met who are into it. There are just a lot of ways that it makes sense to me and interests me. If Alex decides to move here, he could help me out. He's just looking at the idea right now."

"Can you make any money doing it? How much do you have to invest?" Andrew was probing now, and I wondered why. He hadn't taken interest in my professional pursuits or in business of any kind before. Perhaps Alex's possible involvement had aroused his curiosity.

Before I had a chance to answer his question, a tap on the window startled me, and I turned to find Gina Leyton, my neighbor, standing next to the Flex. I fumbled with the switch until the glass drew down.

"Hey, Gina," I said. We weren't close neighbors, but had connected in a variety of ways.

"Hi Abbie." Gina glanced at Andrew.

"This is my son, Andrew. Andrew, Gina Leyton. The Leytons live just up Sugarbush there."

Andrew ducked across, extended his hand out the window, and actually smiled. "Hi, nice to meet you."

Every once in a while they come through for you, these young men.

Turning back to Gina, I said, "I heard you're heading to Arizona for the winter."

"Yeah, the girls are much more likely to visit us there than here." Gina wasn't a chatterer, but here she was, leaning on her elbows into my window, all friendly like.

"So I met Julia Reiss," I said. "She's staying out with you?"

"Yes, she is. It's working out real well. She takes good care of the animals, and she's a quick study. She's working for Sally in town, but she's also doing some pruning and winter chores for us."

This was intriguing. Gina Leyton was an accomplished person, and reputedly demanding of people she worked with.

"So is she here for Thanksgiving?" I asked, suddenly feeling Andrew's impatience next to me.

"No, she actually left today for Ohio, but she's coming back late tomorrow. I guess Friday and Saturday are big days at the store and Sally needs her."

"Right, well you-all have a great Thanksgiving." I leaned

back and was preparing to pull away, when Gina added, "We're doing a giving thanks ceremony in the labyrinth Saturday night if you and your clan want to come. We'll start around seven, weather permitting, and do a bonfire afterward."

Gina knew I had a thing for anything Celtic, and I'd been intrigued with the huge labyrinth she and her husband had built in the field next to their house. The new age, upscale version of a corn maze, I guess—but it hooked me.

"I'd love to do that," I said. "I'll see if I can talk anyone else into it. Thanks, Gina."

She stepped back and I pulled away.

"Who were you talking about?" Andrew asked as soon as we were back on the road.

"A new girl who moved up here and is working at Dolls and More in town. I've run into her a couple of times. She actually rowed in college in Ohio. I told her you were a rower. She looks like she's about your age, but I'm not sure. I was thinking of inviting her for Thanksgiving, but I guess she went home."

"Yeah, I heard. All right, let's see a guy about some cider! Does this thing go any faster than a bicycle?"

I laughed. "It's got six cylinders, but I'm sure I've never exercised them to your satisfaction."

Andrew enjoyed his first-ever American-brewed hard ciders at Tandem Ciders. They had names like Honey Spy, and Scrumpy, and Little Woody, and the tasting room was warm and inviting. We joined a small but enthusiastic group of tasters there . . . early holiday revelers.

"This stuff's okay, Mom," Andrew said, elbows on the bar, head tilted in his unique, ingratiating way.

"Well, good!" I smiled back at him. "Wouldn't want to put a lot of work into something you hated, would I?" I sipped my mug of Early Day cider, savoring the tastes of the five apples that went into its mix, and then added, "Thanks for checking this out with me. Makes a great start to the weekend. I've been thinking about all the different things I have to be thankful for . . . You're going to be a great dad, you know. It won't be easy, but you guys will be good together raising a kid. Here's a toast to that!"

Being part of a nest of love for a new baby boded well for this holiday. Our glasses clinked and a moment of joy bloomed at my center, absent any conditions or contingencies.

Chapter 13

Streams of sand skittered up the beach in the strong south wind, giving texture to the tableau of bluster, unexpected warmth, pounding waves, and slices of light separating tracts of rain. How often I reveled in these singular moments' dramatic artwork of weather and lake; they felt created just for me.

On this Saturday afternoon, I faced the gusts' full force as I ran from the point down the beach toward the stairs that led to the road back home. Just now, the sun shone anew through a slash in the roiling clouds, sending gold beams in a band across the water to my right and gilding the cresting waves before they pounded into stones along the water's edge. Further across the lake, to the west, a curtain of rain undulated with the wind, and to the south another pool of light shone from a hole in the overcast. It was a weather symphony with a master conductor.

Thanksgiving dinner had gone remarkably well, with the only unexpected guests being two Australian shepherd mixes that showed up with Alex. True to form, he'd found them on a pet rescue website and impulsively driven an hour the same day to pick them up. They were on a three-week trial with him, and they were certainly enlivening the weekend with a dose of chaos and entertainment. While I always wished that Alex would think more carefully before making such choices, I missed having dogs around, and these two were sweet and more or less well behaved.

All the cooking I'd done ahead left me the time on Thanksgiving morning to greet the kids with pancakes and eggs as they appeared one by one—Seth and Alex from their long drive, Carrie and Andrew from their long sleep. The pleasure of sons who care about good food and are willing to help prepare it led to a long, leisurely afternoon of last-minute cooking interspersed with watching football and walking the dogs. The meal itself and the evening that followed featured lively conversation, all of us catching up on each other's lives and memories of Thanksgivings past. As I did every year, I repeated the story of my immigrant grandparents' first Thanksgiving in New York. Momentary tightness seized my chest as I wished they could be here to share this night. My grandfather would have made a special fuss in the form of a dramatic toast to Carrie and Andrew, who had brought the most exciting news to the table. That same grandfather had established my habit of collecting conversation topics tailor-made to the dinner company at hand. My grandmother's simple but delicious recipes had informed my own culinary interest, skipping the generation of my mother, who detested cooking of any sort. I did miss my own parents, badly at times, but Thanksgiving had belonged to my maternal grandparents, and my connection to them formed an important part of my identity, as well as my love of the holiday. The warm comfort of their sheltering home and their abiding support had influenced what I'd sought to provide for my own children.

The wind picked up and the paisley swirls of blowing sand rose from the flat beach to make hissing sounds against my running tights and nylon jacket. I slowed and turned toward the massive wooden staircase that ascended the fore-dune, fell to a short valley, and then traversed the face of a taller sand ridge. I ran up to the first landing, taking in the expanse of the lake, beach, and dunes as I caught my breath.

Seth had mentioned a woman friend and their discussion about Thanksgiving plans more than once since he'd arrived, earning him the teasing scrutiny of his brothers.

"So does this 'just a friend' have a name?" Andrew asked, stuffing a bite of herbed biscuit into his mouth.

"Yeah, her name is Sophie," Seth answered easily.

"Where is she today?" Carrie asked.

"She's with her family in South Bend. They're Israeli, but they've lived here a long time, so they're into the American holidays too."

"Whoa! Jewish to boot. That'll light Dad up," Andrew teased.

"I can't imagine not coming home for Thanksgiving," Seth said. "It just wouldn't feel like Thanksgiving. I suppose you just have to make adjustments when you become a part of another family, huh?" He turned to Carrie, who looked around before she answered.

"It isn't the same with my family split up as it was when we were little and all together. Sometimes it's hard. It makes you realize how important your family is, though," she said.

I smiled at Carrie and reached across the table for her hand. "Just think, next Thanksgiving we'll have a little baby-cakes to be thankful for. It's more family; a new family."

Seth raised his glass for a toast. "To Mom and Dad, for keeping us connected and cooking great food. Happy Thanksgiving!"

Nuggets. These were nuggets to rejoice in.

Seth continued, "I actually thought of inviting Sophie to come up and then drive back to Chicago with us Sunday. I wasn't sure if that would work at either end, but it looks like she could come." He looked at me questioningly.

"Absolutely. It's fine with me if everyone else is okay with it." I stole a glance at Alex, who would be the only single with this new plan, but his green eyes were clear and amused. It struck me then that he'd probably heard all about Sophie already. Smart boy, that Seth.

We all turned to Steven, who had been remarkably silent. His smile was wide and predictable.

"There is something I thought of doing on Saturday," I said. "I'm not sure who wants to join in, but Andrew and I ran into Gina Leyton and she's hosting a party at her labyrinth Saturday night. I'd like to go. Should be some great cider, a bunch of neighbors, some folks from town . . ." I let my pitch fade a bit to take the pulse of the group. Steven didn't know the Leytons well—hadn't been around for much of my contact with them. No one said anything, so I continued. "Technically, they use their labyrinth for walking meditations, but this sounds more like a relaxed excuse to give thanks with friends. There should be some people that I'd be interested to meet, and this young woman I've started to get to know who's living out there will be there, so if there isn't another plan afoot—"

"Well, it's not like there are dozens of alternatives for the evening," Alex broke in. "Leyton is the guy that raises Australian cattle dogs, right? Those would be fun to see."

"Yeah, he does breed Australians. How did you know that?" I asked, surprised.

"I met him fishing one day last summer. The perch were practically jumping into my boat and he cruised by to chat. We had a nice talk."

Maybe if I could interest Alex, the others would follow. "They've gotten into all sorts of things with their farm. They had some longhorn cattle, and they're growing this super antioxidant berry and all kinds of things. She does a personal training business too. He used to be the superintendent of schools for the whole state of Alaska before he came and did it for Northport. And he and I were first-year teachers together a hundred years ago. I lost track of him until he showed up here as a neighbor. This is a second or third life for both of them."

"That sounds like a pattern going on here," Andrew chimed in. "All you old people doing your second and third lives."

"Charming, honey. You could offer that description to the Chamber of Commerce." I smiled at Andrew.

"I'd go," Steven said finally. I threw him a look of gratitude.

"Oh, okay. This I have to see. Dad going all woo-woo at the labyrinth." Alex was revving up for a major tease, but Steven shook his head.

"Always have to be ready to try new experiences, and I've got to stay on top of all Mom's little cults she's getting involved in up here."

That produced the desired hilarity among the kids, and I let it pass because it meant we'd all probably get to the Leytons.

I turned to Seth. "Hopefully Sophie will get up here in time for dinner. Then you can decide if you want to come or not, okay?"

"Yeah, I'm thinking she may even come tomorrow, so no problem."

My heartbeat now slowed to a normal pace, and the sun no longer played hide and seek as the cloud cover tightened over the vast lake. I turned from the dune toward the road and resumed my run.

Sophie did come on Friday, in time to join us for our informal but joyous Sabbath dinner of turkey matzo ball soup and sandwiches—a good use of our leftovers. Smart and outgoing, she fit easily into our small group, accepting Alex's Scrabble challenge, helping out in the kitchen, and detailing her background in answer to Steven's thorough questioning. I'd hardly had time to spend with her so far, but I liked what I saw, and was particularly pleased for Seth. He'd always had good friends who were girls and there had been two who were more than friends, but no one since he'd graduated from college and gone to work.

I had a feeling I'd see more of Sophie, but for now, she

was adding good energy to the weekend party, and had gone off with the other kids for a day of walking the beach, checking out the town, and enjoying the unseasonable warmth of the dramatic day.

I returned from my run feeling sandblasted and exhilarated. Steven was napping under his iPad with a sleeping dog on either side of him. I put the finishing touches on pumpkin tarts to bring to the Leytons while I drew a bath for myself. The tarts done, I lit a diffuser with lavender oil I'd gotten from a local grower and sank into the hot water in the old claw foot tub. The heated, scented water drew tension from muscles challenged by the physical work and the stress of preparing meals, anticipating needs, and running. The buoyant comfort of a bath never failed me. If only things were always this pleasant. *Stay in the moment, Abbie.*

Dark comes early in November, and the clearing sky brought beautiful moonlight, shining stars, and dropping temperatures to end the unseasonable warmth. We'd brought two cars to Leyton Farms, across the mile-plus distance by road through apple orchards and fields. I observed our unloading from the cars as we might have looked to others: five vibrant twentysomethings and two salt-and-pepper parents, all tending toward the tall and lean except for Carrie, who was pint-sized in a land of giants.

Luminary bags circled the perimeter of the labyrinth in the field next to the Leytons' lofty home, and we moved as one toward the groups of guests visiting quietly. Tables bearing hot cider, tubs of iced beer, local cheeses, herbed breads, and Gina Leyton's own Saskatoon berry jam were set up on the near side of the carefully plotted circular walkways. Several barrel drum fires provided welcome warming stations. I found a spot for my pumpkin tarts on one of the tables. I'd just set them down when I felt a tap at my elbow. I turned to see Julia Reiss smiling at me.

"Hey Julia. Happy Thanksgiving. You made it back. How was your trip?"

Julia looked momentarily surprised, perhaps because I knew she'd been gone, perhaps because I seemed delighted to see her.

"Oh it was great, thanks. Short but sweet. Happy Thanksgiving to you."

Julia looked as if she were going to say more, but just then Gina Leyton called to the assembled group to gather around the entrance to the labyrinth. She welcomed us and gave a short background and introduction to those who wished to do the meditative walk. I'd heard her describe the eleven-circuit, medieval, Chartres-style maze before, and how walking it represented an archetypal symbol of finding one's own true path through life.

The animated guests slowly quieted so that it was easier to hear Gina's concluding words. "We want to thank you all for coming and sharing this beautiful evening with us. You're so much of what we have to be thankful for. Walk the labyrinth, grab some treats, gather around the fires, and enjoy." Polite applause followed and a few guests began their slow circuits along the grassy paths, while others returned to their conversations. Alex, Seth, and Sophie made their way toward Julia and me.

"Julia, let me introduce you to my kids," I said.

Alex reached us, and before he could make the contemptuous comment about Celtic spiritual pathways that I knew lurked behind his raised eyebrows and half smile, I pulled him close and said, "This is my son Alex. He's visiting from Iowa. Alex, this is Julia."

Alex extended his hand to shake Julia's, and I could see him eyeing her appreciatively. "It's nice to meet you." He turned to me for some identifying information.

"Julia is staying here and helping the Leytons out, and she also works at Sally's store. You know, Dolls and More." I turned to Seth and Sophie. "And this is my son Seth, and his friend Sophie. They're in this weekend from Chicago. This is Julia."

"Hi." This time, Julia extended her hand. She studied my two sons' faces and looked back at me for a long moment.

"Sophie wants to walk the labyrinth, Mom," Seth said.

"I'll come," I offered. "I haven't done it in a while. Let's see if we can get Dad to come. I don't think there have been any anti-labyrinth articles in the *ABA Journal* lately, do you?"

Both the boys smiled.

"Good luck with that, Mom," Alex said. "This I have to see." He shook his head and I began to scan the crowd for Steven.

"I can take you through," Julia volunteered. "Gina's actually taught me a lot about it so I can give people a guided tour if they come while she's out of town." She sounded eager.

I smiled. "Sounds great."

On our way toward the entry stone, I located Steven and moved into the small circle of men around the cider bowl, Alex on my heels.

"Hey, Dad, it's time for your journey onto your life's path," Alex said. "Are you ready to walk with us through a grass maze in the pitch dark and trip over other people while you do it?" Alex clapped Steven on the back and got low chuckles from the assembled men.

Steven looked to me. He appeared skeptical at best. He turned to Seth and Sophie, and then caught sight of Julia Reiss.

I introduced Steven and Julia remained rooted where she stood, eyes locked on him, until the silence became noticeable.

"Hi," she finally said in a small voice. "Should we start?" As she turned, she stumbled over the uneven ground, then stopped to regain her balance. The poised young woman had vanished.

"Come on, Steven, just try this once," I chimed in. "It's a pretty night for a prescribed walk through centuries of meditative tradition! Julia will be our fearless leader."

Julia led us to the beginning of the path and began our tour in an official voice. "Labyrinths are serpentine paths for the purpose of walking with a quiet mind and focusing on a spiritual question or prayer. Lots of different religions use them as a form of meditation. There's only one path to the center and then back out. Some believe it focuses a person on the route to inner truth, and with that solid grounding, we make our way back into the everyday world. Other people just enjoy following the twists and turns and the different symmetries. So we can start one at a time, and give each person space to go at his or her own pace. Does anyone have a question?"

"Yeah, I have a question," Alex said.

A pit formed in my stomach. Alex knew how to be appropriate in social situations, but if someone struck him as false, he could go after that person with a subtle vengeance. I desperately hoped he hadn't put that particular bead on Julia Reiss.

"Yes?" Julia responded. Her smile disarmed me, and I hoped it did Alex as well. She was just trying to help Gina Leyton. She shouldn't have to bargain for emerging from the labyrinth in one piece.

"You seem to have done this a lot. How do you use your walk in the labyrinth?" I was interested by Alex's question, which was charming, if challenging and too personal. I breathed a little easier, thinking it was unlike Alex to venture on such an intimate inroad in front of other people, let alone with someone he'd just met. Could he be flirting?

Julia's eyes traveled to each of our faces in the dim circle of light from the luminaries. She seemed to make a decision; she tossed her dark curls back and faced Alex squarely. "I have a really big question in my life right now, and I use the labyrinth to concentrate on possible different paths to get to an answer. I'm not very good at sitting still and thinking, and I'm not a big meditator, so it's nice to walk and think." She turned back to the rest of us. "So, are we ready?" She had taken charge now, and seemed ready to move our motley crew through this experience.

We lined up like good grade school students, but Julia drew Alex to the front.

"Why don't you start?" she asked.

Brilliant. Let him define his own way of managing this out-of-character event and don't give him the opportunity to observe and judge the rest of us. The changing up of positions took an awkward moment to accomplish, but eventually we were lined up again.

One by one, we stepped onto the close-cropped grass, edged with perfectly flush brick pavers. Julia had all the young people go through before Steven and me, and we watched them step purposefully along the path, which snaked and coiled in even loops and turns. When Sophie entered the first turn, Julia guided Steven to the entrance stepping stone and spoke clearly: "Start at a comfortable pace and stay on the grass; don't think about it too much, and your feet will take you the right way." Steven looked at me askance, but he did as he was told, and I soon followed him, with Julia behind me.

At first, watching the others loop back and forth distracted me. I remembered that once you were in the labyrinth, it seemed bigger and more complicated than it looked from the edge, but I also quickly recognized the point where I really did feel as though my feet had taken over and I didn't have to focus on where I stepped any longer. I hadn't chosen a prayer to say or a question to answer or even a general topic to think about. I opened my senses to the delicious, cool clarity of the night, the defined path, and the collective presence of my family engaged in a refreshingly alternative way of being together. I met Steven as he walked toward me on the adjacent path and silently I reached to touch his sleeve. His upturned face and unfocused stare told me that he was far away in his thoughts. I smiled. Steven didn't easily let go of the here and now.

On the next traverse, on my other side, Julia stepped like a dancer up the pathway. I thought to catch her eye, but it was trained on Steven. She walked briefly in parallel with him, as if she were studying his every move, until she nearly tripped again at a turn.

The pleasurable trance of the walk eventually overcame my curiosity about others' experience, and I arrived at the center of the labyrinth lifted out of concern for anything other than a feeling of well-being. As I drew several deep breaths, it occurred to me that the metaphor of a sure step along a clear path appealed to me. Exiting the center, I found my way back through a second set of loops and turns. Steven moved up, down, and across ahead of me, studying his feet this time.

When I emerged, he was waiting for me.

"Well? How did you like it?" I asked. I looped my arm through his as we walked toward the desserts.

"You know I don't really get into stuff like this, but it's a gorgeous night and a walk under the stars is a treat, even if I was worried my size twelves wouldn't stay on the path."

"It is beautiful, isn't it?" I agreed. "I really enjoyed this."

"That's predictable," said Andrew, who had already sampled the goodies and was no doubt staging himself close to us in order to begin the request to leave.

"Yeah, I guess it is," I said. I looked up at Steven. "So I want you to go do your thing and interview Julia Reiss. I haven't quite figured her out, and I want to know what you think. She certainly seemed to be interested in you. I think she was analyzing your labyrinth skills tonight." Steven was an expert at drawing out peoples' stories, both at work and in his private life; he had a knack for doing it in the most disarming way.

"It looks like Alex may beat me to it," Steven said, pointing subtly over my shoulder. I turned to see Alex engaged in conversation with Julia. They both laughed and set off across the parking area to a large pole barn with a number of dog runs adjacent to a side door. Stan Leyton was already near the barn door, with other guests in tow, and I imagined the dogs were going to be roused from their evening rest.

"Well, Alex is Alex"—I smiled at Steven—"but the right tool for the right job here. I want a Steven Stone interview."

Chapter 14

We passed the remainder of the evening at the Leytons' pleasantly, chatting with neighbors about whose orchard needed replanting, whose medical conditions had resolved, and what predictions were possible for the winter that lay ahead. The farmers' preoccupation with weather had deepened the past season after a freak thaw followed by hard freeze in the spring had destroyed more than half of the year's cherry crop. With a business plan for hard cider production in the works, my interest in these conversations was no longer casual. Charles Aiken's careful pruning session just before the thaw and storm had minimized damage to his young trees and they'd come through well. As the trees were only now coming into their bearing years, keeping them sturdy and healthy was a priority.

Doug Moran, whose orchard lay at the south end of our property, dug the toe of his work boot into hard dirt surrounding one of the fire barrels, the flickering shadows of firelight accenting the furrow between his eyebrows. "I'll be pulling out the front five acres of cherries in March. Would have waited another year but the freeze caused too much breakage."

Our family had picked in that orchard for years, resulting in many a cherry pie and bottle of vishnik, a cherry liqueur prepared from an ancestral Stone family recipe. Visions of empty land—or worse, houses—on that corner crowded my mind.

"You'll replant though, right?" I asked, perhaps too urgently.

"Yup," Doug answered.

I resisted the urge to plant a kiss on his weathered cheek. How I depended on my stoic belief in this land I romanticized, and that these generations of farm families stubbornly held to.

In due time the party wound down and the chill chased us home. The young adults found their couches, board games, and electronics, and leftovers made appearances in sandwiches accompanied by cookies and beer.

I followed Steven to the room we loved the most. The den on the south side of the house had a semi-circle of windows, providing a view of the old orchard and the lake in the distance. An autumn moon shone halfway up the clear sky over the massive maple standing in the lawn between the house and the field. Blue light cooled and softened all the features of the landscape and the darkened room around us.

Steven sank into one of the pair of oversized easy chairs I'd bought thinking they would work well for reading stories to grandchildren one day. I was making my way to the matching chair when he reached for my hand and pulled me toward his lap.

I squeezed into the space next to him, half on his lap, and he began to absently scratch my back with his pinned arm.

"That was pretty fun," I said, then waited, hoping to gauge my husband's reaction to any of the varied people and activities of the long day. I felt content and was enjoying this intimacy. He remained quiet, so I continued, "Sophie's been a good sport, don't you think? Seth seems comfortable and happy around her. She's handling the other boys quite well."

"Yeah," he said, "I like her. You know she comes from right near Kfar Vitkin? She knows Mira and Shaul's boys and went to the army with Tomer."

"You're kidding. Sometimes I think everyone in Israel knows everyone else."

Steven's cousins lived on a small collective in an out-of-the-way spot near the city of Natanya. We were close to those cousins, and to their children, and it was fun to think that this new girl knew them. "So she went back to serve in the army? I thought her family had been here a long time."

"Yeah, she and her brothers all served. I wonder if that complicates citizenship? I guess her mother is American by birth."

"Hmmm. So do you think she's serious about medical school?"

"Sounds like it. She seems smart enough and I like her attitude about it."

I smiled into the darkness. Steven shifted his weight and I started to stand up, but he pulled me back down. I swung my legs sideways over the chair so I was sitting more comfortably on his lap. I grazed his lips with my own and sank my head onto his shoulder, happy to watch the moonlight play over the landscape.

"I had an interesting chat with Julia Reiss." Steven's voice rumbled through his chest into my ear.

"Really. Interesting how?"

"Do you know where she's from?"

"Somewhere in Ohio. I know she rowed for OSU."

"Right. She's from the Dayton area. Yellow Springs, actually. It's where Antioch College is."

"Why do I think they don't have a rowing team at Antioch?"

Steven ignored this comment. "Her mother works in the placement office at the college, helping students arrange their required cooperative work placements. It's a pretty unique program. Been around for a lot of years. I remember friends going there when it was a hippie mecca."

"I've certainly heard about it, but I've never been there. I've only ever driven through Dayton when we used to go to Cincinnati. What does her dad do?"

"He's a wood worker. Teaches at the college and does the art fair circuit. He's been to the Ann Arbor Art Fair a number of times. Brought the whole family once."

I settled further onto Steven's shoulder. "Did you learn anything more about her family?"

"She has an eighteen-year-old brother, and it sounds like her grandmother has been a close part of her life." This all matched information I already had about Julia.

"But what's she doing up here?"

"I actually had a hard time keeping the conversation on her. She did a fair job of interviewing me. Asked me a lot about us, and our kids; how long we'd been married, how old the kids were. She basically repeated what she said at the labyrinth. She liked vacationing in northern Michigan as a child, so thought this would be a good place to come and sort out some kind of personal issue she has. The job and the living situation fell into place, so for now, it's working for her."

"Huh. She didn't give you any clues to what she needs to sort out?"

Steven paused. "Not really." He absently twirled a strand of my hair around his finger. A burst of laughter from the next room seemed to bring him back to our houseful of children. "Come on, it sounds like they've got Pictionary going out there. Let's go watch."

I unwrapped myself from the chair and headed toward the noise. In our family, there is no mere watching a game of Pictionary, and soon Steven and I were assigned to teams. Across the dining table, Alex's face was lit in the soft lamplight. Steven produced one of his fractured interpretations of a clue that resulted in a preposterous line drawing, which caused Alex to break into laughter, lifting the mask of strain that often infused his features. The joyful boy shone through, something that never failed to make me giddy. Seth and Sophie teamed well together, frequently guessing the clues first.

The game ended well after midnight. Andrew and Carrie headed to bed first, the exhaustion of early pregnancy trumping the desire to extend a rare evening with all the brothers in one place. Alex posted the best Pictionary artwork on the refrigerator before securing a spot on the sofa in the den to watch a movie on his laptop. Seth and Sophie took a moonlight walk, and Steven and I climbed the stairs to our room upstairs.

I looked at Steven as I slid into bed and noticed that his face still had that far away look. "You seem a little preoccupied," I ventured. "Are you okay? I thought the evening went really well. Didn't you?"

"Yeah, really well. All the boys seem like they're in pretty good shape, and I like Sophie," Steven replied, his face clearing for a moment.

"But?" I waited.

"No buts," Steven said quietly. "It's been a long day. I'm looking forward to some sleep."

Sunday dawned brilliant and cold. Everyone but Steven had to leave for home, and the typical flurry of packing, loading, and good-byes occupied most of the morning. Alex took the dogs for a walk to avoid the chaos; he would make the trip back to Iowa over two days and wouldn't leave until midafternoon. As always, I experienced a deflated sense of not having gotten quite enough from the kids' visit mixed with relief at getting my life back. I'd grown accustomed to the paradox and felt no guilt.

Sophie and Seth left first. When Andrew and Carrie's car rolled down the driveway a half hour later, I set off into the late-morning brilliance to find Alex. I hoped to talk more to him about my ideas for setting up a pressing and aging operation, and I also wondered where he'd gone with the revelations of his birth family's medical histories. We hadn't had much time alone since he'd arrived.

I knew he would likely have started off on the road leading from the back of the house through the woods to Cathead Point. We both loved the log cabin there, with its view of the lighthouse across the bay to the east, and the Fox Islands in Lake Michigan to the west. If I'd calculated correctly, Alex would be sitting on the front veranda in one of the Adirondack chairs, watching the dogs careening wildly in the dune grass among the boulders—many of which were massive Petoskey stones, the unique, fossil-patterned indigenous rocks coveted by collectors.

Sure enough, after hiking the quarter mile to the point, I rounded the front of the cabin and spied Alex seated comfortably where I expected to see him. I hadn't expected to see Julia Reiss occupying a second chair on the porch, however. I felt a stab of irritation. I wanted this time alone with Alex.

Deep in conversation, they didn't see me approach until the dogs bounded toward me in a flurry of brown and white fur and flailing tails. Alex turned but remained seated, and for a moment I hesitated, uncertain whether an interruption would be welcome. But I wanted these last moments of visit with my son, so I moved closer.

"Hey," Alex called.

"Hi Mrs. Stone," Julia said.

I mounted the broad wooden steps to the solid deck wrapped around three sides of the cabin. The window blinds were drawn, separating us from the comfortable, solid wood furniture, collection of antler lamps, bent-twig stools and end tables, and old quilts and woven blankets stowed in the loft bedrooms inside. Brilliant sunshine danced on the waves ruffling the surface of the lake in front of us. I sank into the chair next to Julia and closed my eyes, waiting to see if they would continue their conversation.

"So what does an orthopedic PA actually do?" Julia asked. "Like, do you do surgery?"

"We do a lot of intake diagnostic work, and yeah, we scrub into surgeries, and then we do a lot of follow-up care." Alex warmed to the attention but remained low-key. He leaned forward in his chair and, with classic Alex savvy, diverted attention from himself, asking, "So, what brought you up here?"

His question surprised me. While Steven often elicited people's life stories, Alex didn't. Just as he'd done the evening before at the Leytons', he was becoming uncharacteristically personal with Julia.

Squinting through half-closed eyes, I saw Julia turn toward me, but I remained silent and unmoving in my chair.

She hesitated, and then spoke quietly, her words floating in the whisper of breeze and the warmth of the sunbathed gallery. "I've discovered some things about my family history that shocked me and left me with a lot of questions. I'm really close to my parents and they don't know what I've discovered. I haven't figured out if I want to get into it with them, or how, and I just thought it would be better to get away and sort things out for myself first. I've always loved it up here so I just decided to take some time. I lucked into the job and a free place to live."

My eyes were open now and turned toward Julia, who leaned back in her chair, her knitted headband uniting the blue of her eyes with the sky into which she stared.

I looked at Alex, but his impassive expression said nothing.

I sat up. "Families can get complicated, can't they?" I didn't want to say more.

"I guess so," Julia said. "Maybe we could talk about that sometime."

This unnerved me a little. Had Steven talked to her about our varied paths to forming a family? I doubted it. Had Alex spoken to her about finding his birth family? I doubted that even more. I began to feel the November chill as the sun climbed past the roof edge. Suddenly, I wanted this girl off my porch. Her interest had begun to feel invasive, and I still wanted time with Alex before he left.

Luckily, he took this moment as a cue to rise and whistle for the dogs.

"I've got to start heading homeward," he said. "It was nice to meet you," he said, nodding at Julia. "Hope you find what you're looking for."

Julia turned to me and laid her gloved hand lightly on my arm before stepping down to the sand. "Bye, Mrs. Stone. I'll see you at the store." Then she turned to Alex. "Bye. Have a safe drive." She loped into a gentle jog, and we watched as her slender form grew smaller along the water's edge.

"That was interesting," I began, uncertain how Alex would code what had just transpired.

"Sounds like she's like all the other weirdos up here trying to solve life's problems," he said. "But she is gorgeous."

Nice, Alex. Way to reduce an emotional revelation to its lowest common denominator.

"Did you guys talk much?" I tried to remain casual, but Julia's incursion into our family had become more mysterious in the past twenty-four hours, not less.

"We talked about dogs and fishing. Why are you so interested in her?"

"I don't know. She just sort of pops up out of nowhere here, and she seems to want to know a lot about us." My answer sounded a little lame, even to me.

"Well, I've got to get going. It's going to be a mess driving in holiday traffic."

"I can make you some lunch while you pack and load. Are you going to try for Alice's tonight?" My sister Alice lived on the north shore of Chicago and of all our extended family members, she was closest to Alex.

"Yeah, it'll be a long seven hours."

We walked in silence for a moment, the dogs snuffling under the leaves for creatures and sticks. I faced Alex. "If you have any thoughts about my business plan so far, I'd be interested to hear them."

"Okay . . ." Alex answered, his intonation suggesting an uncertain degree of enthusiasm.

"As in, I want to know if you'd be willing to go over a preliminary floor plan for a pressing operation in the cider house, and whether it seems workable to you. I'd also like a better sense of how seriously you're thinking of making a move back to Michigan—like seriously interested, casually interested, or just flirting with the idea to please your mommy. Wait, cancel that last one, I don't think that's one of the real choices . . ." I'd intended this as a little joke, but the irritation evident in the hard set of Alex's jaw suggested my humor had failed. I plowed on. "Can I send you ideas and will you tell me what you think?"

"I said okay." Alex's voice rose in some irritation.

"Okay *what*, Alex? I'm not interested in bugging you. I look forward to your input, but I'm not dependent on it." Not for the first time, I wondered why I wanted to pursue this prickly son of mine for my fledgling business—but I did. I knew his organizational and mechanical talents as well as I knew his limitations. He could analyze and design an operation with an eye toward efficiency and productivity as if he were a trained engineer. What I didn't want, any longer, was to tiptoe around his edginess.

"Okay, I'm in for helping you figure out how to arrange your press and the whole aging operation in your cute little garage, and I'll help with the chemistry if you need it. But Dad's already on my case about not throwing away my life to move up here." Alex's sarcasm and eye roll told me all I needed to know about his response to Steven's input.

Even so, I pushed on. "I'm assuming you'd never move here just for this business. I'm just hoping that if you decided to relocate to this area and you found a job you really liked, you might be willing to help me out some. This is a no harm, no foul proposition. And to be honest, as far as Dad's concern goes, when was the last time you made any life decision because your parents wanted you to?" This produced a smile.

"I don't take lightly that Dad's not all into this with me, and I know it's going to mean a division of my time and energy, but I think I can make this small business work, and I want to try it."

By now we'd emerged onto the wide swath of driveway that curved around the back of the house. Alex gazed at the cider house. He began to talk rapidly. "If I were you, I'd lease time with someone else's press for at least the first year, until you get your recipes down," he said, "and just invest in the fermenting and storage equipment. Or get a commitment from someone for producing fresh cider while you're experimenting so you can support the cost of the press from the get-go. And you better have a clear and flexible deal on the growing with Charles Aiken and his son." He turned to face me. "As Dad is also quick to point out, I'm not in a position to commit one way or another to helping. It isn't even a business yet. Exactly what you're planning to start up is something else you ought to figure out."

I stopped and looked at Alex and shook my head. He *had* been thinking about this all the while. In typical fashion, he'd analyzed the essential elements and highlighted important decision points with impressive accuracy. Something shifted at my center, and I knew with conviction that I would take the next steps to make hard cider. With or without Alex's direct employment, I knew I'd have his sound advice and technical acumen at my disposal in some form or other. The two of us looked again toward the cider house with its new roof. Alex turned back to me and I grinned, raised eyebrows inviting him to share my mounting excitement.

"You're nuts," he said, but he said it with a smile.

Chapter 15

Winter hit hard and fast in the second week of December—not unusual for northern Michigan, but still catching off guard those of us clinging to the pleasure of the mild weather that had lasted through Thanksgiving. The snow had begun four days earlier—a mass of roiling clouds that blew in off the lake, accompanied by plummeting temperatures. The first icy onslaught had whipped around in the wind, stinging unprotected cheeks and eyes like needles. Then the front had settled over the peninsula and dropped a foot of snow in twenty-four hours. After another day and several more inches of fluffy white stuff, the storm had passed, and this morning had dawned clear, sunny, and frigid.

The lake no longer pounded out rhythms to the falling snow, and the softened fields, laced tree branches, and muffled sounds combined to create a winter wonderland that never failed to thrill me. No snowbird behavior for me; I loved northern Michigan in the winter precisely for its harsh beauty and isolation. Short days and long nights brought me inward, forcing a welcome shift to indoor work with my hands, reading, planning, and dreaming. In another week,

I would head downstate for the obligatory round of holiday parties and family gatherings. For now, however, I remained up north and determined to use the week to make some decisions about my cider venture.

Charlie Aiken drove up the driveway at 9:00 a.m. on the dot. I'd asked him to come for a "what if" meeting. His young trees were at least a year away from a full crop of apples, but I was ready to lay out for myself what would be required if he grew, I pressed and fermented, and his son James bottled our hard cider.

I had Charlie's own tea recipe brewing in the pot, and had laid out dried fruits and nuts alongside fresh muffins on the old maple kitchen table.

"Hi, Abbie," Charlie greeted me as he shook the snow off his jacket and hung it on a hook by the back door. "Looks like we're finally going to get some winter."

"Bad driving?" I asked.

"A little slippery but nothing outrageous," he said.

"I've got some tea for you, and I've set us up in here." I moved my laptop and set his tea across from where I sat. "I hope this doesn't sound like I'm getting too far ahead of the game, but I've been making some calls and getting some estimates, and I'm feeling like I have to make some choices if I'm going to move forward with this business."

I hadn't meant to jump into the conversation so quickly and seriously. I still wasn't used to the way people (read: men) did business up here. Any major decisions were preceded by a cup of coffee and a requisite amount of conversation about the weather, the high school football/basketball/baseball team, and an exchange of local gossip.

"No, no," he said, "it's not too early at all. Why don't you start by telling me a little more about what you have in mind?" Charlie's expression was impassive, his voice neutral. A jolt of queasy cold wormed its way through my gut.

I'm not ready for this meeting that I asked for. I don't even really know this man . . . I've spent all this time working on assumptions about our current and potential working relationship that aren't necessarily his assumptions at all. What was I thinking? That we would talk about how we each feel about things and then come to some mutual understanding, or kick the can down the road a little more to keep this in the realm of fantasy?

I'd opened a negotiation, and Charlie Aiken was a skilled businessman. All of Steven's misgivings and warnings swarmed around my head like a cloud of gnats. Then Steven Stone rule number one in a negotiation shot out of the buzz: Always get the other guy to put his cards on the table first—as Charlie had just tried to do.

"Actually, I was hoping you would tell me what you have in mind," I said, "where you are in your business plan and whether you've given any thought specifically to the pressing/fermenting part of the process."

Charlie Aiken's eyebrows arched almost imperceptibly. I chose to interpret this as appreciation for my parry rather than amusement. He sipped his tea before saying, "Our four acres of apples are still a year or two away from full production. We're committed to the growing side of things, and then we'll probably tool up for the bottling and distribution, either here or downstate. What happens in between is still an open question."

Back in my lap.

"You know," I said, "in all this time we've been talking, we haven't ever really talked financials. I've done a little research, and the equipment alone for the cider press will be $20,000."

"Who'd you talk to?" Charlie asked.

"Goodnature in New York. It seems they provide equipment to a sizable number of operations around the country. I liked the people I talked to."

"Yep, you've talked to the right folks."

"Look, Charlie, I know in your mind you're partnering with James, and I'm not sure how it would work even if you were willing for me to be a third. What if instead, at least to begin with, you granted me an exclusive contract to process your fruit?" Though my mind was working like an out-of-control sewing machine, gobbling up the fabric of my sketchy plans as I tried to keep my credibility clear of the needle, my voice remained calm. I looked straight at Charlie and more words came, as though pulled through me from a more knowledgeable, savvier source. "I'm thinking of a ten-year contact." *Do I even want to be in this business for ten years?* "That would allow me to amortize my investment in the equipment."

Charlie's eyebrows rose again, and I could see him working to absorb this idea. "Would your son join you?" He was thinking of the ten-year span also.

"I'm not sure. I wouldn't do this based on his decision, but it's a possibility. I've begun the reconstruction of the building out back that I think will be suitable for a cider house. What I need now is a clearer sense of where I'm going with this project and, like I said, what you're thinking about it." There was more, much more, that I wanted to discuss: what he knew about regulatory changes that would impact production, whether he thought shipping downstate for bottling would be cost prohibitive. But for now I just wanted a gauge on Charlie's internal plan, his vision for our collaboration. I knew he'd bought an old press from a defunct cider mill, but I also knew that aside from some sample home-style brewing, he hadn't done anything with the barn or the equipment to gear up for real production, and I doubted his setup would be efficient or economical for a modern cider operation.

He was silent for a long moment. I took comfort in the fact that I saw no signs of retreat or discomfort in his expression.

"That could work," he said. "If this cider thing takes off anywhere near as much as the craft beer movement, there'll be a demand for pressing and fermenting facilities." He fiddled with his teaspoon and looked as if he would say more, but didn't.

"So where do we go from here? Should you and I meet with James? Do you have a sense of what he thinks?"

"Meeting with him would be a good idea. I think he's ready to do the next step of concrete planning, and to be honest, we have to if he's going to be more than a silent partner. Why don't you sketch out as much as you've worked out and we'll do the same? Then the three of us can get together and compare notes."

I sat back in my chair. I wasn't exactly certain of what had just transpired between us, but I felt like we'd made progress. Charlie relaxed a little as well, and as he finished his tea, we chatted about the rumors of development plans for some of the unused buildings in our sleepy town and the forecasts of harsh weather to come in the next several weeks.

For the following half hour, I showed Charlie the cider house renovations and fielded several guarded questions from him about Steven, whom he'd still never met. Was Steven going to retire any time soon? Was he thinking of spending more time up here? I hoped my perfunctory answers and enthusiastic redirecting of our conversation to the improvements in the shed signaled to Charlie that I would consider and act upon any business venture, including our potential association, independent of Steven's plans. I quashed a momentary irritation. *Would Charlie have asked about my wife's plans if I were a man?* In a brief moment of guilty recognition, I realized that he would have asked—and that if he had a wife, I'd wonder whether she would be on board.

When I waved Charlie's truck down the driveway close to noon, I saw the plow had come through, making his trip to the main road less hazardous. I spent the next couple of hours ticking off chores in anticipation of leaving for several weeks. I shut down the upstairs, having restored bed linens and thoroughly cleaned after the full house at Thanksgiving. I liked the cocoon feeling of living entirely downstairs during the winter, when Steven rarely came north. Occupying the small original bedroom, sleeping next to the kitchen, I rarely strayed into the other living areas of the house.

In mid-afternoon, I headed into town for some last-minute holiday shopping which I always liked to do at the few local shops that stayed open all year. After my meeting with Charlie Aiken, I wanted to talk to Sally at Dolls and More. She'd mentioned at one of our Thursday night knitting sessions that her sheriff son knew someone who worked with the state liquor control commission. After the first of the year, I would start the research I needed to do on hard cider regulations.

Town was quiet on this weekday afternoon, and after a trip to the grocery store, I headed across the street to Dolls and More. I found Sally arranging a display of fabric dolls fashioned by members of a doll-making class she'd conducted over the last few months.

"Hey Sal, these are beautiful."

The dolls, which filled an entire wall of tables and display shelves, showcased the talents of a dozen women. Representing holiday themes, literary and children's characters, or just fanciful creations, they were dressed and accessorized in beautiful ensembles of sewn, knit, beaded, and embroidered costumes, with faces drawn, painted, and sculpted to perfection. Sally looked pleased, and I marveled again at her one-woman creation of this fiber-arts outpost in our little town.

We chatted, and I got her son's contact information so I could ask him how to proceed. As I hadn't checked in with her since Thanksgiving, we caught up on our families and particularly about Andrew, who Sally knew had a job in law enforcement.

"He probably knows, but my son Steve says there are more open jobs in the sheriff's departments statewide than there have been in five years. Who knows when that'll happen again?"

"Thanks for the info. They're still hoping to stay somewhere downstate. They've just announced they're pregnant, and they've got some good job leads. I don't think I'll get them up here yet."

Just then, the door to the storage room at the back of

the shop opened and Julia Reiss emerged, an open box loaded with bags of yarn nearly hiding her. Sally started toward her, but Julia said, "I've got it, Sally, I'm good."

I hadn't seen Julia since the day at the log cabin with Alex, but I'd thought of her often.

Sally turned back to me. "What's your older son doing out in Iowa again? Is he talking about moving back this way?"

I'd only told Sally the bare minimum about my plans for the cider business, and even less about Alex joining me, so I navigated carefully around my answer, particularly as Julia had now joined us, stacking yarns in shelving only a few feet from where I sat.

"He's a physician's assistant in an orthopedic practice. He's always talked about wanting to come back to Michigan, but he doesn't have any current plans."

Julia continued to stack yarn, but she'd adopted a listening posture.

"Seems like anymore, I see more PAs than doctors," Sally answered. "Maybe he can find a job around here, now that the economy is finally picking up."

I saw my chance to shift topics. "So I've heard. Sounds like the town is finally going to get some new development. I just hope we don't end up with a zillion new condos along the lakeshore."

Sally filled me in on what she'd heard about a new restaurant and entertainment facility with bowling lanes that just sounded too fantastic for our town, but would provide a needed boost for year-round residents and tourists alike. Of even greater interest, a West Coast venture capitalist with Michigan roots apparently planned to develop a goat farm and cheese making operation not a mile away from my house.

Producing artisanal cheese along with hard cider was an idea I'd had for making my farmhouse property purchase productive. My heart sank for a moment at the idea of someone else pursuing the cheese opportunity. On the other hand, a boutique farming business close by couldn't hurt, and I had my hands full with formulating my plan for the cider alone. I'd have to google this guy. Get in touch, maybe.

As I prepared to leave, already wondering when I'd find the time to make all these contacts and analyze what I'd recently learned, Julia stopped stacking yarn and joined me at the table of dolls.

"It was fun meeting your family at the Leytons' over Thanksgiving," she offered, sitting next to me.

Sally registered surprised interest as she, too, stopped her positioning of doll arms and legs and laid down the T-pins in her hand. Julia hadn't, then, already told Sally about that night.

"I thought everyone enjoyed the evening." I turned to Sally and said, "Gina Leyton invited some neighbors for a labyrinth tour and bonfire the Saturday of Thanksgiving. I actually talked my boys into going, and they had fun. Julia met them all and gave us a guided tour. She managed to get all my guys to try it and repress all their snide remarks."

Sally wasn't your labyrinth kind of a person. "Uh-huh," she said vaguely.

Julia smiled, however, and seemed pleased at my compliment. "Seth looks a lot like you."

"Do you think so? I've always kind of thought he looks like both of us." Seth was tall and thin, and had dark, curly hair, just like Steven and me. He had Steven's eyes but my narrower face. The other two boys were also tall but decidedly departed from our looks, with their bulky builds, fair hair, and broad faces. Was Julia fishing to confirm which of our children were adopted and which were biological? I'd grown used to trying to work around people's curiosities about our "blended" family. Today, however, my patience with that dance was thin.

"My two older sons are adopted, so that's why they don't look much like us," I said with more vehemence that I intended.

Julia had no response to this information beyond saying, "That makes sense. Well, I really liked talking to Alex. How old is he?"

"He'll be twenty-eight in September."

I watched Julia settle into herself with this information. I hadn't anticipated her unusual interest in us. Perhaps she saw Alex as a dating prospect. Why not? He was good looking, had a good job, and she had no way of knowing about the aspects of his personality that sometimes made his mother worry for his future. *Still*...

"And the other two are younger?" Julia asked.

"Yep. Andrew is twenty-five and Seth is twenty-two." And then I thought to ask her, "How old are you?"

"I'm twenty-five too."

Sally had moved off to the front of the store to take care of a lone customer who had wandered in, and I decided to counter Julia's questions with my own.

"I know the Leytons have left for Arizona for a while, and you're out there alone. After New Year's I'll be back up here, and likely by myself, so if you ever need anything, or just want to visit, let me know."

For the second time that day, I had surprised myself with something that seemed to spring forth unbidden from some part of me not directly under my volition.

"Wow, thank you. I will definitely take you up on that," said Julia, a pensive smile lighting her beautiful face. "That's very nice of you."

The call from Julia came well before New Year's. Only two days later, she phoned.

"Mrs. Stone? Hi, this is Julia. I wonder if you have some time today for me to come over. I kind of want to take you up on your offer."

She sounded uneasy, but also somewhat urgent. I had a lot to finish before leaving in two days' time, but I could manage it, and decided I wanted to. Curiosity overcame resistance.

"Sure. I'll be here all day. When's a good time for you?"

"I could come now, if that works."

"Okay. I'll see you soon."

Half an hour later, a small Toyota pickup made its way between the stone pillars and up the long drive to the house. People on the Leelanau Peninsula didn't drive little red Toyota Tacomas, and I wondered if the truck was heavy enough to get through the wallop of snow likely to be dished up in a Leelanau winter. But it suited Julia well, and she hopped out and made her way to the back door with loping grace.

"Thanks for seeing me," she began after we'd settled with tea in the outsized chairs in the den. The day was dull but no snow fell—it was a day to be nestled into an uphol-stered chair in a warm, cheery room.

Wisps of uncertainty and then resolve seemed to travel across Julia's face like cats' paws on the water. I waited and then asked, "So, how are things going?"

Her beautiful blue eyes filled with tears, but still she didn't speak. I certainly hadn't expected tears, and I worked to mask my discomfort with a neutral expression. With dif-ficulty, I remained silent, and sat quietly.

Julia drew a deep breath and spoke at last. "Remember I told you my Mom had me when she was really young, and she and my dad didn't get married until later?"

"Yeah, I do remember that. You spent a lot of time with your great-grandmother, who taught you to knit, right?"

"Right. Well, my parents recently decided to move into a house that has a workshop my dad can use as a studio, so he doesn't have to leave home to work. I thought it was a little late for that, but whatever."

I realized that this was the first time I'd heard Julia sound like a typical twenty-something. Until now she had seemed more grounded, more articulate, less likely to pro-duce an eye-rolling, gum-smacking barrage of *whatever*s or *you-know-what-I-mean*s than other young people her age.

As if she'd heard me, she resumed, her voice tame and measured. "My parents hired me to go through their attic and basement and sort things to purge that they didn't want to move."

"Mm-hmm," I said.

"When I went through an old file cabinet, I found a folder with a bunch of information and some correspondence from an attorney." Julia gripped her fist and seemed to shrink right before my eyes into a frightened child. She was rowing on a river of distress, fighting to stay afloat. "I guess my mother arranged to be artificially inseminated and be a surrogate mother for a couple who couldn't have children. There were letters from three different men, and correspondence about a contract, but I never found a contract." She hesitated as her voice constricted to a near whisper.

I shut my eyes for the briefest moment. I felt a prickle of dread race up my arms, across my chest, and into heat on my face. Before thought, even, the heat, and the sudden absence of oxygen. *She is going to say something terrible now, and I will hear it, and then I will have to do something about it, whether I want to or not.* There was no stopping Julia and I forced my eyes open and looked directly at her. She spoke again, quietly, her fear radiating into the room.

Her eyes looked haunted. "I didn't even know what surrogacy was. I had to look it up. And then I thought, okay, my mom needed money and she thought this would be a way, and then"—Julia's voice thinned and she gulped for air—"there was the part of the correspondence where they asked about her sexual relationships and she said she was in a relationship with my dad . . . but that he was sterile . . . he'd suffered some sort of trauma."

Now, Julia was crying softly. Her courage seemed to have deserted her. In a near whisper, she finished, "One of the three letters asking my mother about surrogacy was from Steven Stone."

Chapter 16

Julia Reiss left my house. I threw on running clothes and took off for the beach. A treacherous veneer of ice made running on the sand a bad idea, and I knew better than to run this rattled. *Not a good day for a fall. I have to keep my wits about me.* My father's face suddenly rose in my thoughts and the sob that had been threatening escaped as I gasped for breath. I so missed him, but I could never have turned to him with this one. His skill had been to point to the joy of the everyday, not shoulder the intractable. He liked his problems simple and solvable. Still, I missed his comforting presence and his steady belief in everyone's ability to overcome the challenges, pain, and disappointments of daily life. A tear burned to ice on my cheek in the cold.

This cannot be happening. This girl . . . Steven's? NO. Summon strength, Abbie. Come on, FEEL IT. Each pound of my foot on the sand brought up past traumas that stabbed at my heart like shards of glass. The years of infertility, the indignities of treatments, the failures of procedures, the struggles to adopt, the house fire, the agonies of nearly losing Alex. We'd met those challenges. Now it should be our time, *my* time to follow my dream. *And now this??*

It became nearly impossible to breathe. The sun glared momentarily on the wave-textured water and the beach, as if illuminating Julia's revelation with an icy clarity. I stopped, heaving in the air, and looked out to the lake for another living soul or sign to anchor me. *We are a family. I built this family with Steven. Feeling love should be saving me right now . . . should be shielding me. Why isn't this working?*

I resumed my run and a half-mile down the shore, I reached the staircase of the old beach cottage where we had started our life on the Leelanau Peninsula. I pounded up the 102 stairs that scaled the dune, frigid air clutching at my lungs. I turned to the lake once more—always my solace, my inspiration—but shades of grey suddenly shrouded it, listless waves licking the snow, ice barely formed along the shore.

Thoughts continued to tumble in my head. *We tried surrogacy with a woman in Ohio twenty-five years ago. She told us it didn't work. I couldn't handle trying it again. So we went another way, and ended up with the three children we loved and raised. Who is Julia Reiss to come out of nowhere with this speculation that Steven fathered her, intruding into my life and my family?*

I paced the top of the dune, disturbing the pristine blanket of snow, turning every word, every contact with Julia, over and over. *She's terrified . . . and also fascinated. Does she think she belongs to Steven— to us?* I swept the snow from the sand under my feet, trying to quell the rage mounting in my chest.

I had been able to make some comforting noises, to ask her where she wanted to take this information. She answered that she'd only confided in me—that she had been too confused and frightened to talk to anyone else. She said that she felt such relief to have been able to tell someone, but that she was sorry to burden me.

Sorry! She's sorry? Does she have any idea what this means?

I had looked at her from a great remove, a skill I have learned so well over the years. I can look at someone, respond sympathetically, and be elsewhere in a deep freeze of emotion, willing myself to perform in the needed way until later,

I kept pacing. *What will I say to Steven? What will Julia say to him?* My heart lay like a lodestone. I still couldn't draw deep enough breaths.

I stopped stock-still. *Is there any chance at all that Steven knows? That he's known about a child in Ohio all along?* My legs collapsed and I sat on the sand and snow, grabbing my knees, rocking back and forth.

No. Whatever else he is, he is honest. He doesn't lie. He's so sure of what is right and wrong, and he acts from that place.

I stood up, beginning to shake with cold. In nearly thirty years of marriage, I'd never had occasion to question Steven in this way.

I took a last look at the lake, willing myself to draw strength from its calm majesty. The cottage behind me slumbered in the winter grey but sheltered me from the wind, if only for a few moments. I would freeze if I didn't start moving again.

I stepped around the back of the cottage and slid down the hill to the driveway, where I high-stepped through drifts up to the road—which, mercifully, had been plowed. I began to jog back toward the farmhouse, method returning to my feet and my thoughts.

I had promised Julia that I would speak with her again before I traveled downstate. Now I promised myself a day to think before I made any decisions about what to say. My feet rolled heel to toe over the light snow cover, the grippers stretched over my running shoes keeping me tethered to the road. What I needed now were emotional grippers. And a plan. *Tell her what you're going to tell her, tell her, tell her what you told her . . .* This old formula for making sure someone gets a message had stood me in good stead all my working and family life. But what would the message be?

Weak shafts of sun stretched to the earth between cloud banks as I traversed the road between the lake and the farm. Passing through the pillars that framed the drive, I tried to formulate my next steps. I would learn as much as I could about Julia Reiss and her parents. I would wait to query Steven. *No overt challenge.* I would tell no one else anything, just yet.

Early dusk settled outside the kitchen window, putting to sleep the landscape and drawing me to the heat of the old kitchen stove. I cursed the slow internet service as I clicked through the screens on my laptop with their paucity of information about Julia Reiss. Her family obviously hadn't bought into the exposure of their lives on social media.

As Steven had learned from Julia, Aaron Reiss was indeed a woodworker. He didn't have a website, but mentions of his shows appeared on gallery sites from around the Midwest, and he'd garnered a handful of awards. More and deeper research revealed that Julia's mother, Fiona Phelan, worked as an administrator at Antioch College and had authored numerous essays and articles on the use of internship and other hands-on educational experiences in college curricula. The very Irish name might explain Julia's black curls, porcelain skin, and deep blue eyes in a new way. Of course, Steven's hair was dark and curly when he had a head full. *Don't go there, Abbie—not yet.*

Nothing I read gave me the information I really needed.

I turned, in the fading light, to thoughts of how I could do the sleuthing from Steven's end. Did he have any records from our days of considering surrogacy? Could I ask him? The ring of the telephone made me jump. Steven.

"Hey, hi there."

"Hi . . . I just got home and wanted to check in. What's going on up there?"

What's going ON? You tell me, Steven. Is there something you want to say about what happened in Ohio twenty-six years ago? For a bad moment I wanted to scream and cry into the phone. The moment passed.

"I'm just trying to wrap things up here so I can come down, probably the day after tomorrow. How are you doing?"

"I'm good. I just bumped into Jack Gunn. He was in

court today with the Benches. They sentenced that kid to life in prison."

This news jolted me from thoughts of Julia. The Benches. The neighborhood family who'd lost a child to a violent crime. Their yearlong horror had moved another painful step. "Oh my God, finally. What an ordeal. I can't believe it took this long. Maybe the Benches can move on."

"Jack said Harvey Bench seemed to perseverate during the whole hearing on the private investigator's testimony, even though that came to light a year ago. He kept saying they never would have gotten the conviction without it."

"Maybe hiring the investigator made him feel like he had a hand in bringing justice to Laura's death."

In the silence that followed, I guessed Steven's thoughts were the same as mine—how the police investigation of the fire that took our house twenty-two years earlier had been ludicrous. If we hadn't had three children under six, if I hadn't been twelve weeks post a thirty-three-hour labor and a C-section, if we hadn't been suddenly homeless and possession-less from the total loss of the fire, we might have gone the route of a private investigator to further attempt solving the crime. Instead, we took our lawyer's advice and concentrated on rebuilding our home and our life.

Steven had resumed talking and it took me a moment to get back to Harvey Bench. *Losing a child.* The enormity of it washed over me and suddenly dovetailed with all the shock and confusion of the last twenty-four hours.

We were both quiet for a moment, and then Steven sighed and said, "I'm hungry. I'm going to forget about working out and go make myself some dinner."

"Okay. Do you have something to eat there?"

"Yup, I've got some leftover fish, and some rice, and I'll make a little salad. I'm good."

"Okay, well, I'll be home soon. Everything else all right?"

"Everything is fine. Be careful driving home, okay?"

"I will. Love you."

Steven made a loud smacking sound before hanging up. After thirty years, he was still incapable of "Love you too," but that kissing sound worked.

I sat for a long time, looking out the kitchen window, now reflecting the light from the room against the darkening snowscape of early evening. *A private investigator.* I didn't know how to discover Julia Reiss's true parentage, and I realized I didn't want to know how. I wanted someone else to do it.

Meanwhile, I would tell Julia that we had to move slowly. I wanted to keep the ripples she'd started in my family's dynamic from becoming a tsunami. I needed to think.

Uneasy, I moved across the kitchen to prepare my own meal and work out the delicate dance of what to say to Julia in a day's time.

Chapter 17

"Hey Norm, it's Abbie Stone," I said into the phone. "I have a little research project. I'm looking for a private investigator, someone who can work in Ohio. Do you know of someone good? Or someone who will connect me with someone good?"

I'd made myself call Norman Tripp first thing, before I had the chance to second-guess my decision or lose my nerve. Norman had been an attorney, taught criminal law, and occasionally helped us navigate our sons' scrapes with the law. He was an old friend, and though he wasn't exactly on speed dial, I knew I could rely on his expertise, his discretion, and his Rolodex.

Norman offered to check on a PI and meet with me when I returned to Ann Arbor. I put the phone back in the charger and waited. In less than ten minutes he forwarded a contact to me. I heard the ping of the email arriving on my laptop and immediately googled Martin Pappas, whose office was located in Dayton, Ohio, and who had a website that took forever to load with our sluggish internet. When the site finally appeared, I saw the tag line *When You Need to Know the Truth*, which caused me to sit back and stare out at the snowy landscape.

Did I need to know the truth? I dropped my head into my hands and kneaded my forehead. If only I could turn back the clock to a "before" setting—before I knew Julia Reiss. No, I'd been down that avenue before, yearning to go back in time, and it never worked, not even for a moment of grace. Grace lay in learning what I needed to know and finding a way to live with it. I found that Martin Pappas specialized in locating people, gathering evidence, and interviewing witnesses and suspects. He also provided "truth verification" with the use of a voice stress analyzer instrument. What did this mean? We weren't talking about criminals here.

Doubt seeped in and I went to the coffee pot to stall. The liquid courage I really wanted lived in the scotch bottle, but I wasn't going down that road.

I had to phone Julia and tell her something, though I wasn't sure yet what to say, and I had to head downstate tomorrow. My resolve returned. The more truth I could excavate about this whole mess on my own, the better I could confront whatever came next.

A new ping sounded at the laptop. I returned to my seat and saw Alex's name. *You still up north? Call me.* I wondered if the momentary feeling of dread I got when I received a cryptic message from this child would ever be replaced by the simple pleasure at the contact that usually followed. At least if he was emailing me, he wasn't likely in a police station or a hospital. Experience, however, had made me wary. I considered, as I paced across the kitchen and tapped his number into the phone, whether to ask him what he knew about private investigators. Alex had done his fair share of searching for hidden people during his time in the military and while he searched for his birth parents. Before I could decide whether to ask, Alex answered the phone.

"Hi Momma." His voice sounded guarded, absent the lazy greeting that usually signaled a catching-up conversation. He had something on his mind. I drew in a breath and braced myself.

"Hey sweetie, what's up?"

As though he'd drawn it from me, Alex breathed out the sigh that wanted to escape my chest and my heart sank. *Not now, Alex . . . not NOW.*

"Well, how would you like another grandchild?"

I sat heavily. For the second time in as many weeks, the race of needle pricks climbed my arms and my heart began to pound.

"What?" It came out a hoarse whisper.

"You heard me. Remember that girl I told you about?" Alex's words were like precision knives, cutting his sentences into staccato pulses of anger. "The one I liked and thought could be the real deal until she told me she wanted nothing to do with a country life?"

"Haley?"

"Haley. She just called me today and told me she's pregnant. She told me she's having the baby, and if I don't want anything to do with it, that's fine, but she's having it." Alex's voice became thin and hard. "She told me the birth control failed. She didn't even want to hear what I thought."

I couldn't breathe, much less respond, and the silence sucked every thought that tried to form into a vortex of panic. *Why is this happening? Is it true? Oh God, not after everything Alex's been through!*

"Mom!" Alex commanded.

"Jesus, Alex," I whispered. That released a torrent of fury that only registered with me in small snatches.

"I don't want to have a child right now . . . Haley is moving to her parents' town . . . She'll keep her job in Des Moines and work from home . . ."

"Alex. Alex, stop. Give me a minute here. Are you sure it's yours?"

The moment the words were out of my mouth, I regretted them. I'd spoken the first thought that registered as I tried to quell my panic.

Alex stayed silent for the shortest moment, and then

answered in a tight voice, "The timing is right, and she says she wasn't with anyone else. When I asked her anything, she got all pissed off and told me she was prepared to have this child without any input from me, if that was what I wanted. So then I asked her if we should reconsider our relationship in light of the baby, and she said no!"

The hurt in his voice cut to my heart. I'd heard it when this girl had left him weeks ago, and now the pain had cut deeper and mixed with the rage of a caged lion.

"Oh, god, Alex, I can't believe this is happening." It was all I could start with, and I knew he understood that I couldn't believe it was happening to him, but also to all of us. "Alex, you have every right to be upset right now, but you have to think hard and be careful here. There's so much at stake. You're going to figure this out. You're going to figure out what the right thing to do is, but you can't make any decisions while you're so angry."

"What do you mean figure it out? What is there for me to figure out? I don't have any choice because—"

"Alex," I cut in. "You have lots of choices to make here, but you can't and shouldn't until you get over this shock and can think. Have you told Dad?"

"No. I thought he was up there with you."

"He's been downstate for the last two weeks."

"Oh sorry, I haven't been keeping track of your separate lives." His sarcasm bit, but I ignored it.

"He'll be home tonight, and I'm driving down tomorrow. Call him."

Alex's rant continued, until every angle of his shock and intolerable circumstance had been repeated and flayed open and his voice was hoarse. I soothed him and tried to find the words to build a scaffold against the panic and dissolution I felt in us both. When I thought I could, I asked, "When's your next shift?"

"Tomorrow at seven."

"Can you get a workout in? Get something good to eat and then get a good night's sleep?"

"I know what I'd rather do. Drive down to that—"

"Alex, I mean it. Go for a run or go to the gym. Call me again if you need to. I'll be here all evening. And let Dad know . . . Okay? Can you do that?"

I heard the barest grunt. "We'll see."

"I'll call you later if I don't hear from you, okay? It's going to be okay, Alex. Somehow, this is going to be okay—"

"Right, good-bye." And he was gone.

Chapter 18

Ann Arbor during the university's winter break felt almost ghostly in its quiet. The population decreased by thousands of vacationing students and faculty, and thousands more townies also spent the holidays elsewhere. I reveled in traffic-free streets, copious parking spots, and immediate seating in restaurants. No longer tied to our children's or my own academic calendar, Steven and I often stayed put over the holidays and prowled the spots that were too crowded when the university throngs were in town.

Seated comfortably in just such a spot, a popular coffee shop with exposed beams and a brick interior, I nursed a cappuccino and scanned the scattered patrons at other tables and in easy chairs. On the dot of our appointed meeting time, Norman Tripp sauntered through the doorway and headed my way.

We'd known each other through many lives, our connection harking back to heady days of youth. Our close network of friends and spouses had confidently worked and played, fueled by enthusiasm and drugs and an expansive sense of optimism that we, along with the rest of our self-actualized generation, would open the world to the best of everything. We were so sure we knew what that would be, what things meant. I rarely saw Norman, but when I did, the bond was strong and deep.

"Abbie Rose!" Norman's eyes crinkled with just the touch of sardonic humor that I found so appealing and comforting about him. He didn't take himself, or anyone else, too seriously. I rose and our long hug produced flushed grins in us both.

"Nor-MAN," I answered, and shook my head. The man simply didn't age. Trim and fit, he had a bit more salt and pepper in his beard now, but he still looked entirely comfortable in his own skin and exuded the charm he'd always had.

"Beautiful as always, Abbie Rose, a sight for sore eyes."

"Thanks so much for helping me with this," I said. "The right man for the right job, I always say."

Norman's face took on an alert expression. No small talk. No asking about each other's families. We'd get to that later, perhaps. I had followed our initial phone conversation with a brief explanatory email that had indicated only my need to research a family issue. Norman had offered to meet, and I'd taken him up on it. In three days' time I had an appointment with the investigator, Martin Pappas, in Ohio. Now, I wanted Norman's help to work out my investigative strategy. He checked all the boxes of someone I could trust, who wouldn't judge me, wouldn't be shocked, and could think dispassionately and help me do the same. I'd been right to choose him for this role, but I was nervous, and his keen look signaled that I had to make the next move.

I took a sip of coffee and a deep breath. "So you remember, Norm, that our means of putting together a family was complicated, right?" I began.

"I certainly do," he answered wryly. His family also had both adopted and biological children. We'd become friends in our early twenties, long before children, and so we'd intersected through more relationships, events, and personal challenges than most other people I knew. We didn't dwell in our pasts, but we were important memory keepers for each other. I didn't have a lot of preparation to do with him.

"When my infertility was diagnosed, we eventually considered surrogacy," I said. Norman's brow lifted very slightly, but he said nothing. "Steven wanted a biological child. His only brother chose a life path unlikely to lead to children, and his father survived the Holocaust but lost many family members. So Steven wanted to carry on his family heritage." I paused. *Am I being disloyal to Steven to reveal this here? No. I need help. And Norman will abide by attorney-client privilege.*

"My infertility shocked us," I continued. "We met so late. We were under a lot of pressure, and felt we had to proceed with adoption, do in vitro fertilization, and consider every other way to have a family, because we both really wanted children—many children." Norman's look of studied interest revealed nothing more than his attentive listening, so I proceeded. "After the first in vitro attempts failed, Steven researched and wanted to try surrogacy. The whole concept was in its infancy, and since I was willing to adopt and truly wanted to have Steven's child, I thought, *Why not try this?*"

I stared at Norman, but still his face remained impassive. He waited for me to get to my point. Why couldn't I?

"I need another coffee," I said, standing abruptly. "Do you want anything else?"

"I'm fine," Norman answered.

I walked to the coffee bar. *Why go through this whole history? Why not just talk about Julia Reiss and her claim, and summarize in one sentence why I need to hire Martin Pappas?* The answer wafted over me with the aroma of freshly ground coffee. I needed to own what happened to me during that time—the damage, and my own failures. Any plan going forward had to account for all of it.

In two minutes I returned to Norman and sipped my coffee in silence. I found his eyes and forced out the confession that had all these years been sealed in the lockbox of my own anguish.

"I agreed to attempt the surrogacy arrangement. We made one attempt, but it didn't work." I battled rising tears. "When it didn't work, I told Steven I couldn't handle another try." My voice rose in urgency. "To me, surrogacy didn't turn out to feel at all like the adoptions we had pursued. Purposely producing Steven's child with another woman's egg and womb and then knowingly taking the child away from that woman—and paying her for her trouble—just didn't work for me. It felt too much like a business deal."

I searched my cup of cappuccino for a route out of the baseness I felt. "I know now that sounds hopelessly idealistic and self-serving, and it hurt Steven deeply, but I could only think of how hard it would be for me to explain it all to a child. How could I describe another woman's willingness to produce and then relinquish a baby—purposely, and for money? By then we had adopted Alex, so I understood something about bonding to a baby. The whole thing just didn't sit well with me."

I paused and Norman sipped his coffee, his eyes not leaving mine. My voice thickened. "We had a really rough time. Steven felt frustrated and betrayed. He felt if I really loved him, I would be supportive of his need for a biological child. Even after the in vitro worked with Seth, in some ways I feel like he never quite forgave me. But we both moved on, and loved and raised our three boys with everything we had. I sometimes wonder if I'd feel differently now, after all we've been through, and with how much the world of infertility and making families has changed." The memory of those years, the shredding of trust and intimacy caused by treatments and adoption procedures and considering all the alternatives, came rushing in with a familiar sucker punch to my chest.

Straightening, I took a breath and forcibly exhaled. "Then, a month ago, this twenty-five-year-old girl showed up in Northport, wondering if perhaps she isn't Steven's daughter—her mother applied to be a surrogate and this girl found paperwork listing Steven as a potential father. She never had reason to believe her parents weren't her biological parents, but that same paperwork makes it clear that her father is infertile. She has an adopted brother. The timing makes sense. And I'm the only one she's told about this." I leaned across the table and looked straight into Norman's eyes. "I want to get a lot more information about everything and everyone in this situation before I blow my whole complicated family apart. That's why I want to hire a private investigator, and anything you can help me think about to pursue this would be really welcome."

Norman watched me for a minute—waiting to make sure I was done, I guessed. When it was clear that I had no more to say, his eyes left mine for the first time since I'd begun talking, and he looked into his coffee cup. I let him think. While he did, I pulled out a legal pad and a pen.

"All right, Abbie Rose," he said, "it sounds like your immediate need is to figure out what you're going to ask Marty Pappas to do three days from now, but I've got some other questions for you before you go down this road."

"Okay, shoot." I had asked for Norman's thoughts, and now I would hear them.

"I'm sure you've already thought a lot about this, but I want to present two possibilities to you before you go any further."

"I'm listening."

"Suppose this girl is either scamming you or is just barking up the wrong tree with this claim, and what you want to do is basic damage control."

"Exactly," I broke in.

Norman held up his hand. He wasn't finished. "So you send Marty in to what? Find a birth certificate? Her birth certificate will list the man she's known all her life as her father, I'll bet anything. Find evidence of a legal contract? If the girl's mother told Steven the pregnancy didn't happen, there would likely be no further correspondence, though we don't know that for sure. And this girl says all she found were letters from surrogate prospects, right?"

"Right."

"Okay, now suppose—and this is hard, Abbie"—Norman leaned toward me—"suppose she is right, and in the best of all worlds, Steven really didn't know. Are you prepared for all the possibilities of what that will mean? The legal ramifications? The impact this will have on your boys, and on Steven?" Norman's look of tender concern unnerved me even more than my own fears already had.

"No, I'm not prepared," I choked out in a whisper. "I don't want anything to do with any of this—but what choice do I have? I'd rather face what I'm going to have to deal with than not know."

Norman straightened up in his seat. "Okay," he said quietly. "If you're sure, let's figure out how to accomplish that." He began to scribble notes on the paper in front of him, and I began to breathe more easily than I had in days. An hour later, I left the coffee shop and walked into a cold morning with a sheaf of papers and the outline of a plan.

Bless Norman.

Chapter 19

Turtle Creek, Ohio, probably looked like any other central Ohio town in January—wide, well-paved roads, bare trees, tidy homes, small businesses, and absent much outdoor activity because of the cold. In Michigan, on a day with leaden skies like this one, there would be a tension of waiting for snow, or recovering from it, and a deep bite to the cold—but here, two hundred miles to the south, it was simply a mild winter day.

At noon, I would meet with Martin Pappas in Dayton to discuss his part of my investigation. For now, though, I had a bit of my own sleuthing to do. I'd told Steven I would attend a knitting workshop in Ohio today, but the "workshop" was of my own making.

The Flex fit right into the fleet of trucks and SUVs in the ample parking lot of a small strip mall. Empty concrete flower boxes lined the sidewalk outside storefronts, and American flags fluttered in the cold wind. I parked in front of Fine Fibers Knit Shop and grabbed my knitting bag. A belt of bells at the door alerted a pleasant-looking woman who appeared to be in her midfifties as I walked in, and she immediately greeted me.

Though unremarkable from the outside, the well-stocked shop measured up to my favorite fiber art haunts. Bins and shelves with an ample assortment of yarns, arranged by variety and color, shared the space with well-crafted knitted samples. My workbag dangled from my arm as I took it all in, and the saleswoman gave me time to do so.

"Is there something I can help you with?" she finally asked.

"I do have a question, and I always look for knit shops when I travel, so I thought I'd stop in."

"Sure. Let me know when you're ready." With that, she turned to unpacking new yarn into a nearby display.

I moved off toward the sales counter, stopping as I went to finger some lovely hand-dyed cashmere wool in heather green. I had plenty of knitting projects to work on at home, but I could rarely resist the pull of beautiful yarn.

Fine Fibers's website had revealed interesting information when I'd checked it out the evening before. I'd found a robust blog, schedule of classes, and full array of yarns for sale, signaling a savvy online component to this business. A mother/daughter class to make a knitted cowl caught my eye and rewarded my decision to research this shop. The cowl had been designed for the instructor's granddaughter and they both appeared in a photo, each modeling beautiful, lace-patterned cowls, in a deep blue to match the granddaughter's arresting eyes. The instructor was Margaret Phelan, and the granddaughter was, unmistakably, Julia Reiss.

I worked my way around the store and back to the proprietress, who by now sat knitting in an easy chair next to the sales counter. She put aside her work and rose as I approached.

I started tentatively. "I checked out your website and downloaded the pattern for the lace cowl. I started it with some yarn I had at home, but I've gotten stuck on one of the directions and wondered if I could get some help, and now I'm afraid I'm also stuck on that beautiful green yarn. Do you by chance have any more of it?"

"Oh, I'm so glad you liked it. That is a wonderful pattern. Margaret, the designer, isn't here this morning, but I'd be happy to help you, and yes, we do have that yarn. Come on over to the work table and let's see what you have there, and I'll grab some of that yarn for you. I'm Esther, by the way."

"Abbie," I responded. So Midwest, so classic, this friendliness and casual familiarity among women who love to work with their hands. I wasn't sure whether I was more disappointed that Margaret Phelan wasn't there, or relieved that I wouldn't have to figure out what to say to her.

"You sit down here, Abbie, and I'll be right back." Esther pulled out a classic teacher's chair at a beautiful wooden table occupying most of the length of the shop's side wall.

She returned in a moment with two balls of the green cashmere yarn, which she handed to me. Its soft beauty filled me with pleasure. Overcoming my discomfort at this knit store subterfuge, I pulled my work and the pattern from my bag and commented, "This is such a beautiful pattern, and I couldn't help but notice how the yarn in the cowls matched the girl in the picture's eyes." *How lame did that sound?*

Esther seemed not to notice my reaching for information. "Oh yes, Margaret's been knitting around those eyes all of Julia's life. Julia's her granddaughter, and her eyes are just as gorgeous as that yarn."

"Lucky Julia," I said. "She must have a bundle of pretty clothes."

"She does. And she makes many of them herself. And when her mom gets into the act, it's quite something. Three generations of great knitters there."

I then asked Esther my question. It wasn't a real question—I'd followed the pattern easily—but I'd chosen something to ask about the European abbreviation that Margaret Phelan had used in her pattern. Esther quickly explained and I continued to work the pattern, hoping to draw her into more conversation.

"This is a gorgeous table. Not your usual knit shop utility version."

"Isn't it nice? Margaret's son-in-law made that for us, back when we were in our old shop downtown. We didn't want to part with it when we moved out here. It kind of reminds us of where we came from too."

"Wow . . . pretty talented family."

"Oh they are, and a good family too. Good people." *Of course they are.* Esther reached for a binder at the other end of the table and flipped through it, then showed me a photo. "This is from our shop's event this year for the fiber festival. There are Margaret and Fiona and Julia, all wearing their own designs. Three generations of talented designers and knitters. And here's Aaron, Fiona's husband, showing off his table and some of the lamps he's carved that he brought in."

There they all were—the three Phelan women and Aaron Reiss. Fiona and her mother were of medium height and had classic Irish features, though not at all like Julia's. Margaret's red hair was pulled back into a careless, loose bun, while Fiona's was short, straight, and spiky. Both women had fair freckled skin and green eyes, and their knitted sweaters and scarves were muted shades of green and amber brown that set off their coloring beautifully. Julia stood an easy head taller, with her tumble of dark curly hair—*Steven's hair,* I thought, and this time I couldn't whisk the idea away. She was tall and slender—*like Seth.*

Stop it, Abbie Rose!

Aaron Reiss appeared to be stocky and only a little taller than his wife. He had a broad, open, pleasant face and a shaggy mop of straight brown hair and brown eyes. I forced my gaze away from the binder. I wanted that photo.

"Where are you from?" Esther asked as I turned back to my knitting.

Suddenly uncertain how to answer, I hesitated. "Ann Arbor," I said finally. This woman knew Julia Reiss, knew her family, and probably knew that she'd moved to northern

Michigan. Or perhaps none of them knew, but I didn't want to risk making that connection.

"Interesting town," said Esther.

"Yep, it is that." I set my work down. I reached for the green yarn and stood. "Can I settle up with you for these?" While Esther made her way across the store, I repacked my workbag, and quickly snapped a photo of the picture in the binder with my cell phone. What more could I think of to ask Esther? My brain went blank and I moved to the sales counter to complete my purchase. Then it came to me.

"If I wanted to talk to Margaret Phelan about designing a project, is there a way I could contact her? I didn't see her information online." I braced myself for Esther to recommend that I contact the store again, even as I worked to suppress distaste for my disingenuous questioning of this nice woman. Instead, luck and Margaret Phelan's business savvy were with me. Esther handed me a business card from a stack on the counter with an attractive logo and Margaret Phelan's email address and phone number printed on a background graphic of an Irish knit shawl.

With nearly an hour left before my meeting with Martin Pappas, I skipped the highway and made my way more slowly toward downtown Dayton, by turns giddy about and distressed by what I'd learned at the knit shop. I'd gained a preliminary sense of the real people who stood behind Julia Reiss. They were no longer faceless antagonists. Doubt crept into my resolve to find the truth about Julia's biological father as quickly as possible. I was doing all of this behind her back. The upheaval that would be visited on her family, as well as my own, began to weigh more heavily. Perhaps I should try to persuade Julia to let this matter rest. Perhaps she would respond to my desire to avoid the anguish her pursuit would doubtless bring to all involved.

She needs to know. I would need to know. I DO need to know. My conviction that learning the truth and managing how that information emerged would help minimize its negative impact on my family returned forcefully, and I wove through the streets of downtown Dayton toward Martin Pappas's office.

He turned out to be nothing like my preconceived notion of a private investigator, neither ruggedly handsome nor disheveled and quiet. I'd watched too many TV shows. Tall, blond, and middle-aged, Martin Pappas was clean-cut and dressed with casual elegance. Soon after he ushered me into his spacious, tidy office, we were seated in comfortable leather chairs facing each other across a glass coffee table.

I nervously summarized what we'd already emailed and spoken about, adding what I'd just learned at the knit shop. Pappas then shared his preliminary work. As Norman had predicted, Julia Reiss's birth certificate named Aaron Reiss as her father. Pappas had found hospital records listing Fiona Phelan as unmarried at Julia's birth. Due to potential Rh factor incompatibility, another form listed Julia's blood type as A-negative. No adoption proceedings regarding Aaron or Julia Reiss appeared in Ohio courts. Pappas had traced the years of Fiona's employment at the university and Aaron's workshops, residencies, and courses in art centers, galleries, and colleges. The families' criminal and driving histories were unremarkable. Pappas had bulleted on a results sheet all that he'd found to date, and had efficiently laid out my options for continued pursuit of the information I wanted. He could keep digging (it would become more expensive), but he believed the clear course was to secure DNA samples from Julia and Steven, in order to determine whether Steven was Julia's biological father. Any other route to secure that information surreptitiously and quickly seemed to him fraught with problems of legality and reliability, not to mention time and cost. He went on to describe how easily samples could be collected from cups, straws, cigarette butts, etc.

After handing me his report, Pappas leaned back in his chair and said, "Mrs. Stone, I've secured this first round of information as we discussed, but I think it's important to ask yourself again what it is you want to have happen and what you expect the consequences to be."

"I want to know if Julia is my husband's daughter," I answered, annoyed at what seemed to me so obvious.

"Yes, of course," he said. "But from hearing you talk, and with your conviction that your husband has no knowledge of having possibly fathered Julia, continuing to pursue this information without telling him—or Fiona Phelan, for that matter—has consequences. Each of them could feel betrayed rather than protected, as I think you see yourself doing."

I squeezed my eyes shut for a moment. His points challenged my resolve. But I'd made my decision. "There is enough upheaval in my family right now," I said. "I don't want to introduce more if I don't have to." Another notion suddenly entered my thoughts. "For whatever reason, Julia came to me—not to her mother, and not to Steven. Maybe that gives me the right to manage this shock my own way. Maybe it doesn't, but that's kind of where I am with it at this point."

"All right. As long as you're going into this with your eyes open, I think we have a plan." Pappas went on to detail the DNA collection process.

Fifteen minutes later, I left Pappas's building and crossed the street to stagger through the cheerful crowd of shoppers at the 2nd Street Market. Lunch seekers had Mediterranean, Italian, and Indian food vendors to choose among, and even in January, local farmers, dairies, and bakeries had fresh and preserved foods for sale. Food and coffee aromas wove a sensory net around my jumbled thoughts.

I purchased a cup of coffee and stared at the paper cup, realizing it could serve to provide someone with my DNA. I'd just arranged with Martin Pappas that I would secure samples from Julia and from Steven. He would stand by if I wanted him to acquire a surreptitious sample from Fiona

Phelan. In the final analysis, I'd been unwilling to authorize that invasive step with a woman I'd never met and who had no inkling of what her daughter had set in motion. Pappas's raising the moral imperatives around betrayal deepened my own concern and added to Norman Tripp's warnings. My hand shook as I brought the coffee to my lips. Suddenly I wanted to be home—back in Ann Arbor and dealing with the mild frustrations of caring for others, then back to the farmhouse and figuring out how to devote myself to the dream of my own business, in the northern place of my heart.

Chapter 20

"Good news, Abbie. Congress just passed regulations that ease taxes on hard cider producers and add pear cider to the craft brew side rather than the wine side. Won't take effect until later in the year, but this is good for our future. Give me a call when you can—I may have a bead on a collection tank. I left a message for you at the house, but you can ignore it. Didn't know exactly where you were. But by the end of this week, James will be back up here, and the three of us can have a sit down. Talk to you soon."

Charlie Aiken's voicemail on my cell phone reached across the entire state to replace the leaden feeling of moral decrepitude I'd battled all morning, ever since leaving Ann Arbor. On my way north, I'd mailed off Steven's nail clippings and a swab from a drinking cup to a DNA lab, and I'd resolved to collect a sample from Julia in the next few days.

Charlie's enthusiastic words drew me north through the quotidian landscape of mid-Michigan. I'd asked him to sort out his business options with his son, and he'd apparently done so. I, on the other hand, felt anything but sorted out. I hadn't even formally put together my part of the proposal.

I'd wanted to go over it with Steven, but in the entire ten days I'd been home, I'd barely managed to discuss anything beyond Alex's predicament and the grocery list. All that we couldn't talk about had caged me like an iron lung. So I hadn't spoken about my business at all; instead, I had concentrated on Alex, on holiday visits, on household chores, on working with Steven in safe, common territory. We had passed on a proposed trip to Chicago to see my sister Alice for New Year's. Neither of us felt like being lively at a party.

As if channeling my frustration at our family drama playing against my orderly plan to organize the business of my dreams, Alex's name popped up on my cell phone with the insistent ring tone I'd assigned for his calls.

"Hey honey," I answered.

"Hi Momma," he answered, and right away I heard more calm in his voice than I had at any time in the previous two weeks.

"I'm on I-75 in the middle of Michigan, headed north. What are you up to?"

"I'm on my way in for an afternoon shift." He paused. "I talked to Haley this morning."

"Really. How did that go?"

"We actually had a fairly reasonable conversation."

"Oh Alex, that's great." How quickly the slightest hopefulness brought tears.

"I told her that I'd needed some time to think after our blowup last week, and that I thought we should step back and try to communicate a little better."

There is a God. "Good for you. That can't have been easy. What did she say?"

"She said it really freaked her out when I asked her if she wanted to go through with the pregnancy, and when I asked her if she wanted to reconsider trying to make a go of our relationship. It was kind of like whiplash, and she just lost her temper."

"That sounds like an honest admission."

"Yeah, I think we were both honest. I told her that if this is my kid, I'm going to take responsibility for it. It's not what I expected to be doing at this point in my life, but I'm not going to be a deadbeat either."

"Did you actually say that to her?"

"More or less."

"Alex Stone, you never cease to amaze me. How are you feeling now?"

"What do you mean? I wasn't planning to be a parent and I don't believe in raising kids in two households, so what amazes you?" Irritation spiked in his voice, but absent the venomous energy of our previous few conversations.

"You amaze me because you feel the way you do but were still able to talk to her civilly—at least, it sounds like you did. That'll go a long way toward making this process—"

"Mom, I don't need a cheerleading session here. I just wanted to tell you so you wouldn't be up north drinking scotch and being all depressed."

How well this boy knew me, but his brashness left me breathless. "Thank you. That's very thoughtful. Have you thought about when you'll tell your brothers?" I knew I was pushing it.

"Mom! I'm almost at the hospital. Gotta go."

"Bye. Have a good shift." When Alex needed to be out of a conversation, he needed to be out. I gently performed a neck roll in either direction and eased the tension in my shoulder. Alex had stepped up. I was so proud of him.

The open farmland stretched on either side of the highway as far as I could see under the cloudless sky. Dry roads and minimal traffic made for a perfect travel day, and I set the car to cruise control. *Another grandchild—one I didn't know if I'd ever be able to see.*

I couldn't fathom all that this might mean for Alex's future, but one thought struck me swiftly, causing me to sit up straighter: He wouldn't be coming back to Michigan any time soon. He wasn't going to join me in the cider business any time soon. He would stay and navigate the radically different course his life had now taken. His attention would be elsewhere for quite some time. *Funny how decisions get made for us sometimes.*

I flipped the radio on, grateful, once again, that I'd splurged on satellite service.

"I'd like to welcome Jake and Deborah, who've come to tell us about their website, FertilityIQ.com, a forum for couples experiencing infertility to rate their doctors and clinics and learn more about others' evaluations. Jake, tell us how you came to start this site . . ."

My God, a Trip Advisor for infertile people. I shook my head, the stone of anguish produced during all the years of tests, drugs, surgeries, and dashed hopes weighing with familiar heft at my center. Alex's unplanned child and the appearance of Julia Reiss were throwing me back to that time of fear and uncertainty, of exploding constructs of how to make family or claim family.

". . . and in other news, *New York Times* best-selling author Pat Conroy has died. In a memorial reading today, the words of the author . . ." *Another tortured author that I love, gone.* " . . . Why do they not teach you that time is a finger snap and an eye blink, and that you should not allow a moment to pass you by without taking joyous, ecstatic note of it, not wasting a single moment of its swift, breakneck circuit?"

I wasn't sure I could manage joyous ecstasy right at the moment, but I surely felt like the clock of my life had sped up in these last months, events and changed circumstances flying by like the mid-Michigan flats outside my car window. In the interest of not wasting time, and because checking tasks off my list had always worked as a way to slow down and anchor myself, I placed a call to the Michigan Liquor Control Commission.

"This is Patty," answered an officious sounding voice.

"Good morning. I'm interested in finding out how to become licensed to produce hard apple cider."

"I would first suggest that you go to our website and look at our frequently asked questions."

"I have done that," I answered firmly. "I saw all the information for beer and for wine producers, but nothing specific to hard apple cider. I understand there have been some recent changes."

"I think the changes you're referring to are on the tax side, not the licensing side."

"So you don't have specific licensing for cider?"

"Hard cider is considered to be fermented wine and falls under those regulations. The alcohol content of the final product determines its licensing category, and then also how much you're producing and whether you'll be selling it in an onsite restaurant, but you'll find all that on the website."

"Okay, but can you briefly tell me what the first steps to initiate the process are, and how long it generally takes?"

"Download the appropriate application form," Patty answered, a note of impatience escaping her robotic tone, "and submit it with the required paperwork and fees. After we've processed your application, we'll schedule an inspection."

"An onsite inspection?"

"Of course."

"And how long does this whole process take?"

"Three to six months."

"Thank you, Patty."

So this meant I couldn't work on licensing until my operation was up and running, but it would be good to study the requirements ahead of time. I should have done this downstate, with high-speed internet. At least now I'd started—done something concrete. I turned up the volume of the radio, switched to an '80s music station, and sang my way to the north country.

Three hours later, I stood in front of an open cupboard door with a glass of scotch in one hand and a fistful of potato chips in the other. The late-afternoon sun slanted across the old snow outside the kitchen window. Even with the second floor shut down, it took a long time for the old farmhouse to warm, and the kitchen was always the first room to get there. The ceramic wood stove began to throw out significant heat, but I'd realized the chill I felt came as much from my own inside as from the cold house, so I'd recruited the scotch, and now it was working its magic.

Still, the phone sat waiting on the counter. I downed another swig, picked up the phone, and dialed Julia Reiss.

"Hi Julia, this is Abbie Stone."

"Oh, hi Mrs. Stone, happy New Year." Julia sounded hesitant and didn't say more.

"Happy New Year to you too. I was hoping you could come for coffee . . . tomorrow would be great if you can do it."

"I don't work until the afternoon. I could come in the morning."

"That would be perfect. How about ten?"

After replacing the phone in its cradle, I paused long enough to pour another glass of scotch, flushed with what I'd set in motion and carried by the mixture of energy and dread I was feeling to make yet another move. I dialed again, this time to Charlie Aiken, and arranged a meeting with him and James for early afternoon the following day.

The light was fading quickly. I pulled on boots and a parka and walked along the two-track until I reached the shore of the bay, just in time to catch the last of the sunset rays over Cathead point, sparkling in pinks, oranges, and blues across the frozen shallows. Turning back toward the empty house, lit only at the back, I felt the weight of what I'd taken on. I wasn't often lonely when alone. Tonight, I was lonely.

Chapter 21

Snow fell silently overnight; no whistling wind heralded the four-inch blanket that covered the landscape, softening the morning call of chickadees from nearby pines and providing a daybreak snow shovel workout, when I rose. I cleared a path from the drive to the house at the back and another to the front door, which we rarely used but which drew visitors with its formal welcome. By 8:00 a.m., breakfast muffins were cooling on the counter. I'd reviewed a dozen ways the conversation might go with Julia and had practiced possible responses, but now, I simply had to wait.

She arrived promptly at ten, her truck barreling up the unplowed drive, throwing a fantail of snow. She stopped next to my car, close to the back entrance, and I greeted her at the door. A blast of cold air and her reddened cheeks, ready smile, and shiny curls immediately freshened the whole atmosphere of the kitchen. Nothing furtive, no veil of dread hung about her, leaving me suddenly paralyzed with doubt about my surreptitious plans. *Should I be including her in this, not working around her?* Quickly, Norman and Pappas's words of warning and caution flooded in. Even if Julia had told me the whole truth, I didn't know her, didn't know where she wanted to go with this question of paternity.

I poured coffee and asked about Julia's brief holiday visit to Ohio and whether there was any news at Dolls and More. After only a few exchanges, I took the plunge.

"Did you say anything to your parents, or learn anything more about surrogacy, when you were home?"

The abrupt change appeared to startle Julia, and her fingers tightened around her coffee cup. I'd carefully chosen the decorative disposable hot cups. They were pretty, and Julia Reiss didn't know me well enough to note that I never served coffee in paper cups.

"No," she said. "I wasn't home for that long and we did a lot of holiday visiting." She looked up at me then, and I could see the question in her eyes before she asked, "What about you? Did you find anything out?" I suspected the mixture of pleading and discomfort on Julia's face mirrored my own.

She'd given me the opportunity I'd needed. "I didn't find anything either. We had a bit of a family crisis that came up just going into the holiday, so I wasn't really able to do any searching."

"Oh no. I'm so sorry. Is everyone okay?"

"We're okay. It's just, something's come up for Alex that's quite unexpected . . . and life-changing." The minute the words were out of my mouth, I regretted them. *Sorry Alex.* Before Julia could ask anything more, I pushed on. "Right at this moment, I can't approach Steven. There are too many stresses on our family right now." I took a sip of coffee and Julia waited, silent and unmoving. I leaned toward her, across the kitchen table around which my family had gathered for so many years. "I know how important this is to you, and I am committed to finding out the truth, but I just need a couple of weeks to get through the mess we're in before . . . I stir the pot." I caught myself before saying, "before getting us into another mess." As resistant as I felt, I didn't want to put Julia on the defensive.

Her gaze dropped to her hands and her shoulders sagged slightly, but her voice remained steady. "All right."

"I want you to think about something in the meantime, Julia." I hoped giving her a task would be a hedge against disappointment. "If it turns out that Steven isn't your father, where will that leave you? Will you pursue other possibilities? Will you feel any more comfortable talking to your mother?" I let these questions sink in for a moment, hesitating as a pained look passed over Julia's face. "There's no going back once we know. Even more important, if it looks like he is your father, how will you tell your mother and the rest of your family?"

"Well, she sure hasn't been in a big rush to tell me. And already there's no going back," Julia blurted out.

As cautious as I was trying to be, and as much as I balked at the unwelcome way in which this girl had insinuated herself into my life, my heart went out to her, and her anger. We were, each of us, trying to control a potentially out-of-control situation for ourselves.

"I know," I said, "but just think about it. Remember, this is the woman who's played a pretty important part in what sounds like a really good family that you have, right? Any which way this shakes out, it's going to be hard, but it's going to be okay too. We just have to work to make it okay." I realized this sounded maternal. I didn't know if I even had the courage of my own conviction—I had my doubts about the possibilities—but at the moment, I needed Julia to consider me an ally. She did not answer me but began to make moves to leave, carrying her plate to the sink and looking for the garbage to throw away her cup. I hastily rose from my chair, sending my own empty cup skittering across the table.

"Just leave everything, I'll take care of it, thank you," I said—too nervously but Julia seemed not to notice. She just stared out the kitchen window toward the newly roofed cider shed.

"Does this mean Alex won't come back here to help you with the cider business?" she asked.

"I'm not sure," I said.

"You know, you should try the Saskatoons in your cider," she said.

"Saskatoons?" I asked blankly.

"Yeah, you know, the berries the Leytons grow—they're a type of serviceberry."

"Right, yes, but in cider?"

"My dad's always fooled around with brewing beer and making wine. He's used different berries for flavoring. It might be worth an experiment." She turned to face me. "When are you going to start production?"

I smiled. This girl had some skills. Whether she was trying to put me at ease or just trying to offer something to a project that she knew interested me, her questions countered the distress and uncertainty we were both feeling.

"I think I'm going to start experimenting with production this summer." In the telling, I realized it was true, and the chill at my center warmed for the first time in days. I would announce this plan to Charlie this afternoon.

"That's great," Julia said.

As her truck receded down the driveway, more slowly than it had at her boisterous arrival, I carefully placed Julia's coffee cup, now flattened, in the DNA kit and sealed it. Though my stomach roiled with nerves, my fingers worked with steady purpose. I had no time for doubt now.

Two hours later, seated at my kitchen table once again, I served Charlie and James fresh coffee, tea, and fragrant muffins. I outlined my plan to affiliate with the nascent Michigan Cider Association, to acquire or produce small batches of juice for trials of different cider mixes, and to install fermentation and aging equipment; I laid out the substantial budget I'd developed, with three phases of implementation, beginning with this summer's trial batches; and I asked Charlie and James if I could use the old press in their barn if I needed it, just for the experimental phase. They agreed, and James reviewed what he'd learned about bottling and distribution from his experience producing beer. He would draw up a detailed business plan. He was clearly in.

Charlie, whose responsibility would center on growing the apples, remained mostly silent. We had to wait for the trees to mature before full production could happen. He looked tired for this early in the day, but his few questions and contributions were well targeted and helpful. No one asked about Alex, or about Steven, and I mentioned neither. Our meeting ended with the promise to reconvene in a month. We had no formal contract, but we'd moved beyond talk to action, and my plans for the summer excited me.

The Aikens left and I woke my laptop to email Alex. He knew his way around the world of eBay and equipment auctions.

Hey Sweetie, I know you're preoccupied right now, but will you keep a cyber eye out for cider making equipment for me? Everything beyond the press—growlers, casks, and fermentation equipment. Love you.

Done. I was making headway. Still, as I pulled on boots and a parka, stepped out into the afternoon cold, and crunched my way to the Flex, the needle of my moral compass sent dull stabs into my gut. Under my arm I carried the DNA kit, with the sample from Julia's coffee cup. I still had a chance to turn this discovery over to the principal actors—to Steven and Fiona Phelan and Julia. I could step back.

Forcefully, with less anger than determination, conviction flooded through me once again. *I didn't ask for this, it's none of my doing, but by God if my life and my family are going to be thrown into chaos, I want to know about it and manage it the best way I can.*

Chapter 22

I'd passed the sign, located on the final stretch of M-22 before the blinking light that signaled entry into North-port, a hundred times. Today, the road was desolate in the way of grey icy January mornings in northern Michigan. The dry cold and snowless overcast effectively blocked sunlight and any expectation of warmth. For years I'd thought of stop-ping—of copying the phone number under the words "Tarot Card Readings" and calling to arrange an appointment—but never had. I didn't know the first thing about tarot, beyond a distant notion of a fortuneteller in flowing India-print robes telling inscrutable things about the future.

Then, at Thanksgiving, I'd met Marie Elena during our labyrinth adventure, and just yesterday had seen her in town at the bookstore. I couldn't place where I'd met her, so I'd asked, and our conversation had developed to reveal her work as a poet and healer and, finally, tarot reader. I banished Steven's rolling eyeballs from my mind's eye, wondering if perhaps she could see him anyway, and the thought suddenly popped into my head to try a reading. It had been nearly a week since I'd sent in the DNA samples, and I knew I'd get the results any day now. I could barely function. Why not try a tarot reading when questions of family identity, business ventures, and personal upheaval were at stake? Though mostly a pragmatist, I also believed in instinct. The pull toward any paradigm that might lend clarity to events about to unfold acted on me powerfully.

So I had phoned Marie Elena for an appointment, and now I rolled down her driveway, berms of snow on either side funneling me toward the house. Its warm yellow paint provided a cheery contrast to the grey winter morning.

Marie Elena greeted me in an attractive wool skirt and sweater, not an India print in sight. She led the way into an open central room filled with a mix of antiques, upholstered chairs, and an odd assortment of tables. A fine Persian rug lay on the wood floor. We crossed into a second room, an add-on to the original farmhouse, and then passed through to yet another, smaller room, where the plaster had been repaired and cleanly painted. A serviceable laminate table, two dressers, a bench, and a bookshelf comprised the furnishings, and prints of Buddhist deities graced the walls. A beaded deerskin pouch sat on the table.

Marie Elena seated me and in a gentle voice asked, "What brought you here today? Do you have a specific question you'd like answered?"

"Not really," I said. I wasn't ready to reveal all that had brought me to her.

Did I know about tarot? I didn't, and so she explained that the cards could give me a snapshot of the important forces operating in my life. I still had choices and free will, but a reading could clue me into my life's direction. In pursuit of joy and fulfillment, she said, we sometimes got stuck with one idea of how that should happen. "A reading can show where your challenges might lie, and what energies would be helpful to meet those challenges."

She went on to talk about karma and different lifetimes, and mostly I stayed with her. She must have seen or felt that my earnest effort to absorb it all for the sake of making this a meaningful experience bordered on incredulity, because she soon wrapped up her introduction and proceeded to withdraw a deck of round cards from the deerskin pouch.

"I'm going to shuffle these and then ask you to place your hands on top of the cards and arrange them into three piles."

When I'd accomplished this, she drew seven cards from the three piles and arranged them faceup in what seemed to be a particular order. "If you don't have a specific question, we will simply call your spirit guides to join us," she said.

As much as I was drawn in, my real questions remained unspoken. *Is Julia Steven's child? Will she become his daughter? How will that change our lives? Will Alex be able to manage his impending fatherhood?*

Marie Elena continued to look at me, and I thought a quizzical expression passed fleetingly across her face, but if so, it vanished swiftly. For the next fifteen minutes, she spoke quietly but firmly, interpreting each of the cards.

She called the focus card of the reading the World card. "Your world is about to expand," said Marie Elena, "through events or a new person."

The hair on my arms tingled.

"This will create wholeness and completion," she continued. "The woman pictured on this card is ready to break free and start a new cycle of life."

Another chill passed through me, and I continued to stare at the cards as Marie Elena moved on.

"Your second card is the Chariot. You will be victorious in steering your life direction, and in balancing the spiritual and material planes. You may face unexpected challenges, but you will meet them with calmness, core strength, and ultimate joy."

I stared at the woman in the chariot, and at a second female figure on the card, entirely blue, who bent over the whole scene like the night sky, stars studding her body. She hovered over *an apple tree!*

The warrior woman in the chariot drew me in like a magnet, as did the mysterious, protective blue woman. The card's colorful images danced off the table and into my center and the room receded. Like the circle of women on the World card, the hands of one holding the feet of the next, in that moment I felt surrounded by a fierce but loving energy. *I need to act from my warrior woman center, whatever happens. I cannot act out of fear.*

After what felt like a long time, I returned my awareness to the room and Marie Elena, who looked at me calmly, expectantly. Did she know?

Before I could even formulate a question, she continued. "Your third card is the Justice card. It symbolizes what is fair and just. Because it is tilted so far to the right, you may feel out of balance. Perhaps you're expending too much energy on getting the outcome you want, rather than where truth and justice lie. Perhaps you need to look at a bigger picture."

All control of my thoughts subsided, along with consciousness of space and time, and a vision of Julia rose before me. *Truth and justice.*

"The Eight of Discs," said Marie Elena, pointing to the next card, "suggests that you need to take the time to consider next steps, to patiently wait for opportunities, and avoid mistakes from earlier attempts. You have many talents and gifts, and you can trust in yourself." She moved to the next card. "Your lesson card is the Sun card, a very powerful life card. You have a radiant life force at this time. You will pursue opportunities with the warmth of a loving heart."

I could only stare at Marie Elena as she pointed to a card depicting a community of women acting as midwives to a younger woman, ready to give birth. "This next card suggests that you will have the support of your community, or perhaps be that support, but the tilt suggests you may be hesitant to seek or give the support needed, and to feel part of something larger." Unbidden, Fiona and Margaret Phelan came to join Julia at the edge of my consciousness. Would I need to make community with them for the sake of a child? Would I birth that fully grown child into my family? Or perhaps this signified something about Alex's child. Who would be the village to welcome this grandchild with me? I shuddered once again, but Marie Elena moved on.

"Your last card is the Judgment card. Now is the time for everything to come out into the open. It is a time of change and it may not be smooth, but the outcome will make you happy, and since this is your outcome card, it is very powerful. Because the card is tilted, you may face opposition and harshness from those who do not understand you. Give others time to rest and renew themselves so that healing energy may come to them. In all of this you will find the courage and strength to be the person you are meant to be, because your consciousness flows from unconditional love."

As if to consecrate this benediction, Marie Elena reached both her hands to mine, which were gripping the edge of the table. She gently massaged my fingers up to my wrists. What I'd engaged in as a diversion, a parlor trick, suddenly felt like a tsunami of energy, a beacon of light leading out of the trap of unsettling decisions I'd made to pursue the truth behind Julia's connection to Steven without their involvement. I wouldn't be derailed, but I had some thinking to do about acting from unconditional love.

Wordlessly, I held Marie Elena's gaze, unable to move past the swirl of stunning revelations that had just lodged in me like a flock of birds settling in the branches of a tree.

And still, Marie Elena wasn't finished. "I've done the computations from your birth date to determine your Life card and your Year card. Do you want me to tell you?"

I nodded mutely.

"Your Life card is the Lovers card. You need balance and integration in joining with others. This card can signify a person falling in love, or perhaps a first time making an entirely independent decision, of finding your own truth in your life. It's an important card; it suggests that you may get your heart's desire. And your card for this year is the Crone, sometimes known as the Hermit card. It often comes when there is a crossroads in a person's life, when you need guidance to make a serious decision. It reflects a time of soul searching, of listening to your heart and your intuition to tell you what to do. See how the sun, that radiant, powerful, but sometimes overpowering life force is pushed behind the Crone, allowing the moon goddess to rule emotion and intuition? The Crone has much life experience, as she is older. Her lighted staff helps others find the way, though this may require a period of solitude and reflection. Finding the right path is sometimes lonely work. The Crone stands ready to light the way when others are ready to move forward in a course of action."

Marie Elena pushed the glass of water she'd brought me closer to my hand and quietly rose, leaving me to try and gather myself. As I pulled her payment from my wallet, I thought, *I'll never remember all this.* I snapped photos of the cards with my phone.

I still hadn't moved when Marie Elena returned carrying two sheets of paper. One had a schematic of the seven card positions, along with one-sentence summaries of each of the interpretations written next to each one. The other page listed my life card and year card computations and descriptions.

"Thank you so much," I said quietly. "I think I got in touch with my warrior self." I smiled. Marie Elena smiled back, and led me through the living rooms to the front door.

Outside, even though it was still overcast, the day seemed blindingly bright. After stumbling to the Flex, I sat for several minutes before slowly heading back out to the world, and home.

For two more days, I haunted my email account, cleaned furiously, and knit until my fingers hurt, all in an effort to tolerate the wait for DNA results. We were enjoying what people in northern Michigan call a "January thaw," which means only that temperatures rise into the high thirties or even low forties at midday.

On the third morning, I turned my walk to the mailbox into a long hike around the shoreline and back through the woods, sinking into snow dampened by the warmer temperatures.

By the time I returned, a Crock-Pot full of sweet and sour meatballs had infused the kitchen air with a pungent comfort. As I pulled a spoon from the drawer to stir them, an email ping sounded on my laptop. I sat down and found a brief email that instructed me to go to the website for the DNA lab results.

Perhaps I should have driven to the library in town, which had high-speed internet, but I could not wait, and so— heart pounding, fingers shaking, cursing the tedious progress of the blue line measuring the browser page's slow loading progress—I entered my user name and password.

In the split second before I read it, I knew. They were a match. With 99 percent confidence.

Like a sonic boom, the knowledge knocked me back in my chair. Now I knew. Now I would have to do something. Make decisions. The weeks of what-ifs vanished in the face of this reality.

The ringing phone barely surfaced in my consciousness. I couldn't think of a single person I could talk to at this moment, so I let it ring, and cringed when I heard Julia's voice leaving a message I didn't want to listen to.

The vision of the Tarot cards swam before me. What had Marie Elena said? That the Judgment card meant that everything had to come out in the open—that unconditional love would win the day. I didn't possess a single loving thought right now. No ember of tenderness lightened the stony weight behind my breastbone. *Steven.* I shuddered. *I should probably get in the car right now and drive downstate.* The urgency I felt to speak to him immediately, to offload this terrible knowledge that, unbeknownst to him, lay between us like a tumor, sent me to the phone.

What was just and fair would prevail, Marie Elena had said, but neither justice nor fairness was finding any space in my frozen heart just now. The blinking light of the answering machine also thrust the problem of Julia Reiss front and center, but I couldn't think of her now, and left the message unheard.

"Hello," Steven's rushed, impatient voice made my heavy heart sink further.

"Hey, how are you?" I realized I hadn't spoken to him in two days, an avoidance I now regretted.

"I can't talk now. There's been a breach and a breakdown in all the computer systems at the firm. I have to go in."

"Jesus. Sorry. Call me when—"

"I've got to take the other line." Steven was gone.

I stood looking at the phone for a long moment before crashing it back into its cradle. A rage I'd been holding at bay burst forth with blinding power. *Maybe I just won't tell him. Make up some lie to tell Julia and just move on with my life.* The years of holding down the fort, of managing crises at home for days at a time while Steven worked across the state or left because of a case or a crisis, bubbled up with a familiar sense of my being left holding the bag. *Our* crises were dealt with on *his* schedule.

I knew my thoughts were unfair. Steven didn't know about this upheaval, and I hadn't told him. As a senior partner in the law firm, he had to handle messes. The old process of rationalizing, making allowances, and shouldering responsibility took hold like lava pouring forth from a volcano—sealing the rock of resentment under its fierce heat.

I poured a scotch. It was five o'clock somewhere. Downing a gulp, I surveyed my options. I could wait and speak to Steven later. I could see Julia and break the news to her.

Or—and this thought popped up with the clarity of the perfect plan—I could contact Fiona Phelan. *Yes.* I knocked back another belt of scotch. Her choice had created this mess. Her lap was where I intended to drop it.

Chapter 23

To drive to the middle of Ohio on a January Sunday to blindside a stranger about the paternity of her twenty-five-year-old daughter surely made no sense. Nonetheless, fueled by anger and frustration, I had already traveled two hours south before the sun rose the next morning. The thaw had given way during the night to a knock-down, drag-out snowstorm, so the first hour had been slow and treacherous. Now I sailed down a cleared expressway, considering my listening choices: audiobook, music, or NPR talk, which at this hour might be gardening or a spirituality show. Neither interested me, so I was soon listening to a novel about a young woman in 1940s Chicago whose ambitions gave way to her husband's career. The well-told story reminded me that everything and nothing had changed since those marker years for women my mother's age.

My mother. I shuddered with gratitude that my parents were gone and I needn't explain away yet another deviation in my life from their expected order of things. Leaving that and all other thoughts, I immersed myself in the audiobook.

After another hour, I stopped for gas and coffee, and to stretch my legs. Rural Michigan early on this Sunday morning featured small towns and farmland in the wide spaces between cities, all sleeping under blankets of snow. Where others might see boredom, I found comfort and peace.

Back on the road, I could no longer keep the confrontation that lay ahead out of my thoughts. I had the phone number and address of the Phelan/Reiss household. If I drove straight through—and, buoyed by a large coffee and an Egg McMuffin, I planned to do just that—I would arrive by noon. And then what? I had no plan other than to show up at the house and ring the doorbell. In another hour it would be civilized to phone, to warn Fiona that I was coming . . . but would I? Would I give her the chance to put me off, or to not be there? I didn't think so.

What would I say to her? What did I really want from her? Acknowledgment that the choice she'd made twenty-six years earlier was now going to hurtle her family and mine into chaos? I gripped the steering wheel. *Yes.* Help in talking to Julia and Steven about their relationship? *Definitely.* An apology for her actions? This one stopped me. She had lied—a huge lie, but would I have done differently? In the cold light of a winter morning, speeding down the nearly deserted expressway, I had to wonder whether in her shoes, I might have been tempted to do exactly what she'd done.

Memory carried me back to the time, nearly thirty years earlier, when I'd undergone an exploratory surgery that confirmed my infertility. The surgeon had come into the recovery room with Steven, the two of them obviously having already conferred. I tried to stay on the conscious side of the anesthesia that still bathed me in a cloud of cotton, but I heard loud and clear the surgeon's words: "Your fallopian tubes are badly scarred. You will never conceive children normally."

The months that followed were laser focused on acquiring family in different ways. We applied for adoption, scheduled surgery and in vitro fertilization, and then, as each of these presented barriers of time and failure, considered surrogacy. And I'd asked Steven to take that option off the table after a single attempt.

Meanwhile, Fiona had found herself pregnant and couldn't live with the arrangement either. She made a choice. Would I have chosen differently? Having now adopted two children and finally borne a child myself, would I release a child I'd carried for nine months for a substantial sum of money to help a family have a baby? While I couldn't summon the last measure of grace to really put myself in Fiona Phelan's place, the pit in my stomach told me that she did have a place, and it was one I'd have to reckon with.

I had crossed the Ohio State line now, and weak sun lit the way south on Route 68 to the middle of Ohio, past churches surrounded by small huddles of cars and trucks and fallow fields without the snow blankets of those to the north.

I stopped two towns short of my destination to freshen up. What had Marie Elena said about one of the tarot cards? We're required to pause and consider, to think and be patient, but not to overthink and therefore fail to act. She'd also told me not to be afraid to call on my spiritual guides for help. *Come on, guides. Let's do this.*

Yellow Springs, Ohio, had the quaint but lively air of a small college town. Stately, century-old homes provided an overall impression of grace, while wildly painted storefronts lent character and the alternative flair for which the town was known.

A café already seemed busy with Sunday breakfast, and an inviting bookshop and galleries lined the town's main street. GPS showed my destination lay less than two miles away. The urge to stop, turn around, and leave welled up, but my guides and I continued. I found myself driving through a well-kept neighborhood, past the high school, and then, abruptly, back into farmland. I arrived at my destination in short order, the foot of a gravel driveway announced by chimes from my car's navigation system.

I drove slowly past it. It led back at least one hundred

yards to a home set sideways in a stand of trees and surrounded by gardens on a sizable expanse of property.

A quarter of a mile down the road, I turned my car
around. When I could see the face of the house, I stopped.

Neither a traditional midwestern farmhouse nor a
modern suburban home, the main portion of the house featured fieldstone and brick, with a large extension at the back.
Maybe the rear portion housed Aaron Reiss's wood shop, or
maybe that was in one of the two additional outbuildings that
sat farther back on the property.

I hadn't pulled far enough to the side of the road; when
a pickup truck whizzed by, perilously close, I had to move.
I pulled onto the road and crept up to the driveway. Turning in slowly, I made my way toward the house, my resolve
crackling like the stones under the Flex's wheels. A win-
ter-browned, grassy pullout to the left of the drive provided
the last moment of sanctuary, and I stalled, looking out over
the gardens and the fields beyond. *Do it, Abbie Rose Stone.
Just do it.*

Fiona Phelan opened the heavy oak door with its inset leaded
glass window. As the door swung away from me, I thought,
Aaron Reiss probably made that door.

I recognized Fiona immediately from the pictures I'd
seen of her. Snapshots fail to communicate the depth, the
luminosity of a person's looks. Fiona's green eyes, her fair,
freckled complexion, and short spiked hair radiated energy,
balanced by a subdued expression that spoke of hard work
and experience.

"Can I help you?" she asked, and I realized I'd been
silently taking it all in for longer than was comfortable in
the social contract of a stranger ringing someone's doorbell.

"Are you Fiona?" I asked to give us both a moment.

"Yes," she responded, her eyes already revealing the
attempt to recognize, to make sense of my appearance.

"My name is Abbie Rose Stone. I live in Northport, Michigan, and I know your daughter, Julia. It appears that her biological father is my husband." I'd crafted these words over the last hours, and I delivered them with as much calm as I could muster, my one concession to a mean-girl desire to throw this woman for a loop equal to the one she'd thrown me. Yet I found I took no pleasure in it.

"Ohh," Fiona gasped, grabbing the door with both hands. Her eyes didn't leave mine.

I quelled the instinct to rush to an apology, to soften the blow. I waited. Fiona continued to stare, and remain speechless, as a shiver visibly traveled down her entire body.

The time had come for my next practiced statements. "I know this is shocking, and I'm sorry to bring this to you out of the blue. Julia doesn't know this, though she suspects, and my husband doesn't know at all, but they need to." Again, I waited. My own experience had taught me that people in shock need time to absorb information. I tried to keep that information simple. "For a lot of people's sake, you and I need to talk about how to proceed with this. I assume your family is here. I saw the Winds Café on my way through town. Will you meet me there? Say in half an hour?"

Fiona's stricken face had gone deathly pale, but intelligence and a small measure of self-possession returned to her eyes, which left my gaze and darted around the circumference of the cold space that held the two of us. Then she spoke in a quiet voice. "I'll be there in half an hour."

I needed the twenty minutes it took to drive back to the café and wait in line for a table to settle my jangled nerves and prepare for Fiona's arrival. I looked longingly at the sign that said, "Brunch (n.) the socially acceptable excuse for day drinking," but I settled for a double shot of espresso instead. The menu looked upscale organic, and I ordered a fruit plate with a muffin.

I felt anonymous amidst the animated diners around me, but it suddenly occurred to me that Fiona Phelan wouldn't. People no doubt knew her around here. At least other conversations could mask ours, giving us some modicum of privacy, and I'd asked for a corner booth.

Just as I began to consider whether Fiona would really show, she came through the door wearing a beautiful knit coat with matching scarf and hat. I couldn't help but admire the handiwork. Our metal-studded waitress appeared instantly, and Fiona ordered coffee and a scone.

"How did you find me? How did you know?" she asked the moment she'd seated herself and shed the lovely sweater coat, revealing her jeans and another, finer-knit sweater.

Her sudden question surprised me with its pointed directness; I took a breath before answering. "Julia came to me a few weeks ago," I said. "She discovered some paperwork about a prospective surrogate arrangement that led her to suspect her paternity. I believe she didn't want to hurt you or your husband, but she wanted to know, and she decided to investigate." If Fiona wanted to dispense with niceties and be direct, I could do direct.

She sat back in her chair as though I'd struck her.

"To say this all came as a shock to me doesn't quite cover it, and I'll admit I didn't want to rock the boat in my life until I knew something conclusive," I said. "But DNA results prove that my husband is your daughter's biological father, and the timing of her birth coincides with the one and only time we attempted surrogacy . . . apparently with you." My voice had become more strident as I spoke, the words punching harder as they tumbled out. I had never known Fiona Phelan's name. It wasn't like me to have left all the arrangements to Steven. Perhaps that was a symptom of my malaise regarding the whole process. I closed my eyes and willed myself to a calmer delivery. "I just got the DNA results and didn't want to tell Julia until I'd spoken to you. It's not something I wanted to discuss on the telephone."

Fiona's red-rimmed eyes and pinched face broadcast the pain I'm sure also appeared on my own face. "And your husband?" she asked.

"He doesn't know. I haven't been able to speak to him yet, but I'm going to tell him tomorrow." A lingering doubt, buried deep in the maelstrom of all that I'd learned, surfaced and burst out. "He doesn't know about Julia, right?"

"No," Fiona nearly whispered, and relief flooded through me even as a wave of nausea accompanied her tacit confirmation. Steven hadn't withheld this information, but he did have a biological daughter. Fiona Phelan wasn't going to deny it.

Why? I wanted to scream at her. *How could you have done this?* But I knew why. She hadn't been capable of going through with the surrogacy for the very reason I hadn't been capable of continuing to pursue it: I didn't believe I could bear a child and willingly relinquish her. Some people could, for noble or ignoble reasons, but I couldn't have. In this moment, right now, however, I needed to hear Fiona say it, to tell me why she'd done this to all of us, and she must have seen that in my face, because the next thing she said was, "I'm so sorry."

I could see that was true, in the open, unfiltered pain in her eyes, and in the fear that rushed through her near-whispered words. "I meant to honor the arrangement. I really did. But then I couldn't. It's true I needed the money, and I really wanted to help your family have a child, but then, when I actually got pregnant, I just couldn't do it." She looked to me for help, but I had none to offer. I barely had the strength to listen.

"Aaron and I had been living together for a long time," she went on. "We knew he was infertile. He tried to convince me to either end the pregnancy or go through with the surrogate arrangement, but eventually he saw that I couldn't do either, and he understood." Now Fiona's voice became more urgent and tears welled in her green eyes. "I lied, and I acted in my own self-interest. It was wrong, and I knew it then, but

I couldn't . . ." She stopped. The look of desperation on her face reached through my anger, and my resistance to accepting the choice I knew I might have made myself.

"I've tried a million times to make myself talk to Julia," Fiona said, rotating her empty coffee mug around and around in her cupped hands. "She has a right to know, but she loves Aaron, and he loves her, and I didn't want anything to come between them. I didn't want to derail her life. No one else knows, not my mother or my son. My son is adopted. He's a complicated kid . . ."

I expelled the breath I didn't know I'd been holding in a long sigh. I certainly knew about complicated kids. Fiona had recovered some equanimity, and something softer settled over her features as she looked up at me. She appeared to be finished talking for the moment. Expectation hung in the air.

How is it that life-changing decisions are set in the most commonplace of moments? I knew this feeling—the *I'm-going-to-drop-my-defenses-and-put-myself-at-risk-to-help-a-situation-that-I-don't-want-to-be-in* feeling. And yet the thinning brunch crowd still buzzed at their tables, the weak winter light shone through the windows, the wait staff casually refilled coffee cups and set up empty tables. A man sat peacefully at another corner table, reading the Sunday *New York Times*, like I wanted to be doing in my own home.

I'm going to let this woman off the hook. The realization settled over me like cotton candy: soft, sweet, and promising a sticky mess. The reasons tumbled over each other for attention. We were going to share a daughter in some form or other. My actions would influence whether this fundamental shift in two families would happen more or less painfully. The warrior way here would be to decline to engage in a fight. The two innocent people most affected, Steven and Julia, deserved a dignified process. The hard-won homeostasis of my own family's bonds required every effort to preserve. Everyone's interests were best served by this situation becoming cooperative and well choreographed—Abbie Rose Stone's specialty. I suddenly felt old and tired.

I downed the last of my espresso. "So, where do we go from here?"

Gratitude filled Fiona's eyes and spread across her lovely features like a warm spring breeze. Two women, two mothers, two wives would work together.

"I need to talk to Aaron, and we'll talk to Julia." This Fiona said with conviction. Then, more tentatively, she added, "And I want to know how I can help you. What do you need from me?"

Despite my best efforts, tears spilled onto my cheeks and irony replaced anger as the thought drifted out of my head, *It's a little late for that.*

At 3:00 p.m., we rose from our table, the last patrons to leave as the café closed. Exhausted, I wanted nothing more than to check into my hotel and sleep for several days, though I knew I had to drive to Ann Arbor in the morning. Fiona pulled on her sweater, watching me as I donned my coat. Again, I read in her eyes a map of my own feelings. Could we trust each other? Would any of what we'd planned work? I couldn't cement this collaboration with a hug, which came and went as a possibility, but Fiona reached and grasped my arm in parting. I didn't envy her next hours, or look forward to my own, and for the hundredth time, I wished to awaken and have the last few weeks vanish as a disturbing dream, releasing the clutch in my stomach.

Chapter 24

Alone in the car, I considered whether to drive the four hours to Ann Arbor now and sleep in my own bed. Too tired, and too wrung out, I dialed Steven at home instead. He answered on the second ring.

"Hi," he said, sounding surprised.

"Hey, how are you?"

"Okay, just paying bills. It's been a crazy twenty-four hours here. Where are you?"

I realized he'd seen my cell phone number, and knew I wasn't at the farmhouse. "I'm out. What happened with the computers?" I deflected.

"It turned out the breach was minimal and everything's back up and running."

"That's good. What's your schedule tomorrow? I'm actually coming home. Do you have to go in?"

"No, I'll be here unless I get called in. I have my monthly meeting Tuesday, but I'm not in court again until Wednesday. What's going on? Are you okay?"

Keep it together, Abbie Rose. "Yeah, I'm fine," I answered. "I've got a lot of things to take care of, and I just need some time with you." I heard the catch at my throat and knew that if he did, he wouldn't just let me go, so I rushed on, "I'm going to leave really early tomorrow, so I'm going to bed early tonight. I'll see you around noon. Maybe we can go out for dinner or catch an early movie." I knew there'd be no movie.

"All right," he said, tentative. Blessedly, I heard the other phone line ring. "I've got another call, Abbie, I've got to go."

"Okay, bye. See you tomorrow. Love you." I dropped the phone into my lap, hands on the steering wheel, frozen in the emptiness on the backside of too much intensity. *Hotel. Sleep.* Instead, Alex's ringtone insisted itself into my already overworked brain. *Oh God, I can't do an intense Alex call. But what if . . .*

"Hey sweetie," I said, working to keep exhaustion and misery out of my voice.

"Hey, Momma, how are you?"

Oh how I wish I could tell you. "I'm good. What's happening?" Alex didn't call without a reason, even if only his boredom on the drive to work.

"I had a meeting with a lawyer today. We talked about all the ways I need to prepare if this kid is really mine."

The bizarre coincidence of this conversation about an unexpected child struck me like an ice ball. *If only I could tell him everything right now.* But I couldn't, not until I'd talked to Steven.

"That sounds like a good idea," I said slowly. "Was it helpful?" I'd begun to shiver in the frigid car.

"Yeah, it really was." Alex launched into a recap of the consult, and I listened, offering murmured sounds of attention. Prepared to advise him, I found instead that I could affirm with conviction the well-articulated plan Alex and the attorney had already worked out. He would write a will, organize his finances to prepare for the possibility of child support, and work out possible legal proceedings for a menu of custody arrangement options. While Alex's voice expressed no pleasure, neither did it contain the rancor of so many of his earlier reports.

For the second time, I grasped onto the slimmest ray of hope that Alex's life wouldn't be derailed by this unplanned circumstance. "Sounds like you're covering all the bases, Alex. You're doing a good job here," I said quietly.

I waited for a dismissive response, but none came.

"Thanks, Momma."

"Love you, sweetie." Before the tears could freeze on my face, I started the car and made my way to the hotel.

In the years Andrew had worked on Lake Erie, I'd grown to love quiet early morning drives through northern Ohio, with its sense of rock-solid, middle-America well-being. On this Monday morning, clear, cold, and snowless, the sun rose behind me, bringing barns, farmhouses, huddled storefronts, and the cars and trucks of early commuters into stark relief against empty fields—a true architecture of rural and small-town life.

I switched on the audiobook I'd started on the ride down, promising myself pure escape for the drive's first hour. *The Atomic Weight of Love* worked equally well as a description of my state of mind and the title of the book. The themes of a woman reckoning over many years and eras how to balance her sense of commitment to others, her passion for her work, and the need to be nurtured in relationship were beautifully drawn throughout the novel. Whereas the protagonist in the book carried out these efforts in an introverted, isolated world, however, I recognized that my struggles happened in the hurly-burly of an active family life and many other involvements. Two hours flew by, as if I'd driven through an airless vacuum, until the weight of needing to frame what I would say to Steven intruded and I turned the audiobook off.

Just after ten o'clock, I turned the Flex into our driveway in Ann Arbor. The familiar grey cedar shakes, white trim, and red door felt especially welcoming this morning. I sat gazing at the cluster of towering hemlocks and the copper beech tree gracing the front of the house as though they'd always been there. They hadn't. We'd planted them all after the house fire, more than twenty years earlier. Memories of the agonizing days after the fire helped put Julia Reiss's appearance into perspective. We'd gotten through worse.

I carried my suitcase through the front door, smiling at the small pleasure of a *New York Times* sitting on the front porch. *The advantages of urban living. Have to finish shoveling the walks and driveway.*

Before searching for Steven in his downstairs office, I switched on my fancy coffee machine. I'd not yet allowed myself this extravagance at the northern farmhouse. Armed with a fresh-brewed cup of French roast, I made my way down the stairs and past the leather couches and game-enabled TV that had been refuge to so many teenage boys until Seth finally went off to college. An exercise bicycle, rowing machine, and bench with free weights had edged out some space in front of the TV. Steven and I had truly cast a wide net when it came to the people we considered family. We'd gathered in many of our boys' friends during all their growing-up years. *Will we extend that net around yet another group of people? Or will it tear, leaving us all adrift?*

I found Steven leaning over his expansive, L-shaped desk, studying one of its multiple monitors. While he had an official office at the firm, in reality, the nerve center of his administrative functions and a good deal of his legal practice happened right here, where, at ten o'clock in the morning, he could sit as he did now, in flannel pajama pants and a T-shirt, a giant untouched mug of tea cold on his desk, his tall frame stooped forward, eyes fixed on one of the oversized screens.

I watched him for a moment. Though I was only slightly off to the side of his visual field, he hadn't heard or seen me come in. He never did.

"Hi," I said.

He jumped upright. "Oh Jesus, you scared me. Hi." He looked at his watch. "Boy, you're early."

"Yeah." I rounded the desk, put my coffee cup down, and, as Steven swiveled his chair toward me, leaned in for a kiss. I avoided his gaze as I drew away, grabbing my coffee and staring into its steam.

"Abbie?"

I still couldn't bring myself to look at him.

"Abbie, what's going on? Why are you here? What aren't you telling me?"

I certainly had his attention now, and this man did know me.

"Come upstairs with me."

"Abbie, you're scaring me. Are the kids okay?"

"The kids are fine. I'm fine. But I have an amazing story to tell you. Come on." I pulled his hand, but he resisted.

"Okay, but I have to finish this."

"Nope. You don't. It can wait." I could see on Steven's face that he knew we were now out of any usual mode of interaction. He could get angry and short with me, or he could just go with the out-of-the-ordinary flow and not make it any harder.

"All right, but this is weird," he said.

The spirit guides were with me.

"Yes, it is," I agreed, and led the way upstairs to the kitchen table. For nearly thirty years, we'd shared family information, from the important to the quotidian, while seated around this strong, enduring piece of maple butcher block, only slightly nicked by three boys' punishing use.

Steven warmed his tea in the microwave and sat at his usual place, nervous impatience tightening the expression around his deep brown eyes.

"You remember Julia Reiss, the girl who showed us around the labyrinth at the Leytons' last Thanksgiving, right?" I began.

"Yes, of course," Steven said. "What about her?" He looked at me as though I were a client taking my sweet time providing the information he needed to make a case.

I held his gaze. "She came to see me about a month ago, after Thanksgiving, and after I'd gotten to know her a little at the knit store. She asked me a lot of questions about our family, and then she told me she'd discovered some troubling information about her mother. She didn't know what to do with it."

"Abbie, what does this have to do with me?" Steven interrupted, agitation erupting.

I took a breath and reached out to lay my hand on Steven's. "Her mother is Fiona Phelan."

Steven's eyes unfocused and seemed to search inside his head, but returned to mine in total confusion. "Who?"

He doesn't remember her name. He remembers faces, but not names. Always.

"Fiona Phelan. In Yellow Springs, Ohio. The surrogate attempt." I waited, watching. I moved my hand up to Steven's forearm and felt the smallest jolt as realization spread through him like radiation. "Julia found a document with your name on it, along with evidence that her father was infertile. She did the math. She'd never been told any of this, and wanted to check it out before—"

"Are you saying she thinks I'm her biological father?" Steven's voice cut in, rising incredulously.

"She doesn't really know. But Steven, you are her biological father." I choked the words out.

"What are you talking about?" Steven stood abruptly, his chair knocking into the wall behind him.

"Steven, sit down."

"Don't tell me to sit down. Who says I'm her father?"

"Sit DOWN. I know this is shocking, but I need you to listen to me and talk to me. We've got a lot to get through. Please." My voice had gone steely, but I knew tears weren't far behind.

Steven sank into his chair and dropped his head into his hands, elbows propped on the table.

"This all happened just as everything hit the fan with

Alex. She came to me, Steven. She was scared and a little desperate. I put her off until I could find out more." I hesitated. What came next could be more disaster than I could cope with, but I knew I had to tell the truth, the whole truth. I gripped his arm.

"I tested her DNA, Steven, without her knowing it. And . . . I tested yours too. It's a match."

Tears welled over my cheeks and I bit my lip as Steven raised his head, his mouth agape.

"What?" he said with a gasp.

"Fiona Phelan got pregnant, Steven. She decided she couldn't give up the baby. She raised Julia as her husband's child. He tried to talk her out of it, but when she refused to change her mind, or to tell you, he agreed to raise Julia. They adopted another child. They're a loving family. Julia suspects something but doesn't know what I've discovered yet."

"How long have you known this?" Steven's voice had gone wooden.

"I tried to tell you when I got the DNA results Saturday night. It's when your systems at the office crashed. I decided to go to Ohio and confront Fiona."

Steven stared at me as though I had two heads.

"I saw her yesterday," I said. "She didn't deny any of it. She and her husband—"

"Wait a minute." Steven rose from his chair again, this time pacing the floor around the large, open great room. I moved toward him but he held his hands up, shaking his head, his face gone pale and clammy. He was in shock.

My own heart started pounding. *Oh God, he's going to have a heart attack.*

Abruptly he sat on the large upholstered ottoman in the center of the room. Hitting it rhythmically with his fist, he stared at the floor, then into the snow-covered garden through the glass doors. I sat on the couch in front of him, and at last he looked up at me, his expression shifting back and forth from torture to wonder.

"I have a daughter?" he asked.

Relief mixed with sorrow nearly choked me. "Yeah, I guess you do." He'd said "I," not "we."

Chapter 24

James Aiken's voicemail disturbed me. For one thing, I'd previously communicated arrangements only with Charlie, so I thought it strange that James would phone me out of the blue. And then, his tone sounded subdued. He'd simply asked me to return his call, giving a number with a downstate area code. Something sounded off.

Two more messages from Julia followed his. After three exhausting days in Ann Arbor with Steven and the long ride north, I didn't have it in me to phone either one of them, and put off returning calls until the next morning.

I'd been gone less than a week, but it felt like a lifetime. I now lived in a new reality.

Flipping the wall calendar to February seemed to signify a turn toward spring and provided a pulse of anticipation amidst the drudgery of unpacking and reentering my solitary life. No matter how deeply frozen the landscape out the kitchen window, the six o'clock sky still held light, and longer days were harbingers of the first garden and orchard work—work I looked forward to. In the clarity of morning, I would call James. Then I would arrange to see Julia. *Tomorrow.*

Morning light broke into my sleep with the exuberance of bright sun on snow and water, as if the beams contained so many jewels. In the moments before the day's obligations weighed in, I luxuriated in the stream of sunlight cast across the bed through the uncovered windows and the sparkling snowscape stretching down to the lake. A cross-country ski, before the snow lost its powdery ease, would be in order as a reward for the day's work.

A fire in the wood stove, a pot of coffee, and a list were no sooner in place than the phone rang.

"James, I got back late last night to your messages. Is everything all right?" I grimaced, waiting him to tell me something I didn't want to hear.

"The news is better this morning, but I'm afraid Dad's in the hospital. We thought it was a relapse of his blood disorder; now the doctors are saying it may only be an imbalance in his endocrine system that sometimes happens after the treatments he had. He's going to have a slew of tests. I'll know more tomorrow about whether he needs to be transferred downstate to Ann Arbor, but what he's not going to do is prune trees any time soon, and that's got him more than a little put out."

Welcome home, Abbie Rose. "Oh Jesus, James, I am really sorry to hear this. Man, I bet he's cranky." There are few people I could imagine less suited to lying in a hospital bed waiting for tests than Charles Aiken. "Is he actually feeling ill? Can I visit him? Do you need anything?" *Slow down, Abbie. This may not be your vacuum to fill.*

"You're right about the cranky part. And he's feeling much better. He actually collapsed on Saturday. It's a good thing Melissa was home. Her friends are helping her cover the kids so she can work and see Dad this week. And he wants you to visit all right—with the orchard map in tow. Seems like you're the one he wants to quarterback the spring pruning. He's rounding up help for you, and I wouldn't put it past him to rig up some video feed so he can watch, but I had to promise to reach you just to keep him in that bed." James's laconic voice held a tinge of worry.

"Is he going to be all right?" I realized the stupidity of that question. "Never mind, I'm sorry. One step at a time. Are you up here, or downstate?"

"I stayed up until last night and then had to leave. I'm going to try to come back up later in the week. I know this is a lot to ask, Abbie, and we think we have at least a week or two before we have to start, but this is really about his peace of mind."

"Of course. Well, he may be overestimating my readiness, but we did a pretty good job together last spring." The urge to engage in this challenge thrust up through the distress of the last week, and the out-of-kilter seesaw at my center came into balance, as if I'd been trying to pull down one side and a person at the other end had finally pushed up off the ground. I wanted to do something productive for my cider business, and this would be my opportunity. *Another test.*

"I'll give it my best whirl, James. How can I get the orchard plan?"

James gave a sheepish chuckle. "It's in your mailbox."

I couldn't wait any longer for the reward of a workout ski in this brilliant morning. I'd mowed a trail through the overgrown orchard in the autumn and continued it to the conservancy land across the road. The path swung back to the road along the eastern shore of the point and then down the center to the house. In the heavy powder on the first loop, I felt muscles release their tension one by one as they warmed with the rhythm of two quick inhales and a forceful exhale, all timed to pole plants and lengthening strides. Snow-blanketed pines, woodland animal tracks, and riffled water in the distance where shore ice opened into the big lake all energized me with their serene beauty. Now I could think.

As promised, Fiona Phelan had emailed me after she and Aaron had spoken to Julia. In fact, they'd driven the seven hours to talk to her in person, here in Northport. On the far stretch of my ski loop, I gazed in the direction of the Leytons' farm, imagining what had transpired there only a few days ago. Fiona had restricted her report to three sentences, indicating that they'd explained the whole situation, apologized, answered Julia's questions, and started to discuss whom to tell, and when. Julia had been "understandably upset," and had asked her parents for some time to deal with the situation. Aaron and Fiona had returned to Ohio the following morning. Fiona thought Julia would want to see Steven, and me, sooner rather than later.

Fiona thought Steven should decide when and how he wanted contact with her and Aaron. *I bet she wants to leave it up to Steven.* In all that had transpired, I'd hardly given thought to the future of Steven's relationship with Fiona, and I was in no hurry to get in the middle of that interaction. What Fiona couldn't know was that Steven's priority would be Julia—now and always. He wouldn't waste time on an unrecoverable past. He was not one to dwell on what couldn't be changed. Lucky Fiona, and amen to the good side of Steven's capacity to move on to the next challenge, the next situation to fix.

His initial shock at the sudden revelation, and his attendant giddiness, had since given way to a driving need for information. He wanted to know everything about Julia, about Fiona, about Aaron and their family. Next, he wanted to make arrangements to see them all, to tell our children, to bring the entire maelstrom into our life like tumbleweed in a windstorm.

"Why don't you come up north with me? We can see her together, in person," I'd suggested. "Unless you think you'd rather see her by yourself."

Steven had looked at me in confusion. "Why would I want to see her by myself? She's going to be part of our family, Abbie. She's our daughter."

Now she's ours. The first hints of panic squeezed my chest. "Steven, we don't know exactly what she's going to be. I'm sure she doesn't either. We know that she's your biological daughter, and that's important information for both of you, but—"

"Oh, so that's where you're going with this?" Steven interrupted. "She's just my daughter, and I can go off and do this by myself?"

"That is not what I mean, and do not go off on me right now." My words caught in a sob I couldn't control. "I'm just saying we need to take the time to figure out how all the pieces fit—one step at a time. And I've had as much as I can handle right now."

Steven had backed off, though his face had told me he thought I was behaving unreasonably. We'd waited until the next day to formulate a plan. He couldn't leave work for at least a week, and we both thought the next contact with Julia should be in person, and soon. Reluctantly, I'd agreed to return to Northport and meet with Julia myself, with a follow-up when Steven arrived.

The long ski, paired with a hot bath, had worked magic, and I felt revitalized and hungry. When I stood in front of the open refrigerator, I realized it lacked even the minimal requirements for my solitary existence after a week's absence, so I headed to town.

Cleared snow in small ridges lined driveways and the roads, indicating there hadn't been much snowfall while I was gone. For a Tuesday, town seemed downright bustling, several cars in the grocery store parking lot and more at the hardware store, the bank, and the post office.

I bought my groceries and stowed them in the Flex before heading to the café for a coffee treat and the almond croissant that nobody could make like Danielle. She filled my order quickly, and I could see her accounting papers spread in front of her laptop, so I didn't engage her in a gossip update. I couldn't handle any more gossip on my end anyway, and the juicy news I had, I could not share.

I moved to a corner table and, making use of the café Wi-Fi, checked email and then called the hospital in Traverse City. The phone in Charlie Aiken's room went unanswered.

Looking out the window and across the street, I saw the OPEN sign at Dolls and More. It was time.

Sally called out a hello from the back room when the bells on the closing doors ceased their friendly chiming.

"Hi Sally," I called back, heading toward the studio. Today she sat at a table, putting the finishing touches on a doll.

"Hi Abbie, how are you? Have you made those bunny slippers yet?"

I groaned. "No, the yarn is sitting there reproaching me, but it looks like I'll be able to stay put for a while now, so I should get to it soon. I'm actually looking forward to making those." After asking about her project, a fairy sprite of a figure, I asked, "Is Julia here?"

"No, she doesn't come in until one on Tuesdays. Is there something I can help you with?"

"Oh, no thanks, I just needed to catch up with her. I'll try her at the Leytons'. Thanks, Sal."

The ride back home took me right by Sugarbush Road and the Leyton farm. It was normally a pleasure to visit this property, set on twenty acres and anchored by the custom home the Leytons had built, but today I was filled with dread. As I wound up the driveway, the berry field and pole barn came into view, and then the labyrinth and extensive manicured gardens, asleep now under a blanket of snow. Even in the dead of winter the farm looked beautiful.

I pulled into the circular driveway just as Julia, seated at the wheel of a midsize tractor, finished plowing snow from the cement apron connecting the driveway to the pole barn. She hadn't seen me yet, and I watched as she reversed the tractor through the open doors of the barn and parked it. I sucked in a deep breath and exhaled sharply, feeling perspiration blossom under all my layers of clothing despite the cold.

A moment later, Julia emerged. When she saw me stepping out of my car, she stopped, then turned to close the barn doors before walking toward me. She looked down at the freshly plowed driveway, then back up at me.

"Hi Julia," I said. She had stopped far enough away from me that a hug seemed out of order, so I quelled that urge. "It's been quite a last few days, hasn't it?" *Lame!*

"Why didn't you just ask me for a DNA sample? I already had one, you know." Her abrupt bitterness stopped me. I groped for something to say, for an actual explanation in the tangle of emotions and thoughts that had woven around all the events of the last month.

"I came to you for help to figure this all out. I didn't go behind your back and keep things from you like my parents did. You could have worked with me." By now, anger and pain had constricted Julia's throat and her voice had dropped nearly to a whisper.

"Maybe I should have done that," I admitted. I was tempted to say more—*You came to me out of the blue and dumped this in my lap. This is my life you've disrupted*—but I could see from her hunched posture and clenched mittens that raw hurt governed her understanding. I knew that look, that feeling.

"Look, Julia. You have every right to be upset, to be angry, and feel betrayed. There's plenty of that to go around for all of us." Julia shot a look at me, then dropped her gaze to the ground again and dug her boot toe into the scraped snow and ice. I forced myself to continue, searching for a way in through the barbed wire of her anger. "We could focus on that, and maybe it will take time for each of us to really work out what's happened. But there are other ways to look at this situation. Steven's pretty shocked, but I think he's already more excited and fascinated than upset or angry. He wants to see you really badly. He's willing to wait until you're ready." I stopped.

"What about you?" A spark of fierceness took over the pain in Julia's blue eyes.

What about me? Behind the fierceness lay a real question—about Julia and me. I hesitated for a moment, then stepped forward and rested my hand on her arm. Her breath made short bursts of cloud between us.

"I'm fucking freezing," I said. "Can we go in for a cup of tea?"

Chapter 25

Winter storms, a weeklong thaw, arctic cold, more snow, and Steven's visit for three days formed the backdrop for my effort to plan a spring pruning for Charlie Aiken's orchard. The days flew.

Steven arrived on a Thursday evening the week after I drove north. He and Julia both thought a brunch at our house on Saturday would work for a first contact. Of course, it wasn't really a first contact at all; they had met on Thanksgiving weekend, and had chatted a good bit then. But that felt like a lifetime ago. Steven and I bristled with nervous energy all day Friday. After raising my three boys, I thought I had the rulebook for fielding situations with twenty-somethings fairly well in hand, but the sudden appearance of a twenty-five-year-old child, and a daughter to boot, made for new territory. I had the feeling that bringing Julia into our family would become defined by a sense of "pre and post," the way we'd come to regard our house fire and other far-reaching family events.

I tried in vain to distract myself by charting out the sections of orchard I could prune during the March week for which Charlie had hired and borrowed help. Steven rattled around the house, looking for things to fix. By four o'clock Friday, we'd both given up and driven to the next town for an early movie and a cozy dinner. Steven didn't want to discuss what to say to Julia the next morning. Unlike me, he rarely found value in planning interactions.

On Saturday morning I rose early and prepared my favorite brunch comfort food: an egg, cheese, and bread casserole. I added a fresh fruit bowl, strong coffee, and cinnamon rolls from Barb's Bakery into the mix.

Julia arrived on time, and as she came through the mud-room, shedding her coat, Steven stood and reached for both her hands. It was a good move—not a hug, but an immediate, welcoming touch.

I stared at the two of them as they stood in front of me, and I don't think I stopped staring for the next two hours. How had I gone so long without seeing the distinct resemblance between them? Distraction? Denial? Or was it that we simply don't see what we aren't looking for?

Julia's hands—often the first thing I notice about a person—were long, slender, and strong-looking, just like Steven's. They were both tall and lanky with slender arms and legs, though Julia's posture was more erect and supported the lean, hard muscles of a rower, whereas Steven had the sloping shoulders of a man who bent over computers and leaned in toward clients. Julia's long, loose, black curls reminded me with a stab of nostalgia how Steven's wild hair had looked when I'd first met him in the post-hippy days of the 1980s. Now his curls had greyed and he kept them close-cropped. And although Julia's blue eyes came from her mother's side of the family, their soft, deep set matched Steven's.

I served food and they talked, tentatively at first, and then in a rush, unleashing pent-up curiosity about each other— Julia's family, her schooling, her interests, Steven's work, more details about our children, and then, finally, the future. Julia had set in motion a momentous process, and in a few short weeks had found her way to a measured consideration of the possibilities that lay ahead. Steven seemed ready and willing to travel that road with her. My fascination with watching the Julia-and-Steven show unfolding in front of me alternated with a reserve born of resistance to disruption in my family and a feeling of separation. I had my own questions for Julia, but for now things were—rightfully—all about these two.

"You know, I asked you, when you first talked to me about all this, what you hoped to get out of finding Steven," I finally ventured. "None of us understood the reality then, so now it's really a question for all of us. How do you see this all working out? I mean, can you visualize what your connection with us will look like?" As my words died into silence, I heard their fuzzy, fretful tone. What did I really want to ask?

Julia had the answer she'd come for, and Steven had his enthusiasm, but the future of the various relationships still seemed like a blank slate to me. I wanted to know what each of them expected going forward, but in that moment I realized how ridiculous it was to expect a real answer from either one of them, let alone what my own answer might be.

I thought Steven would throw out some silly pun or joke. He routinely deflected conversation when things turned too psychological. Instead, he rose from the table, said, "Funny you should mention it," and disappeared into the den.

When he returned, he was holding a small box. He placed it in front of Julia, his smile signaling to me that his gift pleased him, and that he believed it would provide some sort of answer to my question.

Julia's eyes sparkled as she opened the box and withdrew a simple silver bangle bracelet. She and I leaned closer to read the inscription engraved with black ink: *When you've got it, you've got it.*

Julia looked up in confusion from Steven to me and then back to Steven. A jolt shot through my chest, sending a lump into my throat, as she slipped the silver circle onto her wrist.

When Steven didn't say anything, I explained. "That's an expression my Dad always used." I cleared my throat but had to wait for the constriction of tears to loosen before I could continue. Maybe Steven was ready to share this intimate knowledge of my father, but my feelings were mixed. "When he died," I continued, brushing my fingers over the engraved words, "my sister made bracelets for the whole family with that saying engraved on them." I could feel Steven's eyes on me, but I couldn't look at him. "My father always celebrated family connection and believed in focusing on the gifts that come our way rather than the barriers."

It surprised me that Steven had thought of sharing my father's words and the cherished legacy they represented. I wished he'd talked to me first. But now he'd brought Julia into that kinship of bracelets, there was no going back. Clearly, as far as he was concerned, Julia was here to stay, and he saw no reason to waste any time before sharing with her this inner-family gift. I knew he only meant well. *Still . . .*

"This is a wonderful gift," Julia said, reaching to put her hand on Steven's. Then, searching my eyes, "I'd like to hear about your dad sometime. You must miss him."

Tears rose again with alarming speed. I did not want to cry, so I threw a smile over the tears, blew out a clipped, "Yeah," and cleared our dishes onto the counter. Then, with the brightest voice I could muster, I suggested, "How about a walk?"

Julia readily agreed, and Steven went to gather his outdoor gear. As though she'd done it in our kitchen a hundred times, Julia rinsed dishes and loaded the dishwasher while I put food away and wiped the table. I felt lost in a Kabuki dance, unable to summon the stylized steps to depict this drama we were enacting. On the surface, we were having a casual brunch with a new young friend, but the deeper subtext included a long-separated father and daughter, old and painful memories, longing for those now gone, and a confusing pathway to the future. I didn't like when the pieces of my life didn't lock securely into each other.

We set off on the footpath, packed down from use, melt, and refreezing. At first Julia and Steven loped in front, heads down, with their long strides, but almost immediately, Julia turned back to me, waiting for me to walk abreast of them. At every turn, it seemed, she wanted to check in, shepherding me into this new connection. I both appreciated and resisted the attention. Having worked so hard to manage this meeting, I found myself intermittently at a loss as to what my role should be.

The trail didn't comfortably allow three bundled people to walk side by side, so I placed a mittened hand on each of their backs. "I'm right behind you. I can hear perfectly well."

We continued across the old orchard, the aged apple trees silhouetted against a pewter sky. With new eyes, I found myself considering the pruning possibilities for these scattered old trees, and the more practical potential of clearing them and planting my own stand of cider apples.

As if she'd heard my thoughts, Julia asked, "These are all old apple trees, right?"

"Yep. I was just thinking about whether to try restoring them or to take them all out and plant a new orchard. I think I'll try pruning and restoration this spring as an experiment. I'm certainly not ready to plant an orchard this year." We were still walking at a decent clip and my last words were somewhat breathless. Perhaps I only imagined Steven's hunching his shoulders a little more and quickening his pace. *Dammit, why do I have to feel like every thought I have about this cider business takes a chunk out of his hide? And meanwhile, we're trotting around the frozen countryside, working double-time to absorb this girl into our lives!*

I tried to focus my thoughts in a more generous direction. After all, this young woman could be working hard to make all our lives miserable. She could be making the whole situation about her alone. Instead, she seemed attuned to each of us without simpering, to hold her own without sucking more than her share of the psychological oxygen from the air around us.

"When are you going to prune?" she asked tentatively. "I could help, maybe. I majored in environmental and biological sciences."

Of course she did. Every other twenty-something kid did.

"I kind of focused on the botany and horticulture," Julia continued. "I don't know that much about fruit trees, but I'd be really interested to learn how to prune." This Julia delivered with more energy. She stopped and turned back to me, while Steven plowed ahead.

I couldn't help myself. I laughed. My efforts to hang back, to give Steven and Julia space to figure out who they were with each other on this first round, had resulted in Julia offering to assist me with pruning apple trees that Steven wanted nothing to do with. "Ahh, that might be kind of fun. You could get a head start in a couple of weeks when I work on the young trees at a friend of mine's orchard. We're going to need all the help we can get there. Then maybe we can work on this old stuff."

Julia cocked her head with the lovely, sky-blue, knitted hat pulled down over her curls, and said, "Okay. That works."

Steven had paused up ahead, and we resumed our walk, companionably silent, until we reached him.

I smiled at him. "How are we doing?" I asked.

Steven smiled but quipped, "Another innocent victim drafted into the cider project?"

Really? Was he listening? I turned to Julia.

"Actually, I'd love to help," she said. "But would you mind if we keep all this new information—about us—to ourselves a little bit longer?" She stopped walking again. "Like, I know you have to tell your sons . . ." Her voice faded. I could see that the process had gotten ahead of her. Her leapfrogging emotions were taking her for a ride, just as mine were.

"Yeah," I said, "let's keep talking about that. I don't think we've figured out how to go public with this, either."

For the rest of the day, Steven couldn't stop talking about how and when to tell our boys that they had a half sister. When Julia left, he wanted to just pick up the phone and call each of them immediately. I understood his urgency to inform them, but I wanted to see their faces, be in the same room with them, when they heard this news.

After we'd eaten a leisurely dinner, we retired to the sofa in the den, glasses of wine in hand and lights extinguished, to watch the moonlit fields of snow.

"You know, we talked about arranging a long weekend to go somewhere warm and take all the kids. Maybe we should do that sooner rather than later, and tell them when we're all together." Steven spoke tentatively, as if trying out the idea as the words came to him.

"I like that much better than calling each of them," I said. "I don't know if they'll all be able to make it, but I think I remember everyone could get away the last weekend in March. Let's try for that." I bit my lip before adding, *By then, I'll have the pruning done.* No sense in raising snakes to beat them down.

"Can you figure something out with them?" Steven asked. "I've got a huge case next week."

I leaned my head back against the deep sofa cushions and closed my eyes. *Sure I can do that.* "Okay."

"And are you sure you want to pull Julia into this cider business? That could add complication."

I sat bolt upright and faced him directly. "She asked me, Steven. She's interested. It may be a way for me to get to know her better. Please don't try to micromanage my connection to her." Before I could stop myself, I continued, "And I know you meant it in the best possible way, but you should have talked to me before giving Julia the bracelet. I felt a little blindsided."

I felt Steven looking at me in the semi-darkness. He sighed deeply before answering, "Okay. I'm sorry. I didn't mean to do that."

The first week of March carried each of the weather elements from February and warmed them ten to twenty degrees. A brief thaw brought rain, and the refreezing a few days later caused treachery as meltwater became pools of glassy ice. Steven returned to Ann Arbor, and Julia took a week's vacation to travel with her family. *Her family. Fiona, Aaron, a younger brother, her grandmother—they are, in fact, a family.*

I plunged into preparations for pruning Charlie's orchard, working out different scenarios based on weather. I reviewed pruning techniques. I conferred with Charlie twice, now that he'd been released from the hospital to a rehab facility, and assured him that all eventualities had been accounted for. We both knew that all eventualities could never be accounted for, but he seemed less agitated in the face of my confidence.

Pruning week began auspiciously, with bright sunshine, cool temperatures, and little wind. I arrived well before our 8:00 a.m. start time, but five men were already at work sharpening tools and gulping last cups of coffee when I drove up. *They're waiting for me.* I tried to appear calm while my heart pounded, and I introduced myself before setting out the morning's plan and directing each helper to a designated row.

Instructions given, I strode to my own line of trees and, pulling my pruner from my tool belt, stood before the first one. After eyeing it carefully, I made a first sure cut, with five pair of eyes watching.

At ten thirty I called a break, pulling out the monster thermoses of fresh coffee and homemade Danishes Melissa had left for us. Just as we were ready to resume our work, Julia's Toyota pickup turned off M-22 and pulled around the drive to the orchard. She hopped out, overalls and work boots signaling readiness to work.

I couldn't help but smile. "Hey there. How are you?"

"Great."

I hadn't seen her eyes look this clear and relaxed since I'd met her. "Good. Are you ready to prune some trees?"

"Yes, I am. Where do I start?"

"I've got four more trees in this row. Why don't you come and work with me? I'd be glad to have another set of hands." Julia smiled and I handed her my backup hand pruners. "If you need a saw, I've got one here," I said, lifting the tree saw from my belt.

We had worked for almost an hour, with my occasionally advising Julia on where to prune and admiring the skill she already possessed. With the lunch break approaching and my arms starting to ache, I tucked my pruners away and turned to her. "There's something I wanted to talk to you about."

Julia turned toward me and looped her arm over a branch of the tree she'd been working on next to me, comfortably resting her back against the trunk.

I smiled at her and said, "How are your parents doing? I've been thinking about your mom a lot, but I haven't been sure how to approach her."

Julia's eyebrows rose, and the ghost of a sardonic smile passed over her features. I realized immediately what she must be thinking: I hadn't had any hesitation approaching her mother two months ago.

I shook my head, smiling again. "I mean now, and moving forward."

Julia looked up into the bare branches of the tree and then off toward the hill that shielded the orchard from the brutal winds off Lake Michigan. She answered in a steady voice. "We all had a good week together last month. My mom's not a big talker, but she and I had some important conversations. We're going to be okay."

"I'm really glad to hear that," I said, and I meant it. "Steven—and I—will want to get to know your family. Keep us posted about when you're ready, and when you think they're ready, for that. There's no rush. We'll work with whatever you think is best. Meanwhile, let's finish these babies."

"Awesome," she said.

I shook my head, smiling, and turned toward my future.

Chapter 26

The idea of a family vacation in Arizona had pleased all my children—we all needed a seasonal break from the Midwest—so the weekend had come together easily.

Carrie and Andrew arrived in Scottsdale several hours before the rest of us and were already in bathing suits by the pool, drinks in hand, when we got to the hotel. Carrie's radiant face revealed her pregnancy as clearly as the baby bump that graced her tiny frame. Alex and Seth had met us in Phoenix, and we'd driven together to this exclusive resort for the long weekend.

I hoped it wouldn't be too long. Dry heat and fierce sun stunned my winter sensibilities. Though wearing only a sundress and sandals, I felt like I still needed to shed a woolly layer of northern Michigan. I sank into the nearest deck chair by the pool to let my body catch up with itself. The infusion of vitamin D and warmth created a current under my skin, as if fortifying me for what lay ahead. Only a gentle breeze off a great lake would have improved the sensation.

I'd arranged for steak and a good red wine in a private room for our first dinner. The meal began with the requisite teasing exchange of news among my three sons. After the banter moved to politics, I cleared my throat and tapped my knife against my water goblet. Five pairs of surprised eyes turned toward me.

"Dad and I are so grateful to be together with all of you, and we want to thank you for making the effort to get here, especially on short notice."

"Hey, pay for a fat bucks resort weekend, and I'm here," Alex said.

The others chuckled.

"I am looking forward to just relaxing and enjoying everybody," I said. "The next time we do this, there may be baby cousins with us."

Carrie blushed and smiled, and Alex rolled his eyes and shook his head, but he didn't look altogether displeased.

"You all know that our family has been at the center of Dad's and my life for the last thirty years, and you also know we had to work harder than most to create it." Andrew went back to eating his steak and Alex tapped his fork on the table-cloth. Seth leaned back in his chair, his head cocked to one side. Steven stared straight ahead, looking for all the world like a deer in the headlights. I waited for Alex to reprise his oft-repeated taunt—that he never had to imagine his parents having sex, since he and Andrew were adopted and Seth was conceived in a test tube. He spared me this time, and I took a deep breath.

"Two new members of the family are on their way, but recently, Dad and I got some news that's a little shocking, and we wanted to tell you all together."

"You're pregnant too." Andrew's deadpan one-liners always made me laugh, and my nervous burst joined the others.

"It's even more mythic than that. As part of our effort to create a family, we tried an arrangement with a woman to be a surrogate parent." I suddenly couldn't bring myself to say "mother." *Do they all know what a surrogate is?* No one looked confused yet, so I forged ahead. "We tried it once, and

the surrogate told us it didn't work. We never tried it again."
I paced my delivery, though every particle of me wanted to
finish disgorging this information quickly. "It turns out that
the woman did get pregnant, and gave birth to a baby girl,
but she couldn't go through with the arrangement to release
the child to us."

Now they were all staring at me. Steven's face looked
as shocked as the others around the table, as if hearing again
what he already knew deepened its impact. Seth sat bolt
upright, the color leaving his face. Alex looked stony and
Andrew breathed out, "What the fuck?"

By now my voice shook. "Right. Well, it turns out that
the child she had never knew about any of this until about six
months ago, which is when she started looking for her biological father. She found me, and asked for my help because
she wasn't sure, but she thought it could be Dad." All the eyes
in front of me widened, and Carrie's hand flew to her mouth.
"It turns out Dad is her biological father."

"Holy shit, it's that Julia girl." Alex rose from his seat
and leaned across the table, his hands planted on either side
of his plate.

Unable to speak, I stared straight at Alex and nodded as
the table erupted with questions. *How could Alex know?* But
then again, Alex always seemed able to divine crucial information out of thin air with lightning speed. For another spacey
moment, I let the questions fly like meteors around me.

"You mean she didn't TELL you?"

"Who is this woman? When did this happen?"

"Could she do that? Didn't you have a contract?"

"How did you figure it out?"

"She can't just waltz in here—"

I turned to Steven and he snapped out of his frozen
state. As if on cue, our waiter appeared and I ordered another
bottle of wine. I realized I'd stood up and had backed myself
up against the wall behind me. I returned to the table and
sat down.

For the next forty minutes, Steven and I relayed the story just as it had unfolded, trying to answer as many questions as we could. My steak went untouched.

That Fiona could have flat-out lied stupefied Carrie. "I mean, I get that once she was pregnant, she wouldn't want to give up her baby, but that's what she signed up for, right? I mean, I could never make that arrangement in the first place."

"Exactly," I said. "That's why I couldn't try surrogacy again."

"Why?" Alex broke in. "It's not all that different from adoption, is it? You didn't have a problem adopting two kids, did you?"

I sighed. "There are important differences, Alex, and at that time there were aspects of surrogacy that I had a hard time with." I picked up my knife and fork and started to eat my dinner. With that question, Alex had come closer than any of my other children to asking about the circumstances, the stresses, and the *feelings* surrounding all those years of fertility treatments, adoption proceedings, and the surrogacy attempt. I'd been somewhat able to share those feelings with close friends, and with women who'd gone through similar means of forging their families. Certainly Steven and I had fought, cried, and celebrated through those complicated times, but he had a low threshold for delving into the emotional reaches of circumstances he could not change. We had been united in devoting ourselves to our family and the energy it took to raise them. So I'd mostly lived alone with the feeling part, the deeper sense of how our challenges had changed my identity as a mother and changed my worldview. It suddenly occurred to me that I'd never talked to my children about my experience of such things—but tonight wasn't the night for that conversation.

Alex and Andrew's raised voices brought me back to the table conversation. They had engaged Steven in a rapidly heating discussion of the legal issues surrounding this revelation. Could Steven sue? Would Julia claim an inheritance?

"Whoa," Steven said a split second before I could step in. "We aren't in a hostile situation here. Julia has good parents that she loves and who love her. And by the way, so do you." The collective eye roll went right by Steven. "She didn't ask for anything more than to understand the truth about her biological father."

"Yet," Alex murmured.

"She's as shocked as the rest of us," Steven continued. "There isn't anyone evil here."

"I don't know about that," Alex said, the force in his voice belying his indifferent posture. "If I were her, I'd be thinking my mother was a downright bitch right about now."

I winced. "I will admit to thinking that way myself while this all developed," I said. "But I went down and met Julia's mother, and got a sense of who she is, and I didn't get any evil out of it. Failure of courage leading to serious dishonesty, yes, but I don't think she's evil. She's got a lot of work to do with her daughter. There's been a serious breach of trust there. I don't envy her those conversations." As I said this, I realized how truly I felt it.

"Oh, so we're the good guys?" Alex pressed, reaching for what had to be his third Coke. His bobbing knee and rapid speech signaled that he'd had enough caffeine.

"Down, boy," I said. "We have no idea where this is all going. There's a lot for everyone to sort out, and there's no rush. So don't get carried away here."

"Yeah, Alex, she had the hots for you and now she's our sister. That sucks." Andrew put his arm around Carrie and grinned at his brother. Alex shook his head but a small smile played across his face. *These brothers!*

After another twenty minutes of questions and discussion it appeared as if they'd exhausted the topic for this first round, so Alex and Andrew turned to planning a golf outing with Steven and Seth the following day, a once-a-year fiasco involving many lost balls, unforgiving golfers in front and behind them on the course, and months-long exaggerated stories of mishaps.

Carrie caught my eye. "Knit shop?" She held out her cell phone with the local store's mapped location.

I laughed. "Absolutely. Let's do that tomorrow."

Seth had been quiet for a long while.

"A penny for your thoughts," I said.

"You always said one reason you pursued in-vitro was that Dad wanted to continue the Stone genetic heritage. I guess now there are two of us." Seth spoke quietly.

"Yep. That's right. What do you think about that?"

"What do *you* think about it?" he shot back at me.

Always thoughtful, Seth was good at checking in with his mother, but this seemed to be about something else. He still looked pale, and his deep-set brown eyes, so much like Steven's, were pools of worry. *Julia is Seth's genetic half sister.* I hadn't really thought much about this fact. We rarely made a point of genetic ties in our family. *What is he asking me?*

"I think she got half of the good stuff you have," I said lightly, trying to joke my way to what troubled him. "The rest we're going to have to transmit through osmosis. I've actually come to like her. She may do some cider work with me. Mostly, I think we just need to get to know her, and let her get to know us. One step at a time here."

Seth twirled the stem of his wine glass. He wasn't looking at me. I thought to move to what I hoped was safer ground. "How's Sophie doing, by the way?"

"She's good," he said. "She's studying really hard for her boards. She's lined up some great clinical rotations starting in July." His face transformed, the color and sparkle returning. *Oh my, looks like she may be a keeper. Plenty of space for her too.*

"Maybe you two could arrange to come up to the lake house this summer if she can grab some vacation days," I said. "I'd love some quiet time with her. And with you." I reached across the table for his hand. "I know all of this is a lot to take in right now. In my better moments, I'm trying to see it as new branches on the proverbial apple tree."

Seth smiled as the rest of the table erupted into laughter at a joke I didn't hear. "That's my mama."

Epilogue

Hugging baby Lily to my chest and watching the sheriff pace back and forth, déjà vu took my breath away. This time, however, the officer was my son, not a fire marshal; the baby in my arms, my granddaughter; and the house before us, my solid functioning cider house, not the long-ago, burned out shell of our family home in Ann Arbor. The twenty-three years since our fire had served up enough additional challenge and complication for a lifetime, but the scene before me brought a flush of gratitude like a hot spring from my center to every part of my body. Good fortune, my own doggedness, and the love and support of my family, however flawed and tested, had brought me to this fulfillment of my dream.

The fruit press inside hummed away, producing the apple must from which I'd age another batch of hard cider. The impossible blue of the sky, set off by a riot of autumn color, ignited all my senses, and I nearly squealed with delight as I squeezed my sleeping granddaughter in her down bunting. I'd kept that blue baby bag since Seth was her age, along with all the sweaters I'd knit for the boys over the years. I'd get to see them all over again on new members of the family.

The machine sounds slowed to a stop and Julia stepped out of the cider house.

"Hey Andrew, when did you guys get here?" They exchanged an easy hug.

"We've been here about an hour," he answered.

"Oh my god, there's Lily!" Julia crossed the yard to stand next to me, pulling the bunting aside to see Lily's full cheeks and turned up nose. "She's so adorable. Her pictures don't do her justice." Julia gazed at the sleeping baby another moment and then said, "We've got another box of Roxbury russets and Kilcherman's said we could get a box of Tydeman Oranges, and that should do for two more batches."

"Great." I said.

"So when will this cider be ready?" Andrew asked. "You know I'm volunteering to be a taster."

"Three or four months," Julia and I answered at the same time. We laughed.

"We might have something interesting by Thanksgiving from the first batch, but for sure by New Year's," I said. "The last batch . . ." I searched for the right word.

"*Sucked* comes to mind," Julia filled in. "Is Carrie in the house?"

"Yeah, she's making lunch," Andrew said.

Julia headed toward the back door.

"So your first batch bombed?" Andrew asked.

"Actually, the first batch was okay, and we're about to put it in bottles, but the next one not so much. I'm still trying to figure out if we had bad juice or didn't wait long enough for it to ferment. We're still working on our recipes."

Telling Steven about the failure of our second test batch had been punishing, but I'd talked through the possible reasons and my plans for a fix. Eventually, he'd actually assured me that any new business would be a series of fits and starts. I still worried about the finances, especially since I'd started paying Julia a salary, but I'd secured my first contract from a local bar based on a tasting of our first batch.

"So is Julia going to be in business with you?" Andrew asked.

"She's learning about it, and I've hired her to help me this fall. She's applying to graduate programs, so she'll be around this fall and maybe even in winter, but I don't know after that."

Andrew turned toward the woods and eyed the path out to the point, his usual preliminary destination when he visited.

"Go ahead," I said. "I've got her." Lily awoke and her eyes scanned the blue expanse, punctuated with towering pine trees, spread out above her. *Such a face. Andrew's face.* I grinned down at Lily, knowing that Andrew saw himself in her; for the first time in his life, he had a family member who looked like him. What could she see at three months? I'd forgotten all the detailed milestones, but Carrie would know. Lily could see her Nani and Papi—that I knew for sure. For the last month when we'd seen her, Steven and I had both been rewarded with the full-face, irresistible baby grins I had always believed contributed to the continuation of the species.

The back door of the house slammed and Julia strode toward me with the phone in her hand. "It's Steven. He wants to talk to you."

"Hey there," I said, jiggling Lily onto my shoulder so I could hold the phone with my other hand. Some skills stay with us. "How're you doing?"

"I'm good," Steven said. "I'm actually on my way up there."

"You're kidding! I thought you weren't coming up until Saturday."

"Well you've got the kids up there, and I hear there's an apple pressing going on. Don't want to miss all the fun. I worked really hard and got anything I couldn't bring with me done."

I caught Julia's eye and mouthed, "He's on his way." To Steven I said, "Fantastic! You should be up by dinner then. Drive carefully."

I hung up and Julia grinned.

"Can you stay for dinner?" I asked. "It would be so nice to have us all together tonight."

"Are you sure?" she asked.

"Yeah, I'm sure," I said. *She still doesn't quite get it. She's family.*

"Okay, I'd really like to," she said. With that, she returned to the cider house, and the sounds of the press resuming soon filled the air.

I walked with Lily down the path to the lake. The kayaks and beach chairs were put away for the season, and the beach arced wildly up the peninsula to the point. I smiled. Steven was on his way to join me for at least a week. Andrew and Carrie's impromptu decision to spend a week's vacation in Northport had drawn him for sure, and he always wanted to see Julia.

Perhaps her interest in my cider business had changed something for Steven; whatever the reason, he had also begun to show an interest that seemed genuine, and at times even helpful. My investment still held risk, but he no longer pressured me to give it up.

Steven and Julia had granted each other an easy, affectionate, demand-free connection. Without formal definition, they'd become close. Making cider together had brought Julia and me even closer. I found myself talking through decisions with her, sharing my hopes and insecurities alike. When it came to her decisions about graduate school and the essays she had to write, I could be there for her in an unencumbered but helpful manner. The irony that Julia and I had the boots-on-the-ground relationship in the family hadn't escaped me, but added to my gratitude. Steven not only seemed not to mind, he seemed to appreciate our bond and even feed from it.

Alex and Seth were both coming for a quick weekend. Alex wanted to take advantage of the last days before Haley went into labor. The two of them had come to an understanding that they weren't going to be together, but that they would cooperate in order to parent the child they had made. Alex had weathered this major adjustment to his life with a new maturity and moral compass that signaled his becoming an adult I could truly admire. He would make a serious effort to be a good parent.

Lily had fallen asleep again in my arms. She would soon have a cousin. Perhaps sometime after that, she would have a new aunt, as Seth and Sophie seemed to be moving toward a commitment. And Andrew and Carrie had already decided that Lily had another aunt as well—Aunt Julia.

Lily stirred and began to make the small kicking and gurgling sounds that presaged hunger, and before I turned back toward the house I looked out over the water, the sun sparkling on its ruffled surface in a broad avenue to the horizon. The tapestry of color and texture brought a contented peace to my center. I hummed to my granddaughter as I headed up toward home.

Acknowledgments

With gratitude, I acknowledge the extraordinary people who helped me bring this book to life.

First and foremost, I thank my husband, and sons and their families for anchoring me in the real world of loving and living.

For years of reading and refining the many drafts of *Hard Cider*, my eternal thanks to Patricia Hoffman and Kathy York, my critique partners, and for her early input, Claudia Whitsitt.

To beta readers whose personal and expert advice made this such a better book, I thank Nathan Nemon, Barry Nemon, Joan Mandel Eisenberg, David O. Moses, Kathe Langberg, and Pamela Grath. A special thanks to my She Writes sisters, who took time from their own work to closely read and comment— Betsy Graziani Fasbinder, Connie Hertzberg Mayo; you are the best!

To those who shared their expertise in hard apple cider, DNA testing, Tarot reading, fiber arts, and legal issues, I deeply thank Nikki Rothwell and Dan Young of Tandem Ciders, Joe Psenka, Steve Redding, Sally Coohon of Dolls &

More, Karen Cross, Marie Elena Gaspari, Rick Leadbeater, Ben Watson, Stephen Wood of Poverty Lane Orchards, Margaret Potter of Goodnature, Norman Fell, Barbara Richardson of the Dayton Knitting Guild, John Wiegand of Mbiz.com, and Michael Pollan, author *The Botany of Desire*.

I also wish to thank the hundreds of readers of *Even in Darkness*, my first novel, for all the kind words and support. And to all the mothers out there who have shared their courage, heartbreak and wisdom from experiences with infertility and raising challenging children—you know who you are— you have my deepest gratitude.

Finally, to the amazing women at She Writes Press whose work on *Hard Cider* has been invaluable, I thank Brooke Warner, Cait Levin, Julie Metz, Tabitha Lahr and editors Annie Tucker and Krissa Lagos.

Author Bio

Barbara Stark-Nemon, author of the award-winning novel *Even in Darkness*, lives, writes, cycles, swims, and gardens in Ann Arbor and Northport, Michigan. Degrees in English Literature, Art History, and Speech-language Pathology from the University of Michigan led to a career as a teacher and speech therapist working with deaf children. Barbara now writes novels, short stories, essays, and articles.

Learn more about Barbara at www.barbarastarknemon.com

Author photo © Chris Loomis Photography

SELECTED TITLES FROM SHE WRITES PRESS

She Writes Press is an independent publishing company founded to serve women writers everywhere. Visit us at www.shewritespress.com.

Duck Pond Epiphany by Tracey Barnes Priestley. $16.95, 978-1-938314-24-7. When a mother of four delivers her last child to college, she has to decide what to do next—and her life takes a surprising turn.

A Drop In The Ocean: A Novel by Jenni Ogden. $16.95, 978-1-63152-026-6. When middle-aged Anna Fergusson's research lab is abruptly closed, she flees Boston to an island on Australia's Great Barrier Reef—where, amongst the seabirds, nesting turtles, and eccentric islanders, she finds a family and learns some bittersweet lessons about love.

Eden by Jeanne Blasberg. $16.95, 978-1-63152-188-1. As her children and grandchildren assemble for Fourth of July weekend at Eden, the Meister family's grand summer cottage on the Rhode Island shore, Becca decides it's time to introduce the daughter she gave up for adoption fifty years ago.

Again and Again by Ellen Bravo. $16.95, 978-1-63152-939-9. When the man who raped her roommate in college becomes a Senate candidate, women's rights leader Deborah Borenstein must make a choice—one that could determine control of the Senate, the course of a friendship, and the fate of a marriage.

Appetite by Sheila Grinell. $16.95, 978-1-63152-022-8. When twenty-five-year-old Jenn Adler brings home a guru fiancé from Bangalore, her parents must come to grips with the impending marriage—and its effect on their own relationship.

American Family by Catherine Marshall-Smith. $16.95, 978-1631521638. Partners Richard and Michael, recovering alcoholics, struggle to gain custody of Richard's biological daughter from her grandparents after her mother's death only to discover they— and she—are fundamentalist Christians.